THIS DARK ROAD TO MERCY

Wiley Cash

faber

This paperback edition first published in 2022
by Faber & Faber Limited
Bloomsbury House, 74–77 Great Russell Street
London WC1B 3DA

First published in the UK in 2014
by Doubleday, an imprint of Transworld Publishers
One Embassy Gardens, 8 Viaduct Gardens, London SW11 7BW

First published in the United States in 2014
by William Morrow, an imprint of HarperCollins
195 Broadway, New York, NY 10007

Printed and bound by CPI Group (UK) Ltd, Croydon, CR0 4YY

A CIP record for this book
is available from the British Library

ISBN 978–0–571–37347–5

For families of all kinds

Where you come from is gone, where you thought you were going to was never there, and where you are is no good unless you can get away from it. Where is there a place for you to be? No place . . . Nothing outside you can give you any place . . . In yourself right now is all the place you've got.

—Flannery O'Connor, *Wise Blood*

Easter Quillby

CHAPTER 1

Wade disappeared on us when I was nine years old, and then he showed up out of nowhere the year I turned twelve. By then I'd spent nearly three years listening to Mom blame him for everything from the lights getting turned off to me and Ruby not having new shoes to wear to school, and by the time he came back I'd already decided that he was the loser she'd always said he was. But it turns out he was much more than that. He was also a thief, and if I'd known what kind of people were looking for him I never would've let him take me and my little sister out of Gastonia, North Carolina, in the first place.

My earliest memories of Wade are from my mom taking me to the baseball stadium at Sims Field back before she died. She'd point to the field and say, "There's your daddy right there." I wasn't any older than three or four, but I can still remember staring out at the infield where all the men looked the exact same in their uniforms, wondering how I would ever spot my daddy at a baseball game if he looked just like everybody else.

It's funny to think about that now, because on the day he decided to come back for us I knew Wade as soon as I saw him sitting up in the bleachers down the first-base line. I'd always called him "Wade" because it never felt right to think of him as "Dad" or "Daddy" or anything else kids are supposed to call their parents. Parents who got called things like that did stuff for their kids that I couldn't ever imagine Wade doing for us. All he'd ever done for me was give me a baby sister named Ruby and enough stories for my mom to spend the rest of her life telling, but she ended up dying just before I turned twelve, which was the only reason Wade came looking for me and Ruby in the first place.

I'd just made it to third base, and I had no problem acting like I didn't see him sitting up there. My eyes raised themselves just enough to spy Ruby sitting on the bench, waiting on her turn to kick. She had her back to the bleachers and hadn't seen him yet; she might not even have recognized him if she did.

To look at Ruby and Wade you wouldn't even know they were related, but you could've said the same thing about me and her. Ruby looked just like Mom. She had long dark hair, dark eyes, and dark skin even in the wintertime. I was just the opposite. My hair was strawberry blond and straight as a board, and my skin was more likely to burn and freckle than tan. Ruby was beautiful—she always had been. I looked just like Wade.

The bleachers were empty except for him, and I looked around the field and saw that none of the other kids had noticed him yet. Up the hill on my right, Mrs. Hannah and Mrs. Davis stood talking out on the school playground. Neither of them had seen him yet. But I didn't have to wait long for somebody to spot him.

"Look at that man up there," Selena said. She was playing third base and stood bent over with her hands on her knees. She was black just like most of the kids we stayed with after school and just about all the kids we lived with at the home. Her hair was fixed in thick braids with bands that had marbles on them; they clinked together when she moved her head. I'd wanted to ask her to fix my hair just like hers, but my hair was too thin to stay in braids, which was fine with me because Selena was taller than me and seemed a lot older than me too, and I was always too nervous to talk to her. "Why's he just sitting there watching us?" she asked.

I didn't know if she was talking to me or if she was just talking to herself out loud. "I don't know," I finally said. She looked over at me like she'd forgotten I was standing on base beside her. I said a little prayer that she wouldn't mention nothing about me and Wade looking alike, and I found myself wishing again that I looked more like Mom, like Ruby.

A third grader named Greg stepped up to the plate, and even though something told me I shouldn't do it, I ran toward home as soon as he kicked it. The ball didn't do nothing but roll right back to the pitcher, and I got thrown out at the plate. I headed for the bench, but I kept my head down and didn't look up at the bleachers. My face felt hot and I knew it had gone red, and I made myself believe I was embarrassed only because I'd been thrown out at home, not because it had all happened in front of Wade.

Ruby sat by herself on the end of the bench, swinging her feet back and forth. When I got closer, she moved that dark hair behind her ears and stuck out her hand and waited for me.

"High five," she said. I sat down beside her without saying anything, and then I bent over and dusted off my shoes. Ruby left her hand hanging just above my knees. "High five," she said again.

"It's only a high five when it's up high."

"All right," she said. "Low five, then."

I gave her palm a little slap, and I looked up and saw Marcus watching me from the infield at second. He was wearing a white Cubs jersey with Sammy Sosa's number and name on the back. The school year had just started and it was only the third Friday in August, but Mark McGwire already had fifty-one home runs to Sosa's forty-eight. Me and Marcus were both rooting for Sosa to get to sixty-two and break Roger Maris's record first. He smiled at me, but I looked away like I hadn't seen him. It made me nervous, and I pulled my hair back in a ponytail and let it drop to my shoulders. When I looked up at Marcus again he was still smiling. I couldn't help but smile a little bit too, but then I heard a voice whisper my name. "Hey!" it said. "Easter!"

It was Wade. He was leaning against the outside of the fence about halfway down to first base. Ruby looked up at him, stared for a second, and then looked at me. Wade smiled and waved us over. "Is that—?" she started to ask, but I stopped her before she could finish.

"Wait here," I said, standing up from the bench.

"Easter," Ruby said. She jumped down like she was fixing to follow me.

"Wait here," I said again. She just stood there looking at me, and then she looked down the fence at Wade. I pointed to the bench and watched her climb back onto it. She crossed her arms like I'd scolded her. "I'll be right back," I said. I looked up the hill at Mrs. Hannah and Mrs. Davis. They still hadn't seen him. I kept close to the fence and made my way down the baseline.

Wade had on an old blue Braves cap, and his hair, the same strawberry blond as mine, stuck out around his ears. Whiskers covered his face and ran down his neck, and drops of white paint were all over his green T-shirt and blue jeans. He lifted his hand where it sat on top of the fence and gave me a little wave. "Hey," he said, smiling. White paint was all over his hands too.

Before I got to him, I stopped and crossed my arms and leaned my shoulder against the fence. Wade didn't need to think I was happy to see him all of a sudden—that he could just show up after school one day and everything would be okay. To tell the truth, I didn't even want to look at him.

"Y'all trying to integrate the Negro League?" he asked. He laughed like his joke should've made me laugh too, but it didn't. He took his hands off the top of the fence and put them in his pockets.

I looked out at the field where the inning was just getting over.

Marcus walked from the infield toward the bench on the other side of home plate, watching me the whole way. His face looked worried, and I wanted to smile and let him know that it was okay, that I knew the man talking to me, that I knew what I was doing, but I didn't want him thinking I was giving him some kind of sign to come over and check on me. I didn't want him meeting Wade. I turned back to Wade, my arms still crossed. "Why are you here?"

He sighed and raised his eyes and looked toward the outfield, and then he looked down at me. "I heard about what happened to y'all's mother," he said.

"You heard *today*?"

"No, not today," he said. "A while ago."

" 'A while ago' meaning you should've come to her funeral, what little bit of one she had? 'A while ago' meaning you should've come and checked on us before now, before they put us in a home?"

"No," he said. "Not *that* long ago."

"Just long enough to do nothing."

"Nothing until now."

"Until now?" Just saying that made me laugh. I unfolded my arms and turned to walk back to the bench where Ruby was waiting on me.

"Hold on, Easter," he said. "Talk to me for one minute—just one minute." He'd taken his hands out of his pockets and grabbed hold of the chain links in the fence.

"I got to take the field," I said, and even as I said it I thought it sounded like something somebody might say in a movie right before something good or something bad happened to let you know whether the ending was going to be a happy one or not.

"I just want to spend some time with you and your sister," he said.

"You can't," I said. "It's too late."

"I know it seems too late, but y'all are all I've got."

Y'all are all I've got: I'd heard Mom say that about a million times, but she'd said it when she tucked us in at night or when she walked us to the bus stop in the morning. Sometimes she'd said it when I found her crying in our old house late at night. She'd pull me to her and hold me like she was trying to make me feel better even though she was the one crying, and she'd rock back and forth and tell me it was going to be okay. When she'd turn me loose, I'd leave her room and get back in bed, where I'd touch my nightgown and feel where it was wet with her tears. I'd look over at Ruby where she slept, and I'd hear Mom's voice say it again: *Y'all are all I've got.* I hated to see Mom cry, but I always knew she meant what she said. I didn't know what Wade meant when he said it; I didn't think he knew what he meant either.

"You don't *got* us anymore," I said. "You gave us up. I've seen the paper you signed that says it; that's why we're at a home, *Wade.*"

He looked away from me when I called him by his name. Then he blinked his eyes real slow. "I know," he said, "and I'm sorry. But that don't mean we can't spend time together."

I looked over my shoulder and saw that the inning had already started and Jasmine had taken my place at shortstop. "Great," I said. "I lost my spot." I turned back to Wade. "What do you think we're supposed to spend time doing?"

"Well," he said, "I don't know. Your baserunning could use a little work." He stepped away from the fence and rubbed a hand down each arm, and then he touched both his ears and then the tip of his nose. "I was over here trying to help you, but I guess you didn't see me." He started rubbing his hands down his arms again.

"What are you doing?"

"I'm giving you a sign," he said. "I'm telling you to stay on base, to stay right where you are. Wasn't no way that scrawny kid was kicking it out of the infield. I still know the game, Easter. I could come check y'all out one day and we could spend a little time out here on the field, tossing a baseball around, fielding grounders." He smiled when he said it like he thought it was the best idea anybody'd ever had.

" 'Check us out'?" I said. "Like a library book?"

"No, not like a library book. I just mean I'd come and pick you up—spend the day with you and Ruby."

"You can't do that," I said.

"Why not?"

"Because it ain't in the rules. You can't just come and get us."

"What kind of place are y'all in?" he asked.

"A home for at-risk youth," Ruby's voice said. I looked to my right and saw her standing beside me, so close that I couldn't believe I hadn't felt her body up against mine. She stared up at Wade like she was afraid of him, like he might be able to climb right through the fence and pull her back through the chain links to the other side.

"I told you to stay over there," I said. My hip nudged her back toward the bench, but she didn't move, and she didn't take her eyes off Wade.

"At-risk youth?" Wade said. "What are y'all at risk of? Is this the kind of place where kids freak out and hurt each other?"

"That ain't what it's called," I said. "That's something she's heard kids at school say. It's just a foster home."

"Great," he said. He pushed away from the fence and put his hands on his hips. "I hope you know y'all ain't going to be in there long. Somebody's going to come and get you—probably adopt both of you together because you're sisters. You'll probably be the next ones to go."

"How do you know?" I asked.

"Because," he said, his voice sounding like I should already know the answer. He looked up at the rest of the kids on the field, and then he looked back down at me. "Y'all are white."

I heard somebody calling my name, and I turned and looked up the hill, where Mrs. Davis was coming down toward us, moving faster than she would've been walking if everything was normal. When she saw me looking at her she waved her arms above her head and hollered my name again. Mrs. Hannah had stayed up on the playground, but she was closer to the school than she'd been before, and I could tell she was watching us and waiting to see what would happen once Mrs. Davis made it down to the field. "They're probably going to call the police," I said.

"Yeah?" Wade said, smiling. "For talking to your own daddy?"

"They don't know who you are," I said. Then I looked down at Ruby. "We don't either." I took her hand and walked back to the bench. I didn't look back, but I could tell by the way she was walking that Ruby's head was turned so she could stare at Wade. "Come on," I said, giving her hand a good yank so she'd walk faster.

Mrs. Davis had made it to the bottom of the hill by the time we got back to the bench and sat down. She walked inside the fence and squatted down in front of me and Ruby. She had light brown skin and short curly hair and wore thick glasses. "Who was that man y'all were talking to?" she asked.

I looked down to where Wade had been standing at the fence, but he was gone. "I don't know him," I said. I put my hand on Ruby's knee. "Neither one of us do."

CHAPTER 2

A re you sure it was him?" Ruby asked.

"Of course I'm sure," I said. That was about the tenth time she'd asked me that same question since we'd seen Wade that afternoon. It was time for bed, but the lights were still on in our room. Out in the hallway, a couple of kids walked by on their way to the bathroom.

Ruby lay in her bed, staring up at the ceiling. She'd put her hands behind her head, and I could see that she'd crossed her ankles under her comforter. "I don't know," she said. "That's just not how I remember him looking."

"That's because you were four years old the last time you saw him," I said. "And we never had any pictures of him laying around to remind you of what he looked like."

She rolled over to her side and propped her head on her left hand, and she looked across the bedroom to where I was sitting on top of my bed and leaning against the wall, waiting to hear him tap on the window beside me, even though I knew he wouldn't be out there for another couple hours. "We don't have any pictures of Mom either," she said.

"I know," I said, "but I'm going to get us some soon."

"From where?" she asked.

"From her mom and dad," I said. "I'm going to write them in Alaska once me and you get our own place. And I'm going to ask them to send us all Mom's old clothes and toys and all the pictures they've got of her—all the stuff she left up there."

"Maybe we should just go live with them," she said. "Maybe we'd like it."

"No, Ruby, we wouldn't."

"How do you know?" she asked.

"Because," I said, "we don't know them, and they don't know us. Why would they want two girls they've never met to come and live with them? Who'd want that?"

"I don't know," she said. "But maybe they have a room that's got all her old stuff in it, and maybe we'd love them once we met them; maybe they'd love us too. Maybe we'd want to stay." I didn't say anything. We'd had this talk before, and I hoped she was finished asking those kinds of questions, at least for tonight.

She lay back down on her bed. She was quiet but her eyes were still open, and I could tell she was thinking about something. "I hope you can get some pictures of Mom soon," she said. "I can't even remember her."

"Bull-honky you can't," I said. "It's only been three months."

"But I just can't picture her," she said. "I swear." I thought about that for a second, and then I thought about how Ruby was only six years old and how three months must seem like a pretty good bit of life to her.

"It's okay," I said. "It's been a while. But she'll come back to you."

"I hope," Ruby said.

"She will," I said. "Go to sleep." I reached out and clicked off the lamp that sat on the little table between our beds, and then I rested my back against the wall. I looked through the dark room toward Ruby's bed.

"You waiting on him?" she asked.

"Yes," I said.

"Do you think he'll come tonight?"

"I do," I said. "Go to sleep."

I hated it when Ruby talked about not being able to remember Mom, but sometimes I hated that I could remember her so good. Whenever I thought about the day I found her, it seemed like I was another person, like another person with a life other than mine had told me about it. But the telling seemed so real that it was hard to pretend that I'd just heard about it from somebody else. I'll never be able to forget that it was me who found her, even though I've spent plenty of time wishing it hadn't been.

Mom always said that she'd named us what she'd named us because those were her favorite things: Easter was her favorite holiday and rubies were her favorite jewels. Me and Ruby used to ask Mom all the time what her other favorite things were, and we'd pretend those things were our names instead. She'd told us one time that her favorite kind of dog was a Boston terrier and that her favorite color was purple. And when it came to music, she didn't hardly listen to nothing but Journey, so I figured that had to be her favorite band. So that's what me and Ruby started calling ourselves; I was Boston Terrier, and she was Purple Journey. Boston Terrier: I'll admit it sounds silly when you first hear it, but if you split it up into a first name and a last name I think it sounds kind of pretty— fancy and a little bit dangerous, like the name of a woman in an action movie the hero can't quite trust but falls in love with anyway. It seems crazy to say we played make-believe like that now, but we used those names so much they almost became real, and sometimes I wanted to call Ruby "Purple" even when we weren't playing. We'd already promised each other that if we ended up having to run away from the home to keep from being split up then that's who we'd become. We'd be Boston Terrier and Purple Journey for the rest of our lives. No one would ever know we'd been somebody else back in Gastonia.

It's easier for me to imagine Boston Terrier and Purple Journey getting off that school bus and walking past Lineberger Park on their way home to a too-quiet house. It's easier for me to picture a girl with a pretty name like that finding Mom and him lying across the bed in her room, both of them passed out. I don't know what his real name was, but he called himself Calico. When I found them he was down near the foot of the bed with his feet hanging off on to the floor; he had on a black T-shirt and camouflage shorts. Mom had her head resting on a pillow and looked like she just hadn't woke up yet; she wasn't wearing nothing but a pair of blue underwear and a big white T-shirt that had a picture of Tweety Bird on it.

I'd gone into Mom's room by myself, but I heard Ruby in the kitchen, opening and closing the refrigerator and looking through the cabinets for something to eat. I closed Mom's door and locked it behind me, and then I walked over to the bed and stared at her chest, hoping and praying to see it move up and down with her breathing. But I wasn't sure if I could see anything or not. Calico was breathing like he was asleep, and I reached out and touched his leg with my shoe.

"Calico," I whispered. He didn't move, and I touched his leg again. "Calico," I said just a little bit louder.

His eyelids fluttered. I reached out and poked his knee with my finger. When his eyes finally opened he just laid there staring up at the ceiling. I watched him for a second, and then I whispered his name again.

His head popped up, and he looked down the bed at me. His hair was long and wild and stood up everywhere. He blinked his eyes real slow like he couldn't quite see me, and then he sat up on his elbows and looked around. When he looked over at Mom he just stared at her like he couldn't quite remember who she was or how she'd come to be lying there beside him. He looked at me again, and I reckon he finally realized who Mom was and that I was her daughter.

"Hey," he said, jumping up from the bed as fast as he could. "We didn't hear y'all come in." He tried to smile at me, and then he looked back at Mom where she was still lying with her eyes closed.

Calico squeezed past me and walked up alongside the bed and bent down and looked at Mom up close. "Corinne," he whispered. He reached out and put his hand on her shoulder. "Corinne," he said again. "Wake up, girl." He looked up at me and gave me a half smile. "She's okay," he said. "She's just sleeping."

There were all kinds of different pills on Mom's bedside table, and Calico moved them around with his finger like he was looking for one in particular. Then he gathered them all up and dropped them into a little white medicine bottle and screwed the lid on. There were a couple of cans of beer on the table too. The first one he picked up must've been empty because he set it back down. But he picked up the other one and finished it in one long drink.

The bed squeaked when he leaned his knees against it and bent over Mom again and put his fingers on her neck. He closed his eyes like he was concentrating, and then he stood up straight and walked toward the foot of the bed and squeezed by me again before unlocking the bedroom door. His hand stayed on the knob like he didn't want to let it go.

"Listen," Calico said. "I'm going to go see about getting somebody to check on your mom. Y'all just wait here, and I'll be right back. Okay? Y'all just wait here." He opened the door, and I watched him walk into the hall. He opened the front door and closed it behind him, and I heard his shoes going down the steps. For some reason, and I can't tell you why, I imagined him running once he got to the bottom of those steps, and I knew he wasn't running for help.

I sat down beside Mom on the edge of the mattress. My fingers touched her throat where Calico had touched her, and I closed my eyes just like he did. After a few seconds I could just barely feel her pulse, and I knew it meant she was still alive and that she'd be okay and it didn't matter whether Calico kept his word or not. The floorboards squeaked, and I looked up and saw Ruby in the doorway. She'd already kicked off her shoes in the living room and was standing there in her socks. A little smear of peanut butter was on her cheek. "What's wrong with Mom?" she asked.

"She's sick," I said, pulling the covers up around her so Ruby couldn't get a good look at her. "But she'll be okay."

"What's she sick with?"

"I don't know," I said. "She's just sick." Mom's eyelids were jumping just a little bit, and I wondered if she was dreaming. "We need to let her rest." When I raised my eyebrows Ruby got the hint and walked back toward the living room. I bent down and whispered into Mom's ear in case Ruby was out in the hallway trying to listen. "You're going to be all right, Mom," I said. "You just rest now and get a little sleep. We'll be okay for dinner."

I thought about walking down to Fayles' on the corner and calling 911 and getting ahold of an ambulance, but after seeing those pills I knew what it meant to find her asleep like this. Anybody who came and found her like that would put her in the hospital and probably arrest her too. I knew for sure they'd take me and Ruby away. I figured if Mom was breathing and her heart was beating, it was good enough to leave her alone and let her sleep. I'd found her like this before, and she'd always woke up a couple of hours later and come walking into the living room like a zombie from a scary movie. Me and Ruby would be watching television or working on our homework or maybe doing both at the same time. "When'd y'all get home?" she'd ask. It would be almost dark outside, and sometimes it would've been dark for hours.

"We've been home for a while," I'd say.

"Okay," she'd say. "Y'all want something to eat?"

I told myself this time wasn't any different from any of those other times, and I tucked the sheet around her even though it was warm in her room, and I closed her door as quietly as I could and walked into the living room and found Ruby sitting on the floor in front of the television.

That night I heated up a can of SpaghettiOs in a saucepan on the stove. Me and Ruby ate in front of the television and watched *Entertainment Tonight*. I hated Mary Hart's big cheesy smile, but I loved her hair: how huge it was and how it didn't move when she turned her head. I wanted hair like that. I liked her name too. It reminded me of Boston Terrier—one of those names you wouldn't think was real until you met somebody who answered to it.

While Ruby brushed her teeth and got ready for bed, I went back into Mom's room to check on her. It was pitch black and hot as it could be, but I could see by the light coming in from the hallway. I walked around to the side of the bed where Mom had been lying that afternoon. She was still in the same spot, and I sat down beside her. I was afraid that she'd gotten too hot with the door being closed and the sheet being pulled up around her tight, but she wasn't sweating and didn't feel warm when I touched her. She breathed softly, so I knew she was just fine, and I knew she'd wake us up for school in the morning like nothing had happened. I leaned over and whispered in her ear.

"Good night, Mom," I said. "Me and Ruby already ate something and did our homework, and I'm getting her ready for bed." She didn't say nothing or give any sign that she'd heard me, but I didn't expect her to. I stood up and started to walk out into the hall, but then I heard her whisper my name. She'd raised her left arm up from the bed and was holding it out toward me like she wanted me to hold her hand. I walked back to the bed and held her hand in mine, and I just stood there holding it and waiting to see if she'd say something else, but she didn't. "All right, Mom," I said, letting her hand rest on the bed right beside her. "You get some sleep."

I went to bed too, but all night long I kept waking up and wondering if I'd heard her moving around the house: the sound of her feet dragging across the floor, doors opening and closing, water running in the sink.

I woke up in the morning just as it was getting to be daylight outside. The house was silent, just like it was supposed to be at that time of the morning, but something about that quiet told me it was wrong. So I wasn't too surprised at how I found her when I opened her bedroom door.

She was lying sideways on top of the bed like maybe she'd stood up sometime during the night and had fallen back across the bed and just stayed that way. I knew she was dead right when I opened the door. She was on her side with her knees bent up close to her and her hands under her chin. Her dark hair was covering her face, so I couldn't tell whether her eyes were open or not, but I didn't move it out of her face to check because I knew I didn't want to see. I didn't even touch her, which seems strange to think about now because I'd give anything in this world to curl up in bed beside her, be able to smell her hair on the pillowcase, feel her scratch my back through my nightgown. But instead I just stood there looking down at her and went ahead and decided that I wasn't going to cry, not then anyway. I knew it was more important to decide what me and Ruby were going to do next.

Ruby must've felt something in the house too because when I went back into our bedroom I found her sitting up in the bed like she'd been waiting on me.

"How's Mom?" she asked. I just stood there looking at her, trying to figure out how I was going to explain what had happened. "Is she better?"

"No, Ruby," I said, "she's not." I sat down on her bed and told her. I told her about how Mom was tired all the time and that was why she was always sleeping. And I told her that Mom's body just couldn't take that tiredness and that she'd finally had enough. Ruby just sat there and looked at me while I found my way through whatever it was I was saying. I can't promise that I quite remember it myself, but I do remember telling her that now wasn't no time to be sad. I remember telling her that there'd be plenty of time for that later, that right now we had to be tough and figure out what we were going to do next to make sure we stayed together now that we didn't have a mama or a daddy like most kids our age.

I asked her if she wanted to go into Mom's bedroom to see her one more time, and I could tell she thought about it awfully hard, but in the end she decided that she didn't want to, and I couldn't blame her. I didn't go back into that room again either.

"Are you hungry?" I asked. She shook her head. "We probably should eat something anyway." I turned to walk toward the kitchen.

"Where you going?" Ruby asked.

"I'm going to the kitchen," I said. "We need to eat something."

"I'm not hungry."

"Okay," I said, "you don't have to eat nothing if you don't want to." I walked into the hallway.

"Hold on," Ruby said. I stopped walking and waited until she was right behind me, and then we went into the kitchen and opened the cabinets and looked for something to eat, but there wasn't nothing there for breakfast. There wasn't hardly no food at all. I looked around and realized that we didn't have anything, and I saw what our house really looked like, and I knew how people would think of us when they came inside in a few hours to get Mom and take us away to wherever we'd be going. They'd see that we didn't have any furniture except for a plastic deck chair and two folding chairs that you might take to the beach. And they'd see that me and Ruby didn't have beds but just slept on mattresses on the floor that had mismatched sheets on them. They'd know that I'd called them from the corner store because we didn't have a phone, and they'd see that even if we'd had food we didn't have no clean plates to eat from. I stood there looking all around that kitchen with a knot in my throat and an empty stomach, and I swear I could hear flies buzzing in just about every windowpane in that house. I just wanted to leave it all behind.

"You think we need quarters to call 911?" I asked.

"I don't know," Ruby said. "I ain't never called it before."

We spent forever looking for those two quarters. I finally found one in the bottom of my book bag, and Ruby found one behind the dresser in our room. The sun had come up all the way by the time we'd gotten dressed and were walking down the street toward Garrison Boulevard. It would be hot later, but the morning felt nice, and down the hill on the right mist rose up from the creek that ran through the center of Lineberger Park. A few people slept on picnic tables under the shelters. They'd been out there all night because they didn't have no place else to go.

There weren't any cars in the parking lot at Fayles', and I took Ruby by the hand and led her through the lot to the corner where a phone booth sat by the sidewalk. The quarters were ready in my hand, but when we got closer I saw that somebody'd come along and torn the phone loose from the cord and taken it with them. They'd yanked out the phone book too. I stood there looking at that cord where the phone should've been, and I held Ruby's hand and asked myself what Boston Terrier would do.

Then I remembered that you could see a pay phone inside the pool room at Fayles' whenever we walked past it with Mom on the way to the library. I led Ruby back across the lot to the store, but when I let go of her hand and tried to open the door I saw that it was locked. The sign said they didn't open until 7:30 A.M. Through the glass, I could see a man inside the store messing with a coffeemaker, and when he heard me tug on the door he turned around and looked at us over his shoulder. He pointed to his watch. "We ain't open yet," he said. I had to read his lips because I couldn't hear him through the glass. Me and Ruby sat down on the curb in front of the store and waited.

"What are you going to say to 911?" she asked.

"I don't know," I said. "I guess I'll wait and see what they ask me."

A few minutes later we heard the lock turn on the door, and we stood up and walked inside. Smelly coffee dripped into a pot, and the man had already cranked up the hot-dog-turning machine. Hot dogs aren't good for breakfast, but seeing them laid out and roasting on those rollers reminded me that we hadn't eaten nothing yet.

I took Ruby's hand and walked through the store, past the counter, and into the pool room. The man who'd unlocked the door was standing behind the cash register, and he folded his arms and stared at us when we walked past him. I figured he was wondering what two little girls were doing alone at the store this early in the morning.

A cigarette smell came up from the carpet in the pool room when I stepped on it. A big window looked out onto the parking lot, and I could see the phone booth that was missing its phone out on the corner by Garrison. The road was starting to get busy with traffic. In the corner of the room was the pay phone hanging on the wall. A stool was sitting under it. A jukebox sat beside it. I pushed the stool up against the wall and picked up the phone. Ruby leaned against the jukebox and watched me. A plastic Coke bottle sat on top of the phone, and an old brown cigarette was floating down inside it.

I dialed 911 and waited. It rung once, and then the operator picked up. "911," she said. "What's your emergency?"

I waited a second before I said anything because I wanted to make sure I used the right words. "I think my mom might be dead," I finally said.

"Okay," the operator said. "Why do you think that?"

"Because she won't wake up," I said. "And yesterday she was in bed sick and she slept all day. She's still there, and now she won't move. I don't think she's breathing."

"Okay," the operator said again. "And where's your mom right now?"

I gave her the address for our house, and then she asked me Mom's name.

"Her name's Corinne Quillby," I said, "and she's twenty-nine years old."

"All right," the operator said, "and what's your name?"

"My name?" I looked at Ruby where she stood staring at me, her back still leaned up against the jukebox. I smiled at her. "My name's Boston Terrier," I said.

Ruby smiled back. "And I'm Purple Journey," she whispered.

CHAPTER 3

I must've drifted off to sleep sitting up in my bed, because the next thing I heard was the sound of him tapping on the window outside. Ruby didn't move, and I figured she was either asleep or pretending to be. I scooted down toward the end of the bed and reached out and unlocked the window and opened it. It was a new window and the frame was made out of plastic, so it slid up easy without making a sound. The window frames in the house we'd lived in with Mom were old and made out of wood. Sometimes we couldn't get them open no matter how hard we tried. I scooted back toward my pillow and waited for him to climb in.

The windowsill was painted white, and even though it was dark in our room I could see Marcus's fingers close around it to pull himself up, and I heard the sound his shoes made when they scraped against the side of the house as he climbed up into our room, first one leg and then the other.

"Be quiet," I whispered.

"I'm trying to," he whispered back.

Once he'd climbed in all the way he walked right to our closet and stepped inside and closed it behind him. I lay down and covered myself up with the sheet and pretended to be asleep. We always did that in case Miss Crawford or one of the other workers heard him coming in the window and opened our bedroom door to check on me and Ruby. I always imagined hearing somebody's footsteps coming toward us, the bedroom door opening, and that crack of light coming in the room from the hallway and lying across my bed. "Easter?" one of them would whisper.

I'd stir in my pretend-sleep like they'd just woke me up, and I'd wait a second before saying anything. "What?" I'd say.

"You okay?"

"Yes, ma'am," I'd say.

They'd peek in the door, see me and Ruby both in our beds, and decide things looked just fine. That's what I hoped would happen anyway. I didn't know what they'd do if they found Marcus Walker hiding in our closet.

I lay there with my eyes closed and waited a few minutes, and then I whispered his name. "I think you can come on out," I said.

I heard the closet door open slowly, and I could just barely see him as he stepped out and walked toward the bed. "Hey," he said.

"Hey," I said back.

He might've snuck in three or four times before that, and we never did much except whisper to each other and tell stories about our lives and our families. We lay down side by side on the bed together one time, and the last time he'd snuck in we'd given each other a quick pop-kiss before he left. I didn't know if he was my boyfriend or not, but I thought he might be.

Tonight we sat on my bed with our backs against the wall. Our feet hung off the side of the bed. It looked funny to see my pale white feet beside his black sneakers in the little bit of light coming in the window. He smelled good, and I knew he'd put on some of his dad's cologne, but I didn't know what the name of it was. We'd already run out of stuff to talk about, but only because he just wanted to know one thing: who the man was that I'd been talking to at the baseball field.

"His name's Wade," I finally said.

"Who is he?" Marcus asked. I took a deep breath to let him know I didn't want to answer that question; I didn't want to talk about Wade at all. "You don't have to tell me," he said. "I just thought it was weird."

We were quiet for a second, and then Marcus's hand slid across the bed. When I turned my hand over he put his fingers through mine. We just sat there holding hands, neither one of us saying a word.

"He's my dad," I finally said. I waited, already knowing what he was going to say.

"You told me you didn't have a dad," he said.

I looked over at him. "Maybe I said that just because I don't want the one I got."

"What does he do?"

"Who knows," I said. "He used to be a pitcher a long time ago."

"Really?" Marcus asked. His voice sounded excited. "Who'd he play for?"

"The Gastonia Rangers," I said, "and a couple of other teams you've probably never heard of."

"Did he make it to the big leagues?"

"Not even close."

"Did you ever see him pitch?"

"A couple times when I was real little, but I don't really remember it." That was the truth. My clearest memory of going to a Rangers game was the last time Mom took us not long after Ruby was born. Rowdy Ranger, the mascot, was going around to all the kids in the stands and giving them high fives. He had on a white cowboy hat and a black mask over his eyes. When he saw me and Mom, he came trotting down the stairs toward us, but right as he reached out his hand to slap mine he tripped over the last step and spilled my Coke all over Ruby. She was just a little baby, and she wouldn't stop crying once she got wet. People around us started fussing, trying to give Mom napkins to dry Ruby off, but Mom took one look at Rowdy Ranger and another look at her sopping-wet baby, and she packed up all our stuff and took us right home. That was the last time I'd been to a baseball game.

"Sammy Sosa used to play for the Gastonia Rangers before he got called up to Texas," Marcus said.

"I know. My dad used to play with him."

"Wow," Marcus said.

"Yeah, and I saw Michael Jordan at the Food Lion."

"Really?" he asked, laughing.

"Of course not," I said. "I don't believe a word my dad's ever told me."

"Sosa hit another one tonight against the Giants," he said. "That's forty-nine."

"He's still two behind McGwire."

"I know," he said, "but he'll catch him."

My palm had started to sweat, and I thought about turning Marcus's hand loose, but then I felt his thumb rub mine real gently, and I decided that it felt nice no matter how sweaty my hand got.

"Do you think your dad will try to get you back?" he asked.

"He might," I said. "But I don't think he can, and I don't want to go with him if he does."

"Why not?"

"It's a long story," I said. Then I said, "He told me today that he's afraid somebody's going to adopt us soon just because we're white."

Marcus sat there and didn't say nothing, but I could tell he was thinking about what I'd said. "He's probably right, you know," he finally said. "I bet y'all would have a better chance of getting adopted because of that." We were quiet for a minute. Then Marcus whispered, "Did you tell him anything about your grandparents?"

"No," I said. "I don't want to think about that. Not yet anyway."

"I know," Marcus said. "I don't want to think about that either." He squeezed my hand, and I squeezed his back. "But what if you have to go?"

"I don't know," I said. "We don't even know them. We've never met them. It's kind of like they're not even real." I looked over at Ruby and thought about what she'd said earlier about us going to Alaska. "There ain't no way it would be a good idea for us to just show up in Alaska."

"So what's your plan?" he asked.

I leaned my head against the wall and smiled. "You really want to know?"

"Yes," he said.

I closed my eyes and told him that I'd do whatever I could to make sure that me and Ruby stayed in the home until I was eighteen because then I'd be able to adopt her and take her with me wherever we wanted to go.

"Where do you want to go?" he asked.

"College," I said. I told him that I wanted to take Ruby with me and get her in a school near the college. We'd both go to class all day, and at night I could get a job because Ruby would be old enough to stay home by herself.

"You think you can take her with you to college?" he asked. "Think she could live with you in the dorm?"

"I don't know," I said. "We could get a little place of our own so we wouldn't have to live with anybody else. Besides," I said, "I'm sick of living with other people anyway."

"My cousin Janae goes to Gaston College," he said. "She's got a little girl who's three. They have an apartment."

"Yeah," I said, "but that's just community college. That's just right down the road."

"What's wrong with that?" he asked.

"Nothing," I said. "I just want to go to a *real* college. The kind you have to pack up and leave home for."

He asked me what I wanted to go to school for, and I told him that I wanted to be a police officer because it was the easiest way to explain it. I didn't tell him that I really wanted to be in the FBI.

"I think you'd be a good cop," he said. "I wouldn't mess with you."

"You'd better not," I told him. "I'd throw the cuffs on you."

He laughed, and then he unlaced his fingers from mine and put his hand in his lap. "Can I ask you something?" he said.

"Yes."

"Why do you only talk to me when I come over here at night?"

"What do you mean?" I asked.

"You don't ever talk to me anywhere else," he said. "You won't even hardly look at me: not at school, not after school. It'll probably be the same way on Monday too."

I didn't know what to say because I hadn't thought about it before, and I didn't know how to explain myself.

"You wouldn't even let me meet your dad today," he said.

"That doesn't mean nothing," I said. "Nobody's met him. I don't hardly know him."

"But you've met *my* mom and dad," he said.

"One time," I said. "I met them one time after school, and you didn't even tell them I'm your girlfriend."

"Are you?" he asked.

"I don't know," I said. "I'm not sure."

"You wouldn't think so by how you act."

"I just don't want nobody knowing my business," I said.

"That means you just don't want them knowing about me."

"That's not what it means."

"Whatever," he said. He climbed down from the bed.

"Where you going?" I asked.

"I have to go," he said. "I've been here too long anyway." He slid the window open and put his hands on the windowsill. He stood there, bent over, looking outside like he was waiting for me to say something, but I didn't know what to say. I'd been wondering if we'd kiss again when he left, and when it looked like we wouldn't it made me realize how bad I'd wanted to. "Maybe I'll see you at school," he said. He put his foot outside and sat on the sill, and then he lifted his other foot through and slid out. I heard him drop to the ground.

CHAPTER 4

Marcus didn't come back to my window the next night or Sunday night either, and I didn't see him at school on Monday because we weren't in the same class. After school was over, he must've gone straight home because he didn't hang around and play kickball with us like he usually did. He didn't have to stay after school like me and Ruby. His mom usually got off work before he got home, and even if she didn't he was allowed to be at home by himself. Most kids my age were, but not me. None of the kids from the home could be there without Miss Crawford or one of the other workers, so we had to hang around after school until someone came to pick us up in the van.

By Friday, I was half convinced I'd never see Marcus again. I told myself that if I ever did see him I'd tell everyone I knew that he was my boyfriend: Ruby, Miss Crawford, even Wade if he ever decided to show up again.

Saturday morning, after breakfast, Ruby hung out with some of the little kids and watched cartoons in the TV room. I stayed in our room and stared at the wall with a Nancy Drew mystery, *The Case of the Disappearing Diamond,* open on my lap, trying to figure out all the things Marcus could be thinking.

I knew I wouldn't be able to concentrate enough to solve the mystery with Nancy if I was just going to sit there and think about something else while listening to the little kids laugh at cartoons a few rooms over, so I climbed off my bed and walked toward the office to ask Miss Crawford if she'd sign me on to one of the computers.

There were two computers in the study room for playing games and getting on the World Wide Web. I didn't ever have any reason to get on the Web, but I liked hearing the loud, fuzzy sound of the phone line dialing. I thought that voice saying, "you've got mail," was pretty neat, even though I'd never gotten an e-mail myself. I'd never had a reason to send one either. I liked getting on the computer for one thing only: Oregon Trail. I'd name two of the pioneers after me and Ruby and play for hours, and once the rest of them died off I'd pretend that it was just me and her in that wagon, shooting at turkeys and deer and floating across rivers on our way out West.

I walked past the computer room and peeked in to make sure one of the computers was open. A boy named Travis who was a few years younger than me was sitting at one of them. I couldn't tell what he was looking at, but he had on earphones and I could hear rap music playing from where I stood; he nodded his head to the beat.

Hopefully somebody wouldn't claim that other computer before I could get back, and I walked down the hall to the office; it was through a door just off the kitchen.

When I got closer I could hear a man's voice, and I stopped in the kitchen and listened at the door. Miss Crawford was talking too, and she was being stern with somebody. Her voice sounded just like she looked: skinny and tough. She was old and had gray hair, but all of us knew she meant business, and nobody messed with her.

"Listen," she said, "I ain't the person you need to be talking to." A file cabinet slid open, and I heard her take something out and slide the drawer closed.

"But they're my kids," the man's voice said. I recognized it immediately; it was Wade. He sounded nervous and scared, completely different from how he'd acted when we'd seen him at the baseball field the week before.

"Not in the eyes of the court they ain't," Miss Crawford said. "Not legally. Their files say you gave them up in 1996, and you don't get them back just because their mama died. You can't just show up after school like you did or come over here on a Saturday morning and try to see them."

"But when I signed that paper they said there was some kind of provision that gave me visitation rights. I remember that. I remember that from when I signed it."

"There might've been," Miss Crawford said. "That's something you're going to have to ask the judge about. Or you can contact their guardian ad litem, Brady Weller. Here's his card."

When I heard Brady Weller's name I immediately pictured him. Me and Ruby had met him a couple times. The first time was the morning we woke up in the home after we'd moved in the night before. He was waiting for us in the living room with Miss Crawford. She told us who he was, and then she led us to the dining room table and left us alone. Brady was tall with short blond hair and bright blue eyes. He was older than Mom, but as soon as I saw him I couldn't help but wish that she'd been friends with guys like Brady Weller instead of Calico. He set a couple of folders on the table in front of him, but he didn't open them. I think he would've smiled at us if we'd been anybody else, but he seemed to know we probably wouldn't feel like smiling back. "How do y'all like your new room?" he asked, leaning forward and putting his hands on the table.

Me and Ruby just sat there staring at the table. But then she looked up at me, and then she looked at Brady. "Our mom's dead," she finally said. Her eyes started filling up with tears.

Brady reached out and put his hand on her shoulder. "I know," he said. "And I was awfully sorry to hear that. But this is a good place to be. Miss Crawford's really nice, and she's really excited about y'all being here. And I'm going to be with you every step of the way."

Wade had gotten quiet on the other side of the door, and he must've been looking down at Brady's card.

"Why do I even have to call anybody?" he asked. "They're my kids."

"I know that, Mr. Chesterfield," Miss Crawford said. "But there's just nothing else I can do for you."

I imagined Wade staring at Miss Crawford with a look in his eyes that begged her to do anything she could do to help him. She must've seen the look I had in mind, because she said, "I'm sorry, Mr. Chesterfield, but this is just the way things have to be."

"I get it," he finally said. "But I don't have a lot of time on my hands."

"I understand," she said.

"So just let me see them today," he said. "I'm not asking for much. Just a few minutes. That's all."

Miss Crawford interrupted him. "I'm sorry, but I just can't do that. I probably shouldn't tell you what I'm about to tell you, but I want you to understand this situation. We've been in contact with the girls' grandparents in Alaska, and they're working really hard to adopt these girls, and so far they've done everything right, everything the court's asked of them."

"Well, that's just great," Wade said. "You need to know that those people haven't ever laid eyes on these girls, not once in their whole lives. But me, I'm *here*. I want them. They're *my* girls."

"I understand," Miss Crawford said. "But that's not how the law works."

"I know how the law works," Wade said. "And I know it never works for people like me." He was quiet for a second, and then his voice came out in a whisper. "Are you going to send my girls to Alaska?"

"I don't know. Maybe, but I can't say for sure. I ain't in no kind of position to make any promises."

I heard the floor creak as Wade walked toward the door that led out to the porch. I heard him put his hand on the knob and turn it, and then I heard the sound the door made when he opened it. But then I knew that he was just standing there because I didn't hear it close.

"I want you to know that I was tricked into signing that paper," he said. "I never would've signed it if I'd known I was giving them up."

"I understand," Miss Crawford said. "And I—" But Wade shut the door and she didn't say nothing else.

I didn't knock on the office door to ask Miss Crawford to sign me on to the computer because I didn't feel like playing Oregon Trail anymore. I didn't feel like doing much of anything right then except being alone. I crept across the kitchen and walked down the hallway, past the computer room with that empty computer, back to our bedroom. I closed the door behind me and sat on the edge of the bed and just looked around at the few things we had in there that we could call our own: the light pink bedspreads covering mattresses that sat up off the floor like beds are supposed to; a closetful of clothes; the board games and books stacked up beneath the table between our beds. I tried to imagine those things far away from here in some bedroom in Alaska, where Mom had told us it snowed so much that it piled up against the windows, where there wasn't no sun for almost half the year and it was always dark just like the nighttime. It was impossible to picture me and Ruby and any of our things in a place like that.

I knew exactly which piece of paper Wade was talking about signing. I'd found it in Mom's room after we'd all come home from the courthouse; it was the last time I'd seen Wade. Mom had made me and Ruby go to court with her, even though I was only nine years old and Ruby wasn't nothing but four. I remember her saying, "I want you both to see what your daddy's willing to do if you ask him nice enough."

Wade was waiting on us when we got to the courtroom. His eyes were swollen and red. He rocked back and forth on his feet, and finally he just sat down in a chair and waited for things to get started. Me and Ruby sat with Mom. She wouldn't let us go over and say nothing to Wade, even though he kept looking over at us and sniffing real loud like he was trying to get us to look at him. We hadn't seen him in a while, and Mom acted like she didn't even see him now. He'd tried to dress up and look nice by wearing a button-down shirt, but it still had the crease marks where it had been folded at the store; it looked like he'd just unwrapped it and put it right on.

I can't quite remember what happened next, and I can't quite remember what the judge said, but I do remember watching Mom and Wade go up to where the judge sat. Mom walked right up there like she couldn't wait to hear what he had to say, but Wade just shuffled his feet and moved so slow that I thought he might not ever make it. The three of them whispered back and forth, and every now and then Wade would turn his head and look over at me and Ruby to try to get our attention. I watched him rock back on his heels, and a couple of times he rocked too far and had to grab on to something to keep from falling over.

But one thing I do remember is watching them sign that piece of paper, and I remember watching as they gave Mom a copy of it. As soon as she got that piece of paper in her hands it was over; we were out the door and walking back down the street away from the courthouse and away from downtown. She didn't tell Wade "bye" or give the judge a "thank-you" or nothing—just gone. Me and Ruby couldn't hardly keep up with her. She put that piece of paper in her pocketbook and took me and Ruby by the hand. "It's just us now," she said. "All we've got to worry about is ourselves—ourselves and nobody else."

When we got home, Mom took that piece of paper into her room and shut the door. A few minutes later I heard her crying.

That night, while she was in the kitchen getting Ruby something to eat, I snuck into her bedroom and found the paper folded up on her bedside table. I picked it up and read all that I could. Across the top, it said *Termination of Parental Rights*. Farther down it said, *In signing this document, I, Wade Chesterfield, hereby relinquish my parental rights to Easter Renee Quillby and Ruby Justice Quillby, both minors . . . Relinquish:* I had no idea what that word meant, but I saw where Mom had signed, and I recognized Wade's signature right by hers. I folded up that piece of paper and left it exactly where I'd found it, and I snuck out of Mom's room and went into our bedroom. My spelling book was in my backpack, and I got it out and flipped to the back where there was a dictionary that we used to look up our vocabulary words. I found it. *Relinquish: to give up; leave; abandon.* That sounded just about right to me.

That night, after Mom had gone to bed and Ruby was asleep, I crept down the hallway to find the one thing Wade had left behind in our house. I opened the closet by the front door just as quiet as I could, and I picked up the bag and slung it over my shoulder and carried it into the bathroom. I closed the door behind me and flipped on the light, and then I looked under the sink and found a bottle of nail-polish remover and a bunch of cotton balls. I sat on the floor with my back against the tub, opened up that bag, and, one by one, took out all those old baseballs that Wade had signed back when he thought he was going to be famous, and I used Mom's nail-polish remover and tried my hardest to take his name off every single one.

Pruitt

CHAPTER 5

The old man taught me how to hit a fastball by setting an empty bottle of Michelob Light on top of a T-ball tee he'd picked up at a yard sale. He tossed me the safety glasses he wore in his shop, and then he stepped back and took a swig from a fresh beer, nodded toward the empty bottle, and said, "Go on and hit it."

The sound of an aluminum bat busting a glass bottle is just about the best thing a six-year-old can hear. The old man stood far enough away so the glass couldn't reach him, and he laughed every time one of those bottles busted, and then he'd open another beer and drain it just so he could set it up on the tee. Beer gleamed on the bat, and my arms and shirt were damp.

After we'd gone through a six-pack he walked into the carport and got another one out of the dirty white refrigerator by the steps. He twisted the top off another beer and set the six-pack down on the hood of the car. "Could you feel that glass on you?" he asked.

When I looked down at my wet arms I saw that it wasn't just the beer that had been sprinkling my skin; little bits of glass had been mixed in too. "Yes."

"Good," he said before knocking back the rest of his beer. He walked across the yard with his open hand out in front of him. "Go on and take them glasses off." He took the glasses from my face, and then he folded them and dropped them into the breast pocket on his union suit. He balanced his empty beer on the tee and stepped back. "Hit it," he said. He crossed his arms and waited. "Hit it," he said again.

"Will you give me back them—" but his hands were on me before the words had left my mouth. My hands tried to drop the bat, but he closed his fingers around mine and gripped it tighter. "Hit it, sissy," he said. He raised my hands so the bat was over my right shoulder. My nose sniffed back a sob and my eyes narrowed to keep the tears from running down my cheeks. He slapped me on the back of the head.

"Crying ain't going to get you these damn glasses back," he said. "Now hit it!" He turned and walked back to the carport and opened another beer and lit a cigarette. My stance was open toward him like he was playing first base, and his eyes were on me like he was waiting to see where the ball would go.

The bat came off my shoulder and swung toward the bottle, but at the last second my face turned away, and the front of the bat clipped the tee and knocked the bottle off into the grass. The old man slammed his beer on top of the hood and stormed across the yard.

When he reached me he bent down eye level. "Why'd you turn your head?" he asked. "You're supposed to keep your eyes"—he left the cigarette burning in the corner of his mouth and plopped his huge hand down on my head and turned it toward the tee—"in line with your shoulders." He swung my shoulders around so they squared with where home plate would've been.

"Okay."

"Okay, what?"

"My head won't turn."

"Bullshit, it won't," he said. He took the cigarette out of his mouth and blew smoke in my face.

"What if that glass gets in my eyes?"

He put a finger under my chin and turned my face so that he looked right at me. "Then close them," he said. "That bottle's there whether you can see it or not."

Another six-pack had been busted off the tee before the screen door on the porch slammed shut behind me. My mother sat on the sofa in the living room, folding laundry and watching soap operas with the sound turned all the way down. "What was all that noise out there?" she asked. She looked up and saw me and dropped whatever she'd been folding. "What in the world did you do?" She jumped up off the sofa and took my hand and pulled me down the hallway toward the bathroom.

She sat me up on the counter and used peroxide and cotton balls to clean the blood while my eyes stared at her in the mirror before they closed to picture those bottles exploding. Even with my eyes closed my body could sense every move her hands made, every time she'd stop and reach for the peroxide, each part of my face or my arms those wet cotton balls were about to touch. When my eyes opened again, the streaks of blood were gone and the counter was covered in pink cotton.

My mother looked at me in the mirror like she was studying my face to make sure she'd gotten all the blood off. She sighed. "I swear," she said. "Sometimes I think your daddy does meanness just for meanness's sake."

But what she'd said wasn't true—not all of it anyway. My father was trying to teach me something valuable about baseball, maybe even something valuable about life itself, and that is this: anything you want to do well you'd better be able to do with your eyes closed.

The old man's lesson has stayed in my mind, and it was still there as my eyes opened slowly into the darkness of another Saturday night at Tomcat's; I scanned the near-empty room from the last seat at the far end of the bar: two middle-aged men with wedding rings on sitting at one table, watching as a tanning-bed blonde—too old to be moving how she was moving on the dance floor—made eye contact and tried to squeeze them for another drink; three local boys from either Belmont or Stanley knocking back Budweisers and screaming at the television where the highlights of the Carolina Panthers' final preseason game played on the TVs over the bar; Guns N' Roses' "Sweet Child o' Mine" blasting from the speakers in the ceiling. It was a pretty regular Saturday night.

Different story in the Boss's office.

He'd come in a few minutes before eleven with his two cousins, Rick and Eddie, and gone straight back to the office and slammed the door, but not before Eddie stopped by the bar and picked up a couple of Bud Lights and a Dewar's on the rocks.

For the next couple of hours the Boss could be heard from his office during the breaks between songs, even though his door was closed, even though the bar hummed with people's voices and the sound from the TVs. Somebody'd been banging something against the inside of the office door; earlier it sounded like a file cabinet had been overturned. Every now and then a "shit" or a "bastard" came from that end of the hallway. He'd never acted like this during my two-month stint at the door.

A shaft of light from the office shot down the hallway before disappearing. Rick walked toward the bar; even in the near dark of the club his forehead looked to be sweating and his face seemed pale. He picked up a cocktail napkin from the bar and took off his glasses and wiped his face. My nose caught a whiff; what had looked like sweat was actually whiskey.

He caught me staring at him. "How in the hell can you see with those sunglasses on?" he asked. He balled up the cocktail napkin and tossed it on the bar.

"What's up with all the noise back there?"

"That's the sound of the shit hitting the fan," he said.

"Something happen?"

"Yeah," he said. "You could say that. You could definitely say that." He picked up another napkin and wiped his face. "Why are you asking?"

"It gets boring out here."

"Lucky you," he said. He sighed, and then he took his glasses off and rubbed his eyes. He put them back on and looked up at the television. "Somebody stole something from the Boss," he finally said. "Something they definitely shouldn't have stolen."

"What was it?"

The television reflected in Rick's glasses: a preview of McGwire's Sunday game against the Braves. Rick stood frozen, staring up at the screen. "You played baseball, didn't you, Pruitt?"

"Yes."

"Does the name Wade Chesterfield ring a bell?"

"Maybe." The skin tickled around my nostrils. A wipe at my nose left a faint smear of blood across the back of my hand.

"If you know where to find Chesterfield, then you should tell the Boss." Rick nodded toward the office. "The Boss might want you to 'talk' to him." He used his fingers to make quotation marks in the air. "Know what I mean?" He stepped back and looked at me. "Seriously," he said, nodding toward the office again. "Go talk to him."

Rick opened the door and walked into the parking lot. The floodlights showed rain dotting the windshields on the cars parked out front. On the other side of the bar the Boss's office sat at the end of the hallway it shared with the restrooms. The strip of light beneath the door vibrated like something was being thrown against it.

No one answered after the first knock. After the second knock the Boss's voice boomed from inside. "What?!" he screamed.

"It's Pruitt."

"Now ain't the time," he said. "Ask Ducky at the bar to take care of it. He's not doing anything."

"This ain't about the club. It's about Wade Chesterfield." A second later the lock popped on the door and fluorescent light spilled into the hallway.

"Well, come on in," the Boss's voice said.

The office light was near blinding after the darkness of the club. To the right of the door, a file cabinet leaned at an angle against the wall, the drawers hanging open, files scattered on the floor below. The desk near the back wall had been cleared, and papers and broken picture frames covered the floor on either side of it. The Boss sat at his desk like nothing had happened, his boots—fancy embroidered cowboy boots the color of stained red cherry—were up on his desk and crossed at the ankles. His black hair and goatee were so dark it was obvious he dyed both. His cousin Eddie sat in a folding chair, leaning up against the wall, his arms across his chest, a fresh hole the size of the Boss's fist in the paneling behind his head. Eddie lifted a hand and pushed his cowlick down on his forehead. Then he combed his fingers through his thin mustache.

"What's up, Pruitt?" the Boss asked.

"Heard you're looking for Wade Chesterfield."

"You know where he is?" He pointed to Eddie. "Because my asshole cousin has been looking for him since yesterday, and guess what?" He turned up his palms and shrugged his shoulders. "Nothing," he said. "So, what can you do?"

"Find him."

"Do you know him?" Eddie asked. The room grew quiet.

"Do you know him?" the Boss repeated. Eddie's smile caught the corner of my eye.

"From the minors, back in the day."

"Was that before . . . ?" The Boss pointed to his eye and let his voice trail off.

"Yes. Before that."

"Is that why you wear sunglasses all the time?" Eddie asked.

My focus stayed on the Boss. "You're not going to find anyone more willing to kill Wade Chesterfield."

"Is that right?" the Boss asked. He smiled and looked over at

Eddie and nodded like he agreed. "Then why haven't you killed him? It would've saved me a lot of trouble."

"You're the first that's been willing to pay for it."

The Boss stared for a second, and then he started laughing. He dropped his feet off his desk and fell forward in his chair and put his hands on his knees. "Are you serious?" he asked. He waited for me to respond, tears in his eyes, then he busted out laughing again, harder than he had before. "He *is* serious," he said. Eddie snickered from his chair against the wall.

The Boss laughed himself hoarse, and then he wiped his eyes and sat up straight in his chair. He took a tissue from a box on his desk and blew his nose. "Jesus," he said, out of breath. "It's been a shitty day. I didn't know how bad I needed that."

"There's nothing to laugh at."

"There's nothing to laugh at," the Boss repeated in a whisper. "Well, I disagree, Pruitt. Your old buddy stole a lot of money from me, and I happen to want it back. What you said is funny because the idea that I'd pay you to do something I can do myself is about the most hilarious thing I've ever heard." He started arranging things on his desk like the conversation was over.

"If you could do it then you would've done it already."

"Good night, Pruitt," he said. "Close the door on your way out."

"Twenty-five thousand to find him. Another twenty-five and he'll disappear forever. He'll be found and killed one way or another; the only difference is that right now you can decide whether or not you'll get your money back."

The Boss leaned back in his chair and smiled. "Well, well, well," he said. "You want to play hit man."

"It's not a game."

"You're right," he said. "It's blackmail. But I'll tell you what, Pruitt. Here's what I'll do: five thousand up front, five thousand *if* you find him, and then five thousand if I get my money back. Another five thousand if he disappears for good. Deal?"

"Twenty-five thousand up front. He'll disappear for fifty. Just like before."

"No way," the Boss said. "No way. I don't have that kind of money just lying around." My hand reached for the doorknob. "Hold on," he said, his eyes closed like he was deep in thought. "Five thousand up front, ten thousand if you find him, and then ten thousand if I get all my money back. Twenty-five thousand if he disappears after that." He opened his eyes. "That's it, Pruitt. Take it or leave it."

I took it.

"You got ten days," he said. "Ten days, and then I'm bringing you back in."

"The take."

"What about it?"

"How much did he get?"

"Enough," the Boss said. He pointed at me. "And you'd better bring back every damn cent of it."

"You don't have any idea how much he took, do you? If you did, you'd tell me."

The Boss leaned back in his seat and stared at Eddie, and then he looked back at me. "Don't push me, Pruitt," he said. "Do not push me."

He picked up a pen and scribbled something down on a pad and tore off the sheet. He handed it across the desk; the name Lane Kelly and an address and phone number were written on it. "This guy knows something," the Boss said. He nodded at Eddie. "But my asshole cousin couldn't find him either."

The Boss unlocked a drawer, pulled out stacks of bound twenties, dropped several into a plastic Food Lion grocery bag, and held it out to Eddie. Eddie jumped up from his chair and walked to the Boss's desk and took it, and then he carried it across the office, refusing to make eye contact until he'd sat down.

I opened the door and the light behind me fell into the dark hallway. Music from the club filled the office. The Boss's voice stopped me from leaving. "So what do you have against Wade Chesterfield?"

My face turned toward him. "Why?"

"It just seems like you want to find him more than I do."

"He stole something from me too."

"Really," the Boss said. "And what would that be?"

I took my hand off the doorknob and lifted my sunglasses. The Boss's smile fell when he saw what was beneath them. "Everything."

The house lights came up at 2 A.M., and the place was cleared by 2:30. My truck sat by the Dumpster in the back corner of the lot, out of the reach of any lights. Movement behind the Dumpster caught my eye. A swift kick flushed them out: the tanning-bed blonde and one of the guys who'd been watching her dance scrambled like rats across the parking lot, the woman laughing, yelling, "Sorry, Pruitt," over her shoulder, the man trying to outrun her like they hadn't been together. They disappeared around the front of the building where a few cars were still parked.

One click of the remote and my truck unlocked, another click and the headlights and the roof lights came on. The plastic grocery bag bounced onto the floorboard after hitting the passenger's seat. The truck's V-8 rumbled itself to life.

It took half a trip around the parking lot to find Eddie's new sil-ver Camaro, the same car he usually drove the Boss to work in. He'd backed it in and double-parked it beneath a light on Wilkinson Bou-levard on the Charlotte side of the lot. I stopped the truck about ten feet in front of the Camaro's bumper, my lights illuminating every drop of rain on the car's waxed surface. Two black thirty-four-inch Pro Stock Louisville Sluggers rested in the gun rack in the truck's back window.

At first, it was only Eddie's face in my mind: his skinny mus-tache, his redneck haircut, the little gold hoop piercing the carti-lage on the top outer edge of his left ear. But then his face blurred into Wade Chesterfield's, the way he'd looked ten years ago. The

Camaro's headlights became eye sockets, the taillights too, and when they busted and the glass and plastic fell to the asphalt, there was the sense of a fading bright light, the world turning black, the feel of something lost forever.

The house sat alone in a dark, wooded cul-de-sac, no lights on inside, the sun coming up through the trees behind it. The .45mm Glock that had been hidden under my front seat was sitting on the dash, my batting gloves lying beside it, the slip of paper the Boss had given me a few hours earlier with Lane Kelly's name and address on it still in my hand.

Once I was outside the truck there were no sounds except for the engine cooling and the birds waking up in the trees around the house. My eyes darted from window to window looking for the slightest movement in the blinds, shadows on the other side of the glass. The house seemed empty.

A detached garage sat at the end of the driveway, the glass panes on its door covered on the inside with a curtain.

Dense woods bordered the backyard, and with my truck parked down the street and out of sight I thought of hiding there, listening to the birds and waiting for someone to come home. But instead my hands slipped on the batting gloves and tried the knob on the back door. It was unlocked, but the dead bolt wasn't.

The first kick shook the house and rattled the windows. The second busted the dead bolt through the frame, and the door swung open and slammed against the wall inside.

Slowly, gun raised, I cleared the rooms one by one—lights were turned on and off, closets and bedroom doors were opened and closed. No one was home. Framed photographs ran the length of the hallway, and my eyes went from picture to picture looking for Wade Chesterfield's face in the dim light coming through the living room windows at the other end. A particular man and woman appeared in just about every picture. I chose the photo that showed their faces the most clearly and lifted it from the wall and carried it into the kitchen.

After the frame had been removed and the picture folded and slipped into the cargo pocket of my shorts, all the kitchen drawers were opened one by one until keys were found—some of them loose, some of them on rings in twos and threes.

The fourth or fifth key unlocked the garage door. It was dark inside and my hand felt around on the wall until it found a light switch. The garage was full of power tools—a table saw, nail guns, air compressors—and a single car: a silver two-door Honda Civic. It was a woman's car with a lipstick-smeared coffee cup in one of the cup holders, CD cases, including Celine Dion's latest, scattered on the passenger's seat.

Lane Kelly's car was missing.

CHAPTER 6

Euphrates Evans was still in the same trailer park down by the South Carolina state line, sitting outside the same trailer he'd been living in for at least ten years. He didn't turn around when my truck came to a stop in the gravel drive fifteen feet behind him, didn't give any sign that he heard footsteps coming toward him. Late forties and still thick in the arms and shoulders, and, except for a little gray hair, no different than he'd ever been. A television sat on a small table in front of him; it was plugged in to a bright orange extension cord that snaked through the grass and up through a cracked window in the trailer. A black cord for the cable ran alongside the orange one. On the television, the Cubs/Rockies game was in the first inning. When my shadow fell across him, Phrate looked up like he'd been waiting on me all morning. He wore a thin red tie and a short-sleeved shirt that was too tight, tucked into a pair of gray slacks: church clothes.

"Well I'll be damned, Pruitt," he said. He stood up slowly, his face wrinkling in pain as he straightened his back. While shaking hands, he nodded toward my truck. "I thought I heard somebody's redneck-ass truck pull up in my driveway."

He shuffled over and picked up a closed folding chair that was leaning against the trailer. He opened it and set it down beside his. "Have a seat," he said. He put his hands on his chair's armrests and slowly lowered himself. "So," he said. "It's been a while."

"Over four years."

"When'd you get out?" he asked.

"February."

"Right in time for spring training," he said, smiling.

"Yeah. Right in time."

"You working?" he asked.

"Over at a bar called Tomcat's on Wilkinson. Weren't a lot of other options."

"Well, it's nice to see you on the outside, man. You look good, stronger than hell." He flexed his biceps. "You still at it?"

"Still at it."

"What you on?"

"Deca. Testosterone. That's about it."

He turned and looked at the television. "Not me, man. Not anymore."

My eyes took in the shirt and tie he was wearing. "You been at work?"

He leaned back in his chair and crossed his legs, and then he straightened his tie.

"Hell no," he said. "I'm at church." He smiled and pointed to the television, where the Cubs were at bat in the top of the first in Colorado. "At least my mother thinks I am." He turned around and looked at the trailer where the cords snaked through the cracked window. "She's inside, asleep, lying up in a hospital bed with lung cancer, hooked up to oxygen." My mind pictured a shriveled, old black woman with Phrate's face, her eyes closed, tubes running into her nose and both her arms. "She can't leave the house," he said, "but she sure as hell wants to know where I'm at all the time. 'My way or the highway,' she says." He laughed. "On Sunday mornings, I'm . . . in . . . *church*."

"It's almost three P.M."

Phrate smiled. "You ain't ever been to church with black folks, have you? If you want to go I bet every one of them in town is still meeting." He looked at his wristwatch. "Probably ain't even got to the sermon yet."

In Denver, Sosa hit one out against Kile. The announcers went crazy; so did the fans. Phrate clapped his hands. "All right!" he said. "Ol' Sammy—that's fifty-four. That white boy better look out; Sammy's getting hot." He reached into his breast pocket for a pack of cigarettes. He shook one out and picked up a lighter off the table. "You know I played with him, right?"

"Yes; 'eighty-seven, 'eighty-eight."

"That's right," he said. He lit his cigarette. "And you were with the—"

"Grasshoppers."

"Okay," he said. "I remember now." He smiled and looked back at the television. "You were something, Pruitt: those quick hands, that nice swing." He stopped talking and looked over like he was seeing my arms and the rest of my body for the first time. "But now," he said, "you should be crushing it with Sammy and McGwire."

"Wade Chesterfield was on that team with you and Sosa."

"Yep. He was. I played with Wade for a couple years with the Rangers before he—you know." He stopped talking and acted like he was taking a drink out of a bottle. He looked at me again. "Why?"

My eyes were on the television, but Phrate's eyes were on me. "Ever see him around?"

"Pruitt, come on, man," he said, "you got to let that go. That was, what, ten years ago? You're not one of those dudes who's on some kind of trip like you see in the movies, are you? Guy gets out of jail and then spends the rest of his life getting even with everybody who screwed him before he went in."

"Why? You worried about why I'm here to see you?"

"Shit," he said. He ran both his hands down the length of his thighs and sunk lower in his seat. He took a drag from his cigarette and exhaled through his nose. "Man, what did you want me to do? Roll up in the front office, turn myself in to the cops because I let you juice my players every now and then? Come on, man. You know it don't work like that."

"How does it work, Phrate?"

"It's a calculated risk, man, and you got hit. The Knights hired you to weight-train the team, not to inject those kids with all kinds of shit. But they knew what was going on, and it's messed up, but that don't mean it's somebody else's fault. It's like stepping into the batter's box. You think Wade meant to do that to you? No way. It's all calculated risk. Nobody knows what's going to happen. Wade could be a deadbeat and a bum, everybody knows that, but he wasn't no headhunter."

"This isn't about the past." The Cubs had ended the inning with a pop fly to right, and the game had gone to commercial.

"Then why are you here?" he asked.

"Just need to know if you've seen him."

"I haven't seen you in years and years, and suddenly you show up asking questions about Wade Chesterfield because you want to know if I've seen him?"

"That's right."

"I ain't stupid, Pruitt," he said.

"Well, then this is a pointless conversation, isn't it?"

Phrate sat there staring at the television until the commercials were over and the game was back on. The camera followed Sosa as he trotted out to right field to begin the inning. Phrate looked over at me. "You still got your bag of tricks?"

"Maybe. Why?"

"Because I might be a whole lot more interested in talking about ol' Wade if you do."

"What do you have in mind?"

"I don't know," he said. "Vicodin, Oxy, Flexeril—anything that might take the edge off."

"Might be some Dilaudid in the truck."

"A dose of that, and I'll tell you everything I know."

Phrate said he hadn't seen Wade Chesterfield in a couple years, but the last he'd heard he'd gone clean, gotten a good job. "I think that girl he was with had a couple of kids," he said. "But Wade wasn't no kind of daddy to them."

"Boys or girls?"

"Girls," he said. "One of them was named something like Sunday or Wednesday or a holiday or something. Might've been Easter."

"Easter?"

"Yeah," he said. "It was Easter. It was definitely Easter."

"What about the other one?"

"I don't know," he said. "But I heard their mama OD'd on something a few months ago."

"Who told you that?"

"We're just talking about Wade here, man."

"Anything else?"

"His real name ain't Chesterfield," he said, smiling. "It's Chessman."

"Why'd he change it?

"Come on, man," Phrate said, laughing. "Why do you think he changed it? You ever hear of a Jew ballplayer?"

"Hank Greenberg, Sandy Koufax, Erskine Mayer."

"Well, maybe Wade wasn't a fan of them."

"Any other family in the area?"

"Not that I know of." He was quiet for a minute, like he'd said everything he'd ever known about Wade Chesterfield. Then he raised his eyebrows. "So, back to our deal."

My doctor's kit was hidden under a gym bag in the floorboard behind the passenger's seat of the truck. Phrate's eyes lit up when he saw me carrying it back to the table.

"Where do you want to do this?"

"Hell, man," he said. "Right here's fine. It don't matter." The trailer to my right had its blinds closed tight, and there was no car parked in front of it.

Syringes and multidose vials lined the inside of the kit. I slipped on my batting gloves before popping the cap off a syringe and plunging the needle into a vial and drawing out 10 ccs.

"Your gloves sterile?" Phrate asked. His laugh sounded nervous.

"They're sterile enough."

Phrate put his cigarette between his lips and stood up and untucked his shirt. Then he undid his belt and dropped his pants a few inches and turned around. The needle sunk into the fatty upper muscle of his right glute just like it had a thousand times before. He winced a little when it went in. "That brings back memories," he said, his eyes already turning glassy. As soon as the needle was out he lowered himself down into his chair, the cigarette still burning between his lips. "Damn," he said. "I wasn't expecting to feel it so—" The muscles in his face relaxed and the cigarette fell from his mouth and landed in his lap. "Damn," he whispered. My gloved hand picked up the cigarette and put it out in the ashtray. Phrate's eyes closed and his head lolled back, his body already limp in the chair.

Easter Quillby

CHAPTER 7

I'd spent Sunday afternoon sitting on the floor in the TV room, watching the Cubs play the Rockies and making a card for Marcus. After Sammy had hit number fifty-four in the first inning, I'd drawn a picture of him waiting on a pitch on the front of Marcus's card, and I'd put a little 54 up in the corner of the picture, and then I'd drawn a little heart around it and used Magic Markers to color it all in. I'd never thought of myself as much of an artist, but that picture surprised me by how good it looked; part of me hated to give it away, but I hoped Marcus would like it. On the inside of the card I'd written, *I'm sorry. Can we talk tonight?* and I'd signed it *Love, Easter, your girlfriend (I hope!).* McGwire hit number fifty-five that night against the Braves, but he did it late in the seventh inning, and I'd already gone to bed.

On Monday morning, just before we left for school, I'd taped up the card inside an envelope and given it to a boy named Damon because he was in Marcus's class.

"What is it?" he'd asked.

"It's for Marcus," I'd said. "Don't read it."

"Y'all like each other?"

"No," I'd said, but then I caught myself and remembered why Marcus had gotten mad at me in the first place. "I mean, 'I don't know.' Just give it to him—please."

I was on pins and needles all day, and it didn't help that it was my week to wipe down my class's tables after lunch in the cafeteria. They called it being a "table helper," but all you really did was fish a stinky, old rag out of a bucket of soapy brown water and wipe down the table after the class was finished eating. The kids in your class lined up against the wall and waited on you to finish, some of them just standing there staring at you. I hated to have all of them look at me while I cleaned those tables, but I hated the pukey smell the brown water left on your hands even more. When it was your turn, a copy of your school picture always hung on the bulletin board in the cafeteria, but somebody'd come along and taken mine down. I asked Mrs. Davis where it could've gone, and she just shrugged her shoulders and said she'd find another one to put back up.

But I'd forgotten all about the smell of those rags and my missing picture by the time school was over, and when Mrs. Davis took us out to the playground I couldn't think about nothing else except finding Damon. I had to wait for the kickball game to start before I could ask him anything. He was kicking second behind Selena, and I walked up to him where he stood against the fence, waiting his turn.

"Did you give Marcus my note?" I asked.

"Yeah," he said, "I told you I would, didn't I?"

"What'd he say?" I asked.

"Nothing," he said.

"Did he open it?"

"I don't know," he said. "I guess so." Selena popped it up, and it dropped just behind second. She made it to first. Damon walked toward the plate; I grabbed his arm.

"But he didn't say anything?" I asked.

"I already told you 'no,'" he said. "Stop bothering me. Dang."

There were already two down when I got thrown out at first after grounding it back to the pitcher. And then, halfway through the bottom of the inning, Selena made me leave my spot at short after I missed two pop-ups back-to-back. They put me out in right field because they said my head wasn't in the game. I told them I was fine, but I knew they were right. Still, it's embarrassing to be put out in right once you get used to playing shortstop.

I stood out there with the sun beating down against my back, knowing that nobody was going to kick it out to right field because none of them was left-footed, and even if they were they couldn't kick it this far anyway. But being out there gave me plenty of time to think, which is exactly what I needed to do. I thought about what I'd heard Miss Crawford say to Wade last Saturday morning about how she'd been talking with our grandparents and that she couldn't make any promises about whether or not we'd be moving to Alaska. And then I thought about all the questions Marcus had asked me about our grandparents, about Wade.

Damon was playing first, hunched over with his hands on his knees in the "ready" position. I prayed that he'd really given that note to Marcus. What had Marcus thought when he'd opened it? Had he liked the picture I'd drawn of Sosa? Would I hear him knock on my window later that night? I needed to talk to him bad, not just about us, but about me and Ruby and about what I'd heard Miss Crawford say. I'd even talk to him about Wade if there was anything he still wanted to know.

I'd half expected Wade to show up at the field again one day after school, but he hadn't. I looked at the fence where he'd been leaning against it, and something caught my eye: a man stood off in the woods, just staring at me. He wore black sunglasses and a black baseball hat that looked brand new. A thick gold chain hung around his neck, and he wore a black tank top too. But the thing that stood out most about him was his arms; they were huge. He walked toward the fence once he realized that I'd seen him, but he stopped before he got too close, and I knew it was because he didn't want nobody else to know he was out there.

"Come here for a second," he said. His voice was scary and high-pitched like a woman's, and it seemed like his tongue was too big for his mouth. "I need to ask you something."

I didn't move. "What?"

He didn't say anything, and I knew he was hoping that I'd walk over toward the fence. "Is your name Easter Quillby?" he finally said.

"No, that's not my name."

He looked at a piece of paper he held in his hand, and then turned it around so I could see it too; it was the picture of me that had been hanging in the cafeteria. He smiled and took off his sunglasses. His left eye was closed, and the skin around it sagged down the side of his face. "Yes it is," he said. "And your daddy's name is Wade Chesterfield."

"I ain't got a daddy," I said, staring at his eye, knowing that he'd shown it to me just so I'd be scared.

"Yes you do," he said, smiling again. "And he's in trouble."

"You'd better get away from here," I said. "I'll scream for my teacher."

"No you won't." He put his sunglasses back on and just stood there staring at me for a second, and then he turned real slow and walked off into the trees. The branches closed around him and he disappeared, and after a second I wondered if I'd seen him at all.

When the inning was over I told everybody that I didn't feel good, and I took Ruby and went up the hill to the playground and sat on the swings so we'd be near Mrs. Davis and Mrs. Hannah. I didn't say anything to them about the man I'd seen because I didn't want them sending us somewhere else before I had the chance to talk to Marcus and figure out how me and Ruby were going to keep from going to Alaska. She swung back and forth while I just sat there beside her, thinking about asking her if she'd seen anything weird: any strange people out in the woods, anything that stood out. But I didn't want to worry her, so I kept my mouth shut. I was terrified, though, and I sat in that swing and stared out over the woods, wondering where he'd gone and hoping he wouldn't come back.

It wasn't a new thing for people to come around looking for Wade. There had been plenty of times when me and Ruby were playing out in the yard and somebody's car would stop and they'd roll down the window and say, "Y'all seen your daddy?," or something like that. There had been plenty of times when I woke up in the middle of the night with headlights shining bright on the wall of our bedroom and the sound of somebody banging on the front door, screaming for Wade. Mom would get up cursing at herself and go out to the front room and yell at whoever it was that Wade wasn't home and didn't even live there anymore.

But something about this time felt different; nobody'd ever come to find us at school before, and nobody'd ever talked so quiet or stood so still when they asked about Wade. And not a single one of them had ever known my name.

That night, after dinner, most of the kids hung out in the TV room and watched the Cubs play the Reds. My bedroom door was closed, but I could hear them cheer every time Sosa came up to bat. Ruby hung out in the computer room and played Oregon Trail. She liked it just as much as I did. I didn't leave our room after dinner except to get ready for bed; I didn't feel like being around anybody because I had too much on my mind. My bed was covered in homework I hadn't finished, but I couldn't stop worrying about whether or not Marcus would come over, and I couldn't stop thinking about the man I'd seen out in the woods. His voice wouldn't leave my head.

Ruby opened the door and walked into the bedroom just as I was closing my math book after finishing some division problems that were due the next day. She kicked off her shoes and pulled down her covers.

"How'd you do?" I asked.

"Okay," she said. "I didn't make it all the way, though. And you died of cholera."

"Great," I said. I slipped my homework into my book bag, climbed off my bed, and dropped the bag by the door. "Are you sure you didn't have any homework?" I asked.

"Yep," she said.

"Well, then I guess we should get ready for bed."

We took turns brushing our teeth in the bathroom across the hall, and then we got into bed; I turned out the light on the table between us. Miss Crawford opened our door a few minutes later and told us good night. I was still hoping that Marcus would come, and I didn't plan on going to sleep, but the next thing I remember is Ruby whispering my name.

"What?" I asked.

"Wouldn't it be fun?"

"What?" I asked again.

"Going on a trip," she said. "Just me and you, just like on Oregon Trail."

"It would," I said. "Go to sleep."

But I must not have slept too soundly because my eyes popped right open when I heard him at the window. I looked over at the clock on the table; it was just a little after one in the morning. I kicked the sheets off me as quick as I could so that he wouldn't tap again and wake up Ruby. I crawled down to the end of my bed and unlocked the window and slid it open. I sat back and waited.

I heard Marcus put the toe of his shoe against the outside of the house to start climbing up, but when a pair of hands came in and grabbed on to the windowsill I realized they weren't his. The hands were white, and they had hair on the backs of them and little tufts of it above the knuckles. I knew the minute I saw them that they were man's hands, and I was too surprised and scared to do anything except watch as they helped whoever it was climb up through the window and into our bedroom. I looked over at Ruby and saw that she was awake and sitting up in bed. She had the covers pulled up around her, and she sat there and stared at those hands too.

But then the light coming in the window showed white paint on the man's hands, and when he put his shoulders through I saw the old blue Braves cap, and by the time he'd pulled his legs through I saw the old paint-flecked blue jeans and the same green T-shirt he'd had on at the baseball field a couple weeks ago. I clicked on the light on our bedside table just as he stood up straight.

"Wade!" I said. "You ain't supposed to be here!"

"Shhhhhh!" he said.

Ruby kicked the covers off her and jumped out of the bed like it was Christmas morning. "Daddy," she said.

"No!" I said. I jumped out of my bed too and tried to stop her from going to him, but she was too fast. Wade picked her up and hugged her to him.

"Hey, baby," he whispered. He squeezed her tight.

"Put her down," I said. "You're going to be in big trouble for this." I moved like I was walking toward the bedroom door. When he didn't sit Ruby down, I put my hand on the knob like I was going to open it. "You need to leave," I said, "or I'm going to holler for Miss Crawford, and she'll call the—" But he didn't let me finish.

"Y'all have to come with me," he said. He stood there holding Ruby and staring down at me. "I'm serious," he said. "You ain't even got time to pack nothing. We've got to go."

"Yeah, right," I said. I gave the knob half a turn.

"I'm serious," he said. "This ain't no joke. You can stay here alone if you're hardheaded, but I'm taking your sister."

Ruby still had her arms around Wade's neck, and I knew her well enough to know it was going to take some real convincing to get her to turn him loose.

"We ain't going to let them send us to Alaska, Wade," I said.

"This ain't about Alaska," he said.

"Then what's it about?" I asked. I let go of the doorknob and put my hands on my hips to let him know I meant business.

"I'll tell you in the car," he said. "But we need to go; I'm serious. It's not safe here."

When he said that, I pictured the man I'd seen standing off in the woods that afternoon: the smile he'd given me, his closed eye, the way his skin looked all saggy on his face. Then I looked all around our bedroom, at all the nice, new things we'd been given after we moved into the home. But then my eyes stopped on the open window Wade had just crawled through, and I pictured something else: snow piled up high enough to pour inside onto the carpet; voices I didn't know that belonged to people I'd never met coming from rooms down the hall in a house I hadn't seen before; the daytime gone as black as night outside our window.

I looked up at Wade where he held Ruby in his arms, and I don't know why, but at the time, leaving with him seemed like the best answer. At the time, it seemed like the only safe thing to do.

I jumped to the ground, and then I turned around and waited for Wade to lower Ruby down from the window. When he held her out to me, I could see that his shirt was wet with sweat around the armpits. Ruby and I were both still in our nightgowns; all he'd let us do was put on some socks and shoes. We stood back from the house and watched Wade climb out of the window and jump to the ground. Three houses down, there was a car parked on the street, and Wade took our hands and led us to it.

"Come on, come on, come on," he whispered. He walked fast, and I could tell he wanted to get as far away from that window as we could. He opened the back door on the passenger's side and me and Ruby climbed in. When I slid past Wade I caught a whiff of him, and I could tell that he hadn't had a shower in a while. He went around to the driver's side and jumped in and started the engine. The radio came on and I heard men's voices; they were talking about baseball. Wade left the headlights off and drove away from the curb. I got up on my knees and looked out the back window at the home, figuring I might be seeing it for the last time. I saw that Wade had left our bedroom window open and one of the curtains was hanging out. There was a little bit of light shining from the window where I'd left the lamp on by the bed.

And then, just as I was about to turn around, I saw something move in the bushes just to the right of the window, and as we went around the curve I saw Marcus step out of the shadows and into the yard. He was pretty far away, and I couldn't tell for sure, but it looked like he was holding the card I'd made for him. I knew that he'd been there the whole time, and I knew that he'd seen us leave with Wade. I wanted to raise my hand and wave, but by the time I did we'd already gone around the curve, and he was too far away to have seen it anyway. I sat down and put my seat belt on, and then I looked over to make sure Ruby had hers on too.

Up in the front seat, Wade clapped his hands, and then he stopped at the stop sign at the end of the street and reached out and turned the radio down. "All right," he said. He turned around and looked at us. His face was sweating, and his hat was dark blue where the sweat had soaked through it. He was pale, and for the first time I saw that he looked scared, but he still tried to smile at us anyway. "Did y'all hear that?" he asked. Even his voice sounded scared. He pointed to the radio. "Sammy got another one tonight; that's fifty-five." He stared at us for a second longer, and then he turned around and drove out of the neighborhood. I saw his eyes look into the rearview mirror like he thought somebody might be following us. "Fifty-five," he said. "It's all tied up."

Brady Weller

CHAPTER 8

The first child I was ever assigned was a newborn baby boy named Stephen. His mama had just come home from the hospital when her boyfriend showed up at the house and shot her twice as she was trying to run out the back door. He went back inside and set the place on fire. And then he shot himself out in the front yard. Maybe he never knew his son was in a crib back in the bedroom. If he did, he sure didn't do nothing about it.

Almost the entire house burned down around that one bedroom before the fire department got there to put it out. But that little boy survived without a scratch on him.

People on the scene said it was some kind of miracle, especially after they found out how that fire had come to be started and what all had taken place that day.

Now, you tell me a child who survives something like that isn't going to do something great with his life. Or mine. That little boy's now living with his adopted family over in Belmont, about ten miles from the place where he should've died. He'll start the first grade this year. There's a little bit of happiness out there in this world, and sometimes these kids are lucky enough to find it.

Some folks find their way to being a guardian ad litem because they feel moved to help kids and families that can't help themselves, but not me; that's not how I got here. I found my way here by trying to undo something that can never be undone, and that will to undo it is probably why I've lasted as long as I have. Six years is a long time to watch families being torn apart, parents leaving their kids behind, babies without names being born into this world already addicted to the same things that got their mamas and daddies in trouble in the first place.

But I didn't always see people as so worthy of being helped, and I certainly didn't see myself as worthy of helping them. I never would've found my way to this place in my life if Judge Shelburne hadn't called me into his chambers a week after my trial had ended. I'd been a police officer and then a detective for almost twenty years, and it was the first time a judge had ever asked to speak with me. I'd just tossed a cigarette butt onto the sidewalk and stubbed it out with my shoe when I saw the judge swing a long black Town Car into a reserved spot across the street from the courthouse. I stood there waiting for him, but he didn't look at me as he crossed the street slowly, cane in hand, not even giving a nod when he passed me on his way inside the courthouse. "Eight minutes, Weller," he'd said over his shoulder. "Plenty of time to smoke another one if you need to."

After going through security where only one of the guards acknowledged me while the other one just stood there with his eyes lowered, I slipped my car keys and loose change back into my pockets and took the elevator up to the third floor. Judge Shelburne's secretary met me in the office and led me into his chambers; it was just like I'd thought it would be: tall bookcases lined with books, a big oak desk, the judge sitting behind it in suspenders, his sports coat hanging from the same rack that held his robe. He nodded to one of the chairs on the other side of the desk, and I took a seat.

It was quiet while the judge fished a cigar out of a box on his desk and clipped off the end. He stared at me through the flame, its light reflecting in his dark eyes. "You look like shit, Detective," he finally said. He took a puff and leaned back in his chair and crossed his legs.

"I'm not a detective anymore."

"The hell you're not," he said. "You don't stop being what you are just because some bastards raise hay until you quit. You think I'll stop being a judge just because a couple jackasses want me to retire? If so, then you'd better think again." He smiled and leaned forward, the sunlight through the window behind him glinting off his bald head. "They'd better think again too. I'll stay as long as the people of Gaston County want me to stay. You should keep that in mind because you're a damn good detective, and you've got a lot of friends in this community, especially from where I'm sitting." He opened the cigar case and turned it to face me. My hand reached out, but I hesitated before picking one up. "These here won't give you cancer as fast as those cigarettes, but at least you won't feel like you're sitting here wasting your time listening to me."

He handed me the cutter across the desk, and I reached into my pocket for my lighter. "Why am I sitting here?"

"Because it's time somebody talked some damn sense into your head," he said. "And it looks like nobody else is willing to do it. So here you are. With me."

I looked at him and took a puff off my cigar, and then I picked a piece of tobacco off my tongue.

"You've been off the job for six months," he said. "What have you been doing?"

"Giving money to lawyers," I said. "You know what happened."

"Hell, everybody in this town knows what happened. But that don't mean you need to plan on living your life like every day is the day after. That's not going to do anybody any good, especially not you. You're half my age, son. What are you going to do with the rest of your life?"

I took another puff off my cigar, and then I held it up and looked at the glowing end. "My sister's husband needed somebody to lend him a hand."

"Doing what?"

"Installing security systems," I said. "A company called Safe-at-Home."

The judge tossed his cigar into an ashtray on his desk and wiped his face with both hands. "Good God," he said. "What the hell? You're used to being the one who gets called to chase down the bad guys, and now you're spending your time answering the phone when babysitters and cleaning ladies get the police called on them by accident."

"What should I be doing?"

"The first thing you should do is stop feeling so damn sorry for yourself and start looking at how you can bring as much good out of this shitty situation as possible." He stubbed his cigar out in the ashtray, and I thought that meant our meeting was over, but I was wrong. "Hear me out," he said, leaning forward, his elbows on his desk, his fingers interlaced like he was fixing to pray. "You probably know that our guardian ad litem program is made up of attorneys and volunteers, and on the volunteer side we could use somebody who needs another chance to do the right thing, especially somebody who knows the law and who's seen the things you've seen. Most of our volunteers are country-club housewives, and these kids deserve more than that."

"Nothing wrong with country-club housewives," I said.

"Not until you drop them down into the middle of a couple of these shit situations. Then they break apart like china dolls. They love the kids, but they can't take seeing them get hurt."

I cleared my throat and sat up straighter in my chair. "Who's going to want me around their kids after what happened?"

"People who don't have a choice," he said. "People who have lost their rights to lay claim to their children, people who may not have deserved that claim in the first place." He stood up from his chair and walked around to the front of the desk and leaned against it, staring down at me the whole time. "Listen, Detective; that boy is gone, it was an accident, and nothing you can do or no prayer his momma and daddy can pray is going to bring him back. You can't live for him and you can't speak for him; but there are a lot of kids out there who need somebody to speak for them, and I think you're just the man to do it."

I said yes to Judge Shelburne mostly because it was the easiest thing to say at that time, and it took me a while to see myself as someone who could ever speak on a child's behalf unless it was my own daughter's. But I got used to it, and the years passed and it became easier and easier, seemed more and more natural. And then I was asked to speak for Easter and Ruby Quillby, two little girls, sisters, who didn't have anybody else in this world to listen to them and give them a voice. And now they'd gone missing, and their voices were even harder to hear.

Helen Crawford, the woman who managed the home where the girls lived, had already called the police before getting ahold of me, and when I got there that morning I saw a young officer filling out paperwork in a patrol car in the driveway and a couple unmarkeds sitting half in the grass out at the curb. I parked behind Sandy's old, beat-up Taurus, the same one we'd once shared back when we were partners.

He was coming up through the yard, carrying a cardboard evidence box with both hands, and when he saw me he raised it like he was bringing me a present and I'd gotten there too soon and ruined the surprise. At forty-three, he was three years younger than me and was just as tall and skinny as he'd ever been, and he wore the same kind of dark dress shirt and the same dark tie—loosened at the neck—he'd always worn. I climbed out of my car and watched him set the box inside his trunk and slam it shut. He turned around and stared for a second at the Safe-at-Home emblem on the breast pocket of my red golf shirt. "I hate to tell you this," he finally said, "but if you're here to install an alarm you're too late for it to do any good." He smiled and put his hands in his pockets.

"Don't think I haven't already tried." I nodded toward Miss

Crawford where she stood at the front door, staring out at the road like she wanted to ask one of us what happened next. "She said she didn't want the kids feeling like prisoners."

"It's better than feeling kidnapped."

"She also said there wasn't enough money."

"It's state government," he said. "There's never enough money. You know that as well as anybody." He sighed. "She told me they're your kids."

"They are," I said. "Since May."

"Well, come on, then." He turned, and I followed him down through the yard around to the left side of the house. We'd been partners for a few years before I left the force. I've heard detectives say that having a partner is like having a second wife or a second husband, and I think I'd have to agree with that. Just like any other married couple, me and Sandy both got the same phone call in the middle of the night and met up at a place where something terrible might've just happened, bleary-eyed and frustrated, hoping that what we found wouldn't be half as bad as the responding officer had made it sound. And, just like a real marriage, if a partnership goes to shit it can feel like a rocky divorce, and sometimes I saw myself as the spouse who'd been left behind, keeping tabs on the ex to see if he'd met anyone new and hoping there was a chance that it could all work out and everything would go back to how it used to be.

Sandy had moved up to detective faster than I had, and I knew he'd dreamed of being in the FBI or at least making the State Bureau. I figured he wouldn't be a detective for too much longer.

We crossed the driveway of the one-story brick ranch and stopped and stared up at an open window covered in black fingerprint dust: Easter and Ruby's bedroom. A plainclothes detective walked by inside. "All the doors were still locked this morning," Sandy said. "And none of the kids have a key, so this is the only way they could've gotten out. We pulled some prints: most of them small, but some of them big enough to belong to an adult."

"Easter wouldn't have unlocked that window unless it was somebody she knew," I said.

"Is that the oldest one?"

"Yep. She's twelve."

"They got any family around here?"

"Their mama died in May," I said. "And their daddy gave them up years ago, but that don't mean nothing."

"Is he a good guy or a bad guy?"

"Hell, I don't know," I said. "He's probably somewhere in between. Most of them are. He showed up at their school a week and a half ago, and he was over here on Saturday morning, trying to see them."

"That's what I heard," Sandy said. I started to walk around to the front of the house. "Where are you going?" he asked.

"Inside."

"You can't do that," he said. "This is a crime scene."

"But they're my kids."

"And you'll see any reports you care to see as soon as we're done writing them."

I looked toward the front of the house, where I figured Miss Crawford was still standing right inside the door. "She's inside there."

"She'll listen to me when I tell her not to touch anything; she's too scared to touch anything anyway," he said. "You don't listen, and you ain't scared of shit."

I stared at him for a second, waiting for him to flinch, but he wouldn't. I dug one of my cards out of my wallet and handed it to him. "Just fax over whatever you've got as soon as you can. Today."

He took the card and looked at it. "You know that's not the rules," he said, smiling.

"When did you start following the rules?" I turned to walk back to the car, and Sandy followed me. I'd been right; Miss Crawford still stood by the front door. I could see the fear on her face. She looked up at me and tried to smile. I waved. "It'll be okay, Miss Crawford. This kind of thing happens all the time."

"It ain't never happened to me," she said.

"Well, I know, but it's happened to other folks, and they . . ." My voice trailed off because I didn't know what else to say. I pointed toward the patrol car in the driveway, where the officer was still filling out paperwork. "It'll be all right," I said. "You're in good hands."

"That went well," Sandy said. He crossed his arms and leaned against the back of his car

"She looks pretty rattled."

"She is. What about you?"

"I've been through worse than this," I said. "And you know all about that."

"Yeah, well, you're not missing anything," he said.

"Is it that bad?"

"Worse than you can imagine," he said. "Unless, of course, you've seen a guy running around town with a sack full of money, about fourteen and a half million. If you have, I'm ready for his description." He reached into his breast pocket and pulled out an ink pen and clicked it open like he was ready to write something down.

"You've still got nothing?"

"Nothing," he said.

"What's it been, ten months?"

"Almost eleven."

"That's got to be killing you."

"It is," he said. "But only because everybody, including the FBI and the Charlotte guys, thinks it should be solved by now." He dropped the pen into his pocket. "I don't get it," he said. "Two guys spend all day driving around Charlotte in an armored car, taking pickups, making deliveries. The last drop of the day, one guy gets out, the other doesn't, and then he drives off and disappears—dumps the truck right on the Gastonia side of the bridge." He held a finger to his head like it was a gun. "Thanks, asshole."

"But that can't be the only reason the Feds are all over you," I said.

"It's not," he said. "Some of the money's been passed here in town. Here and up at the casino in Cherokee, but you can't see anything on the security cameras. The FBI brought in NASA, and they still can't see anything. It's not like we know who we're looking for anyway. The driver definitely had help, but he's probably long gone by now, if he's even still alive."

"Nobody's passing big bills?"

"No," he said. "They knew what they were doing, and they're way ahead of us. It's kicking our ass."

I nodded toward the house. "That's why you should let me lend you a hand on this case. I could take this one off your hands—one less on the books. Just help me out with what you can."

"I don't think so, Brady."

"Come on, Sandy," I said. "I help you; you help me. That's how we work it."

"When, Brady?" he asked. "When do you help me? When do we 'work it' like that? You've never worked anything for me." He jingled his keys in his pocket and turned and looked at the house, and then he looked down at his feet. "I'm sorry. It's just these Feds," he said. "They've got everybody paranoid. They come rolling into town, kicking down doors, asking all kinds of questions, getting up in your face to make sure you don't touch anything. A few days later, they're like, 'Why hasn't anybody done anything? Who's in charge here?' I'm telling you, man, it should make you happy you're out." He caught himself as soon as he'd said it. "I didn't mean—"

"It's okay," I said. "Don't worry about it."

He sighed. "All right. Look, I should be able to send you a few things today. I shouldn't be doing it, but today's probably not the best day to start following the rules, right?"

CHAPTER 9

I spent the rest of the morning back at the office, filling out invoices on new systems and answering phone calls about installation appointments, but the whole time I kept picturing the black fingerprint dust on the window ledge and thinking about what kind of promises or threats somebody would have to make to get Easter Quillby to open that window and crawl out into the night.

If twenty years as a cop taught me anything it's that when folks disappear it usually means, one, they're dead, or two, they don't want to be found. Most of the time, when kids go missing, it's the first, especially after they've been gone for forty-eight hours. After that, the chances of ever finding them, much less finding them alive, grow slimmer and slimmer with each day.

But Easter and Ruby's case seemed like one of the easier ones: two little girls with a dead mother and a deadbeat father, who suddenly reappears out of nowhere, go missing from a foster home. I was about 99 percent sure the girls were with their father, and I was about 99 percent sure that after two days the amount of trouble he'd gotten himself into would start to sink in, and he'd end up trying to bring them back like nothing had happened.

While I worked, my eyes kept drifting to the framed picture of my daughter, Jessica, and me that sat on the corner of my desk. She was eleven in the photograph, about the same age as Easter Quillby. Somebody'd taken the picture on a Saturday morning one fall when her Indian Princess tribe had spent the weekend at Camp Thunderbird out on Lake Wylie, which meant that a handful of little girls had spent the weekend together in one cabin, cutting out vests from huge rolls of felt and earning colored feathers for arts and crafts and horseback riding while their fathers stood around trying to find things to talk about besides their kids and their wives.

In the photo, Jessica sat on one of the camp's horses, and I stood beside her, my hand reaching up and holding the saddle horn like I was guiding her, even though a camp hand was holding the reins off-camera, clearly aware that I didn't know what in the hell I was doing. I'm just standing there, squinting into the sun, smiling for the camera. The night before one of the dads and I had left the camp after the girls had all gone to sleep, the rest of the guys staying behind to sit around and play cards. We'd driven over to a convenience store across the street from the camp and bought a case of beer. Then we went back and sat in the amphitheater by the lake, chugging beers and tossing the empties into the dark near the edge of the water. Jessica was just a little girl in the picture, and now she was sixteen, beginning her junior year of high school, starting to think about college.

She lived with my ex-wife, Tina, and her husband, Dean, in an old, wooded neighborhood where most of the houses were protected by alarm systems I'd either installed or serviced, but I'd never stepped a foot inside Dean's house, but that's not to say he was a bad guy. He was a blue-collar, hardworking family man who'd made his money after opening a construction firm with his brother. Hell, he could've even been me, but he wasn't. He and my ex-wife had been married for five years, and Jessica had been living in that house almost half as long as she'd lived in mine.

Back before the accident, we used to have lunch on Sundays after church at the Cracker Barrel, and then we'd ride through the rich neighborhoods, talking about which house we'd buy once we had the money, even though we knew we never would. I don't know if he lived there then or not, but I know we probably drove past Dean's house a million times.

I haven't gone to church in years, and now I never drive past houses like Dean's unless I have to.

When I came back from lunch, papers were waiting for me in the fax machine's tray. I sat down at my desk and leafed through the pages: a police report with handwriting so sloppy I couldn't hardly read it.

In the report, Miss Crawford said she'd gone in to check on Easter and Ruby that morning because they were late for breakfast; she'd found two empty beds and no girls. Then she saw the open window and called the police. She said both girls had on nightgowns when they went to bed, but she couldn't remember the colors. A pair of sneakers belonging to each of them was missing, but nothing else had been taken. She mentioned their father, Wade Chesterfield, showing up at school and later at the home, describing him as tall and thin, maybe six feet and 175 pounds, with strawberry-blond hair just like Easter's.

But I was surprised by what I found on the last page of the report. I laid the rest of the pages down by the fax machine and stood up and walked out to the reception area, where the sunlight came in through the glass door and front windows. I held the paper under the light to get a good look at it. It was a front and back photocopy of Wade Chesterfield's baseball card with the Gastonia Rangers.

The card looked like something the Rangers might've created for a promotional night at the beginning of a season when hopes were still high. It might've even been a vanity card that Chesterfield had designed, ordered, and paid for himself. The photo was him in his pitcher's windup: a lefty. The Gastonia Rangers, who'd left town and moved to Hickory at the end of the '92 season, were a farm team for the Texas Rangers, and their uniforms were almost identical. Chesterfield was wearing the white home jersey, and even though the photocopy was black and white, his hat was probably blue and the cursive *Rangers* on his shirt was blue with red trimming. The other side of the card listed Chesterfield's stats and his description. He was six-one and, at the time, weighed in at only 162 pounds. It was all there; the only thing I couldn't tell from Wade Chesterfield's card was what he looked like: somebody'd come along and scratched out his face with an ink pen.

I went back to my desk and flipped through the pages, stopping when I found Wade's mug shot. It had been taken in 1995, and in it his hair was an oily mess and his face was splotched with whiskers. I tried to imagine that face, clean-shaven and years younger, atop the pitcher's body.

The cordless phone sat on my desk, and I picked it up and called Sandy's number at the station.

"What's up?" he asked

"Who scratched out his face?"

"Whose face?"

"Chesterfield's on the baseball card: who scratched it out?"

"I don't know," he said. "We found it under the older one's mattress. I guess she did it. Looks like he wasn't in the running for father of the year, not this year anyway." When he said that I looked at the framed picture of Jessica and me sitting on my desk; I imagined finding that photo with my own face scratched out. Something turned in my chest, and I forced the picture out of my mind. I stood and walked to the reception area and stared out at the cars passing by on Franklin Avenue.

"What was he arrested for?"

"DUI," Sandy said. "And that wasn't his first. Hopefully it was his last, especially if he's got those girls with him." The phone grew quiet, and I knew Sandy was staring at his desk, trying to think of what to say next since he couldn't take back what he'd already said. I cleared my throat.

"Okay," I said. "Thanks."

"Hey," he said, "plan on lunch tomorrow so we can talk about all this. I'll give you a call if I hear anything before then."

"Sure," I said. I hung up.

When I turned to walk back to my desk, I saw that a sheet of paper had been left in the fax machine's tray. It was a copy of Easter's and Ruby's school pictures. They'd had them displayed on the dresser in their bedroom back at the home. Unlike most kids, whose parents dressed them up for school photos, Easter and Ruby just had on shorts and T-shirts, and their hair was long and unbrushed. Even though they hardly looked like sisters, there was something in their eyes that told you they'd seen the same things, and I thought about how no one else in this world had a picture of these two little girls displayed in their home, and that the only picture of either of them was on a dresser in a bedroom they'd disappeared from.

There were appointments I needed to make and orders to the manufacturer that needed to be completed, but instead I sat in one of the three chairs in the otherwise empty office's reception area and watched the sunlight coming through the glass door move across the carpet. Every now and then I'd pick up the faxed pages sitting in the chair to my right and flip through them before sitting them down again, but mostly I just sat there, waiting until it was time to leave. I could've gone home already, relied on the answering machine to take any messages that might need taking, but I hated being at my apartment when it was still light out, and I never left the office before dusk, which meant I left pretty late sometimes during the summer. It was the first day of September, and I knew it wouldn't be dark enough to go home for a while just yet.

There was a television in the back of the office, and I thought about turning on ESPN and trying to catch the pregame news of McGwire against the Marlins. I had $250 on him going homerless tonight, but something told me I'd be wrong.

It had taken a couple of years, but I'd learned that this kind of restlessness couldn't be helped; the late afternoon still felt like the beginning of the day to me, and habit made me half afraid to go home until full dark, afraid to make something to eat, to sit down and turn on a game for fear that I'd be called away any minute to tramp along railroad tracks on the way to a dead body or to pick shell casings out of a gravel driveway in a dark trailer park. For years I'd laid in bed beside Tina, wide-awake and waiting for the phone to ring. It never rang at my place now, but that didn't mean I'd stopped listening for it.

I thought about what Sandy had said earlier about Wade Chesterfield not being "father of the year" and his arrests on DUIs, and I wondered if Easter knew about those, wherever she and Ruby were, if she was thinking about those arrests when she'd scratched out his face on that baseball card, if she was thinking about them right now while her dad drove them around God knows where. I wondered if Wade was thinking about them too, if he looked in his rearview mirror at his daughters in the backseat if and when those DUIs popped into his mind, or if he didn't look because he didn't want to take his eyes off the road because a split second had already shown him what could happen if you did.

That's what I'd done: looked at Jessica in the rearview mirror where she sat in the backseat telling me all about the basketball practice I'd just nodded off during instead of watching like the others parents had. We were in the driveway by then, and I'd already found the remote and pushed the button to raise the garage door. I didn't even know he was standing there until Jessica screamed; by then it was too late.

Tina's father was in his last days with a failed liver at the hospital in Chapel Hill, and I'd had to take the weekend off and switch to days so I could be there when Jessica got home from school. Before leaving, Tina had taped a note to the refrigerator, reminding me to do two things: take twenty dollars over to Michael, our neighbors' fifteen-year-old son who cut our grass every Saturday morning, and take Jessica to basketball practice at 7 P.M. on Wednesday night; I'd forgotten about both. Tina had always looked at our marriage as a years-long investigation that she couldn't quite get to the bottom of. I was either the uncooperative witness who never gave the right answers or the suspect who'd stumbled his way into doing the wrong thing.

On Wednesday evening, after splitting a Domino's pizza with Jessica, I'd popped two sleeping pills and knocked them back with a beer, hoping for one good, long night of sleep before Tina came home sometime that weekend. It was mid-October and almost dark at 6:30 when Jessica came into the living room in her tennis shoes, shorts, and sweatshirt and reminded me about her basketball practice through my half-closed eyes.

It was pitch black by the time we got home from the Y. I've gone over and over this in my mind, and every time that driveway gets darker and my headlights seem dimmer. We never knew if Michael was on his way over or if he'd already discovered that we weren't home, but, when I pulled in, he'd been there in the middle of the driveway only because I'd forgotten to pay him, forgotten to do both of the two things Tina had asked of me before leaving town to go be with her dad.

The paramedics were there by the time the responding officers arrived; I recognized them both through the window in the kitchen, where I leaned over the sink and splashed cold water on my face. They stood out in the yard, talking to Michael's parents, two people I'd known well for years, the lights from the ambulance flashing across the four of them. Jessica had stopped crying by then, and she was upstairs in her bedroom, not making a sound, probably wishing Tina was at home as badly as I did.

I knew the officers suspected something when they suggested that I let one of them drive me down to the station for questioning, even though I wasn't arrested. The other one stayed behind at the house. At the station I explained what happened, or what I thought had happened. Most of the eyes I met were looking down at the carpet. They let me decline a drug test, which seemed like a favor at the time, but it ended up the other way around.

I was never arrested or charged with a criminal act, but I was sued by Michael's parents a few months later, which left plenty of time for made-up stories to spread through town about how I'd passed out during that night's basketball practice, how I'd behaved after the accident. At the civil trial, other parents lined up to testify that I'd stumbled out of the gym before driving my own daughter home. A couple guys who'd been at the station that night couldn't remember if they'd smelled anything on my breath or not, but they said they were encouraged not to test me, and didn't because I outranked them.

By the time the jury found against me I'd already been given the option of resigning from the force—encouraged to resign is probably a better way to put it—and we'd already lost a lot of money to lawyers. The realization that we'd be paying back Michael's parents for the rest of our lives was a stark one. But there was still the overwhelming feeling that I'd gotten away with something that I shouldn't have, and I couldn't help but believe that Tina felt it too: I didn't spend a second in jail, I was still alive, my daughter was still alive. In some ways, I *had* gotten away with something. But I still wear that guilt like a heavy winter coat because when something like that happens, when a kid would otherwise be alive if it wasn't for you, you never really "get away with it" because it never really goes away.

If my work or my sleeplessness or our arguing caused rifts in our marriage, then the night of the accident was like a boulder rolling down a mountain and splashing all the water out of a pond that once upon a time only had little ripples to worry about. But we hung on as long as we could. I probably held on longer than she did, probably longer than was healthy for either of us—probably longer than was healthy for Jessica.

The three of us were never the same. Nothing was.

Easter Quillby

CHAPTER 10

My eyes opened to the sound of the car's engine turning off. The sun was coming up, and I saw that we'd parked in front of a Waffle House. Wade was sitting up in the front seat, staring at me like he'd been waiting on me to wake up. Ruby still had her eyes closed beside me.

"Where are we?" I asked.

"We're almost there."

"Where's 'there'?"

"Myrtle Beach," he said.

I looked over at Ruby to make sure she was still asleep and wasn't just pretending so that she could listen to what we were saying. "Are you serious?"

"Yes."

"Because neither one of us has ever been to the beach before, and if you're not telling the truth—"

"I'm telling the truth," he whispered, "and you need to start believing me." He nodded toward Ruby. "I ain't asking you to trust me just for my own sake," he said. "I'm asking you to do it for your sister. You don't know how much she looks up to you and how much she wants to be like you."

"Why are you telling me this?"

"I'm telling you because I'm trying to do right, even if I can't change the past, even if I can't make up for lost time or undo all the things I've done," he said. "I just want another chance to be y'all's dad, but if you've already made up your mind that you don't want me to be yours then I understand. But I'm asking you to let Ruby make up her own mind about what she wants."

"I don't think you've changed at all," I said.

"What makes you say that?"

"Because somebody's looking for you. He came to school looking for me too. I saw him out in the woods. He asked if you were my dad. I said no, but he didn't believe me. He knew who I was."

He took his baseball hat off and ran his fingers through his hair, and then he put it back on. He tried to smile. "What did he look like?"

By the time I'd finished describing the man's eye, his voice, and how big he'd been, Wade's face had gone white. "Do you know who he is?" I asked.

"Yes," he said.

"Is he a bad guy?"

"Yes, but he won't find us." He looked from me to Ruby, where she was still asleep beside me. "We just have to trust each other and take care of each other," he said. "Can you trust me?"

I nodded my head yes.

"Thank you," he said. "We'll be okay, and we're going to have a good time. Who knows, you might even change your mind about me." He smiled, and then he opened his door and climbed out.

"Don't count on it," I whispered.

A couple hours later Wade stopped the car and parked it in front of an old garage he'd found after stopping at a pay phone, and then he turned around and looked at me and Ruby. "If y'all could paint a car any color you wanted, what color would you paint it?"

"Pink!" Ruby screamed. After getting to Myrtle Beach, we'd stopped by a store called Wings, and Wade had gone in and bought us some new clothes while we waited in the car. Ruby'd taken off her socks and shoes and was slipping her feet into a pair of pink flip-flops; neither one of us had ever worn a pair before.

"It might look funny for a man to drive a pink car," Wade said.

"What about red?" I asked.

"Red might be better," Wade said. He winked at me like we were sharing some kind of secret. "Wait here."

"Where you going?" Ruby asked.

"I'm going to see about turning this brown car red," he said. He rolled the windows down a little and climbed out. "Y'all stay in the car."

"Okay," we both said at the same time. We watched him walk into what looked like a little office beside the garage. Ruby opened one of the Wings bags Wade had tossed in the backseat, and I opened the other one. We started going through all the clothes he'd just bought for us: a pink bathing suit for Ruby and a red one for me; two matching white T-shirts with *Myrtle Beach* spray-painted on them, *You Can't Touch This* written across the bottom in cursive. There were shorts too: a pink pair for Ruby and blue ones for me.

Wade had said we were going to the beach next, so we went ahead and put on those bathing suits and then slipped the shorts and T-shirts on over them. It was the first time I could remember putting on clothes that nobody had ever owned before me.

Ruby had gotten quiet, and I knew she was thinking about saying something, but she wasn't sure whether I'd like it or not. "What's Miss Crawford going to do when she finds out we're gone?" she finally said.

"She's already found out, Ruby," I said. "School started a couple hours ago."

"Do you think she's worried?"

"Don't think about that," I said. "We don't live there anymore."

"Maybe we should call and tell her we're okay," she said. Her eyes were looking past me, and I turned and saw that she was staring at a pay phone that sat by the sidewalk in front of the garage.

"No, Ruby, we can't call anybody," I said. "We can't tell anybody where we are."

"But what if they're scared?"

"Do you want to move to Alaska?" I asked. "Or do you want us to be split up and sent to different homes? You want Wade to go to jail?" She shook her head. "That's what'll happen if we call home." She sat back and stared at the headrest in front of her. I wondered what was taking Wade so long.

"It's just—" Ruby started to say.

"Stop it, Ruby," I said. "Stop it. You're the one who was so happy to see him last night. Now we're all here, and there's no way we're going back. So put all that feeling bad for people out of your mind."

A few minutes later, the three of us were sitting on a bench out in front of the garage, waiting for a taxi. Wade had gotten a black gym bag out of the trunk, and me and Ruby had stuffed our nightgowns, underwear, and socks and shoes into the Wings bags. The sun was bright and hot, one of those days where the sky looked white.

Me and Ruby were used to riding in taxis with Mom, and sitting there now waiting on this one almost made me feel like we were right back in Gastonia, right back in our old lives, except that now we were with Wade instead of Mom, and we were at the beach instead of out in front of the grocery store or the doctor's office, waiting for a taxi to take us back home.

"Are we moving here?" Ruby asked.

For a minute I thought Wade didn't hear her, but when he sighed I realized that he was just tired and hot and didn't feel like answering a question like that. "No," he said, "we ain't moving here. We're just staying here for a little while."

"Where are we going to live?" Ruby asked. Wade sighed again.

I leaned forward and looked past Wade at her. "Don't ask so many questions," I said. Ruby sat back against the bench where I couldn't see her. I waited, but she didn't say nothing else.

CHAPTER 11

The taxi dropped us off at a hotel right on the beach. After checking in, we had to walk by the pool to take the stairs up to our room. In the water were a boy and a girl about my age. The girl was floating on a raft that looked like a killer whale, and the boy had on a pair of goggles. They looked up at us. Ruby waved at them, but neither one of them waved back. A man and a woman who must've been their parents were lying on deck chairs. The woman was reading a book; the man looked like he was sleeping.

"I like your raft," Ruby said, but the girl didn't say nothing back.

Our room was nice, with two double beds and a little table with two chairs. A big television sat on the dresser across the room from the beds. Wade went around to the far side of the second bed and let the gym bag slide off his shoulder and drop to the floor. He got down on his knees and pushed it under the bed.

"What's in that bag?" I asked.

He looked up at me, and then he pushed it farther under the bed. "Nothing," he said. "Just some clothes." He stood up and clapped his hands. "All right," he said. "Let's hit the beach."

The clock on the bedside table said 1 P.M. by the time we finished putting on sunscreen and left the room to go to the beach. We walked over to a little restaurant on the pier next to the hotel and ordered cheeseburgers, french fries, and Cokes, and then we took the steps from the pier down onto the sand.

While me and Ruby rolled out our towels, Wade took a package out of a bag and started opening it.

"What's that?" Ruby asked.

"You'll see," he said, putting his mouth on a little, clear tube.

I knew what it was before he even started blowing it up. "It's a raft," I said. Wade blew a big breath into the tube and nodded his head at me. After Wade had given it a few more breaths, I could see the picture on the raft, and I didn't want anything to do with it.

"I'm not playing with that," I said. "It's got a Confederate flag on it."

"What do you have against the Confederate flag?" he asked.

"It means you hate black people," I said.

Wade made a face. "That ain't what it means," he said. He gave it a few more puffs before closing the tube.

"What's it mean, then?" I asked.

Wade put the cap on the tube and held the raft out in front of him like he was studying it. "I don't know," he finally said. "But I know it doesn't mean that."

Me and Ruby sat on top of the raft, and Wade rolled out his towel. We stared out at the ocean, eating our cheeseburgers and french fries. For the first time that day I noticed how tired Wade looked, and I thought about how he'd driven all through the night from Gastonia while me and Ruby had been asleep in the backseat. He must've felt my eyes on him, because he turned his head and looked at us.

"Y'all excited about being at the beach?"

"Yes!" Ruby said. She took a bite of her cheeseburger, and then she picked up her can of Coke and took a swallow. "This is the best day ever!"

"Good," Wade said. "I'm glad y'all are having fun. I want this to be fun." He took the last bite of his cheeseburger and folded up the wrapper while he chewed it. "All we're going to do from now on is have fun." He unlaced his shoes and kicked them off. "That's the only rule from now on: have fun."

CHAPTER 12

All day long, Wade had been saying he had a surprise for us, and after dinner that night a taxi dropped us off in the middle of a busy street full of shops and stores and restaurants. Across the street was a boardwalk full of people: families with little kids, women wearing bikini tops with shorts even though it was getting dark, and groups of teenage girls wearing makeup and walking around holding hands with their boyfriends.

"What's the surprise?" Ruby asked.

"You'll see," Wade said. We followed the boardwalk along the beach until Wade stopped and pointed toward some bright lights over the buildings in the distance. "That's it," he said. "The Pavilion."

I looked up and saw the lights of a Ferris wheel peeking just above the roof of a building called the Magic Attic. A bunch of kids not much older than me waited outside in line to get in. None of them had their parents with them. Ruby yanked Wade's hand to make him walk faster. "Come on," she said. They walked through an arcade toward the street on the other side of the boardwalk.

That night we rode just about every ride in the park, and Wade and Ruby rode just about every one of them together. I told myself that I enjoyed the tilt-a-whirl all alone just as much as I would've with Wade sitting beside me, and up at the top of the Ferris wheel I could see the boardwalk and all the hotels just as good as I would've been able to see them if I'd been sitting up there with Ruby instead of all by myself listening to nothing but the wind and the music from the park way down below.

The haunted house was about the only ride in the amusement park just for kids my age, and when we walked past Wade asked me if I wanted to go in.

"Maybe," I said. He snapped off a couple tickets and handed them to me.

"Go ahead," he said. He pointed to a bench. "Me and Ruby will be sitting right over there when you get out."

"Are you not coming with me?" I asked.

"Ruby can't go in there," he said. "There's no way I'm going to leave her out here by herself. But you go ahead. We don't mind. We might even ride something else."

I turned away from him and walked right up to the haunted house and got in line. To go through the haunted house, you had to climb into a little car that was hooked to other cars, just like they were on the roller coaster.

Somebody laughed in line behind me, and I turned and saw two boys and two girls who were all fifteen or sixteen years old. The boys both had on polo shirts and shorts with their baseball hats turned backward. The taller boy had a huge cup of frozen lemonade with a straw sticking out of it. One of the girls was holding a big teddy bear that a boy must've won for her. It was brown and had on blue jean overalls. The boy with frozen lemonade started laughing when I looked at him. I turned back around.

"I don't know what it says," one of the boys whispered.

"Ask her," one of the girls said. She was laughing so hard that she couldn't even whisper.

"Hey," one of the boys said. He tapped me on the shoulder.

"What does your shirt say?" I turned around and showed him my shirt so he'd leave me alone.

"'Can't touch this'?" one of the girls said. All four of them started laughing. I turned back around so they couldn't see me. "Oh my God," she said. "Who'd want to touch that?"

My face turned red because I felt stupid for wearing that T-shirt, even stupider for thinking it was cool. But it was the only shirt I had to wear, and I hated Wade for buying it for me.

The little train pulled out of the haunted house and the people got out, and I climbed into the first car and pulled the bar across my lap. The tall boy with the frozen lemonade and one of the girls got in the car behind me.

The brakes hissed and the cars started rolling into the haunted house, and as soon as we rolled forward some scratchy Halloween music started playing from little speakers in the walls. A white sheet that was supposed to be a ghost dropped from the ceiling. We rode right under the ghost, and it was hanging so low that I could've reached up and touched it. When I looked back at it I saw the boy in the car behind me stand up and smack it. It rocked back and forth like a piñata. The other boy in the car behind him laughed. The whole haunted house was full of cheap stuff that wasn't scary at all. The only time I jumped during the ride was when I felt something cold hit my neck.

At first I thought it must be water dripping from the ceiling, but when I touched my hair and felt around on the back of my head I knew exactly what it was, but I smelled my fingers anyway: lemonade. The boy behind me laughed and whispered, "Can't touch this," to the girl in the car with him. She laughed too. He sucked up more lemon-ade into his straw and spit it into my hair. I didn't turn around to look at him. I just ran my fingers through my hair and hoped it wouldn't look wet when I saw Wade and Ruby after the ride was over.

When the train stopped I wormed myself free from under the lap belt before the operator could release it. I was the first one off the ride, and I ran down the steps past all the people who were waiting in line. Wade and Ruby were sitting on the bench. Wade saw me and waved. He said something, but I was too far away to hear it. The kids who'd been on the ride must've seen Wade wave at me, and they must've seen that me and Ruby had on the same shirt. They busted out laughing again.

Seeing Ruby and Wade sitting on that bench, both of them in their Myrtle Beach T-shirts with those kids laughing at all three of us, gave me the worst, most lonely feeling I'd had since the morning me and Ruby walked down to Fayles' to call 911. I started running, and I didn't stop until I'd crossed the street, run through the arcade, and hit the boardwalk and couldn't go any farther.

I stood there on the boardwalk and leaned against the railing, the wind coming off the ocean and blowing both my hair and my tears off my face.

Somebody tugged on my shirt. I turned around and found Ruby standing behind me. "You okay?" she asked.

"No," I said. "I'm not." I turned back around and looked out at the beach again, half of me hoping that she'd leave me alone, the other half hoping that she'd tell me that she hated Wade too, that she knew why those kids were laughing at us, that she wanted to go home. She stepped up to the railing and stood beside me.

"Was it scary?" she asked.

"Was what scary?"

"The haunted house," she said. "Is that why you're crying?"

"No."

"Then why?"

"You wouldn't understand," I said.

"I bet I would," she said. "I bet I understand a lot more than you think I do."

"Maybe you do," I said.

"Daddy thinks you got scared because you went in there by yourself. He's getting us some quarters to play video games. He thinks you're mad at him."

"He's not our daddy," I said. "I don't know why you want to call him that."

"That's what he wants us to call him."

"Yeah?" I asked. "What about what I want, Ruby?"

Ruby folded her arms across the railing and lifted her chin and rested it on her hands. We both looked out at the ocean. "But doesn't it feel good?" she finally said. "Having a dad like everybody else? I like it; I can't help it."

"Just don't get used to it," I said. Ruby pushed herself away from the railing and raised her voice, and she might've screamed if the wind hadn't been blowing so hard to push her words away from me.

"Why are you acting like this?" she said. "This morning you said I shouldn't think about home, that I should get used to being with him. And now you're telling me I shouldn't." She was crying now, and I reached for her hand, but she pulled it away from me and backed toward the Pavilion. We stood there looking at each other, and then she turned and ran toward the arcade. I followed her.

Wade was standing just inside, and I could tell the pockets of his shorts were weighed down with quarters. He saw that Ruby was crying, and he sighed and bent down to her. "What happened?"

"Nothing," I said before Ruby could answer. "She got scared because I did." I reached out my hand and put it on her head. "Right?" Ruby lifted her head off Wade's shoulder and turned and looked at me. She sniffed and wiped at one of her eyes.

"Well, all right," Wade said, standing up. He patted the quarters in his pockets. "Who feels like playing some video games?"

Ruby looked up at him. "I do!" she said.

Wade put both hands in his pockets, and when he brought them out he had fistfuls of quarters. He bent down and divided one handful of quarters between the pockets of Ruby's shorts, and then he held out his other hand to me. I cupped my hands and he let the quarters spill into my palms. I tried to dump them into my pockets without dropping any, but a few slipped through my fingers and rolled out toward the boardwalk. Ruby ran after them and brought them back to me.

"What do y'all want to play first?" Wade asked. He kneeled again and cinched the drawstring on Ruby's shorts to keep the quarters in her pockets from tugging them down.

"Pac-Man!" Ruby screamed, jumping up and down.

I looked around the arcade and saw what I'd been looking for. "Can I go to the bathroom?" I asked. Wade looked around until he saw the sign for the bathrooms on the far wall beside the gift shop.

"Okay," he said. "But come back here when you're done."

As soon as I turned down the hallway to the restrooms I saw what I'd been hoping to find: a pay phone sat on the wall right in between the men's and women's restrooms. I used my shoulder to hold the phone against my cheek, and I took out a fistful of quarters and put them all in the coin slot. As soon as I heard the dial tone I called his number and closed my eyes and waited for it to ring.

"Hello?" Marcus said.

"Marcus?"

"Yeah?"

"It's me," I said. "Easter." The line was quiet.

"Hey," he finally said. "I was hoping you'd call me."

"I hope it's okay that I did," I said, putting my hand over my other ear because the arcade was so loud, even though I was all the way at the end of the hall.

"Where are you?" he asked.

"I'm in an arcade," I said, "in Myrtle Beach, with my dad and Ruby. We came here last night."

"I saw y'all leave," he said. "I was trying to come over."

Something made a noise on the other end, and then I heard a voice in the room with Marcus. "Who's that?" I asked. "Don't tell them it's me." But it was too late. His mom got on the phone.

"Easter, baby, where are you?"

"Put Marcus back on, please," I said. My hands had started to sweat, and I could feel my heart beating in my ears.

"Don't be afraid, honey. The police are going to find you; they're looking for you and your sister now. You're somewhere with your daddy?"

"Marcus said they're in Myrtle Beach," a man said in the background. It was Marcus's dad.

"Myrtle Beach?" his mom said. "Okay, okay."

"Please put Marcus back on," I said. "Please." But she wouldn't, and she wouldn't stop talking, telling me it was going to be okay.

"What's she saying?" asked Marcus's dad in the background. His mom didn't say anything to him; she just kept talking to me. But then the line went quiet.

"Hello?" I said. I could hear Marcus's parents talking, but I didn't know what they were saying. "Hello?" I said again. I pictured Marcus's mom standing in the kitchen with her hand over the receiver, whispering to his dad. I didn't know what to do, so I hung up. A few quarters clinked into the change return.

It wasn't until starting back down the hallway toward the arcade that I understood what I'd just done. Everybody in Gastonia probably already knew we were missing. Now Marcus's mom and dad knew where we were and who we were with. It wouldn't be but a couple of minutes before the police would know it all too.

After going through all Wade's quarters, me and Ruby stood out on the sidewalk watching the roller coaster while Wade called a taxi.

Just below the sounds of the roller coaster and the music and the noises of the video games in the arcade was another sound. Ruby heard it too, and we looked around until we found it; across the street to our left was a pitching cage. The noise we'd heard was a baseball being thrown against a rubber curtain; on it was a picture of a catcher squatting behind home plate. A man about Wade's age was pitching, and another man sat on a stool beside the cage where a little screen with red numbers showed how fast the man's pitches were. The first pitch was forty-four, the second forty-seven. A group of people stood around, clapping and laughing.

When she heard Wade hang up the phone, Ruby looked at him and pointed to the pitching cage. "I want to do that," she said. Wade's mouth made a straight line, and he squinted his eyes like he was thinking about something he didn't want to think about. "Please?" Ruby said.

"Okay," Wade said. "We'll go watch." He took Ruby's hand and she took mine, and the three of us crossed the street.

We stood by the cage and watched the man throw a few more pitches before his turn was up. His friends were still clapping and cheering. The man operating the cage looked over at the three of us from where he sat on the stool. He was fat and his butt and his thighs sagged off the stool like his pants had been stuffed with water balloons.

"Y'all want to give it a shot?" he asked.

Ruby looked up at Wade and leaned her body against his leg. "Can I try it?" she asked.

"How much is it?" Wade asked the fat man on the stool.

"Ten pitches for five dollars," he said. Wade fished his wallet out of his back pocket and found a five-dollar bill. He held it out to the man and the man took it without even standing up from his stool.

Wade reached down and put his hand on Ruby's head. She looked up at him. "You can throw five pitches," Wade said, holding up his other hand and spreading out all his fingers. He pointed at me. "And Easter gets to throw five too."

"I don't want to," I said. "Ruby can throw all of them."

"No," he said. "I want to see what you can do. The old man wants to see what kind of arm his daughters have."

Ruby stood at the front of the cage and looked at the picture of the catcher that was drawn on the curtain at the other end. The baseballs the man had been throwing sat in between her and the catcher. The fat man on the stool gestured toward the baseballs.

"Go ahead," he said. Ruby walked into the cage and rolled the baseballs out to where we stood, and Wade bent down and scooped them up as they came toward us. He waited on her to walk out of the cage, and then he handed her a ball. She spun around to throw it, but Wade put his hand on her shoulder to stop her.

"You mind if she takes a few steps in?" he asked the fat man, nodding his head toward the catcher. The fat man just shrugged his shoulders. He held a wad of money in his hand with a rubber band around it. He unfastened the rubber band and rolled Wade's five-dollar bill into the wad.

"It don't matter to me," he said. Wade kept his hands on Ruby's shoulders and walked her about ten feet into the cage.

"This looks good," he said. Ruby reared back her arm and lobbed her first pitch at the catcher. It arced like a rainbow and fell against the curtain just above the catcher's head. I looked at the little screen beside the fat man: the red numbers said twenty-four. Ruby turned around and ran toward me, but she stopped by the fat man's stool and looked at the twenty-four on the screen.

"Twenty-four!" she said to Wade.

"That's great," Wade said. "And you still got four more."

Ruby finished her pitches, and then she walked out of the cage and brought all three baseballs to me.

"Your turn," she said.

"I don't really want to," I said. Wade followed Ruby out of the cage and stood beside me.

"Come on," he said. "It'll be fun." He nudged me with his elbow. "I want to see you sling some heat." I sighed loud enough for them both to hear me, and I set two of the baseballs down and stood up straight and took a step toward the cage. "All right," Wade said, clapping his hands, "bring the heat."

I held the ball in front of me with both hands and stared down the cage at the catcher on the rubber curtain, and then I turned my left shoulder toward him and raised my right leg just like I'd seen John Smoltz do a hundred times. I threw the ball as hard as I could, and it smacked against the rubber about three feet to the left of the catcher's head. I looked at the screen to see how fast I'd thrown it: thirty-six.

"All right!" Wade said. He clapped, and when I turned and looked at him he had his hand raised like he was waiting on me to give him a high five. I reached out and smacked his palm, and I felt my face getting hot and I knew it was turning red, but I couldn't help smiling. Ruby raised her hand for a high five too, and I smacked her palm just like I'd smacked Wade's. I bent down and picked up another ball, and when I stood up straight I could feel Wade standing right behind me.

"Just focus on that mitt. Just imagine the ball going right into it." He leaned over me and put his hands on my wrists, and he raised both my hands up to my chest. "Now, when you bring your knee up, make sure your left shoulder is pointing toward the catcher." I stared at the catcher's glove and imagined the ball smacking right into it. When I turned my shoulders to begin my pitch I realized that Wade had stepped away from me. I brought my knee up just like I had before, but this time I kept my eyes on the mitt and turned my left shoulder in like Wade had told me to. I threw the ball as hard as I could, and this time it smacked the catcher right in his mask. The screen said forty-two. I heard Wade clapping behind me.

"Right in there," he said. "If he took it in the mask it's his fault." I didn't look back at him this time because I was smiling for real, and I didn't want him to see it. I bent down and picked up the last baseball. When I stood up straight I heard another voice behind me.

"Look out!" the voice said. "You can't touch this!" I turned and saw the four kids who'd sat behind me in the haunted house. One of the girls was still holding her big stuffed teddy bear, but the tall boy must've finished his lemonade because he had his hands in his pockets. The shorter boy standing beside him laughed, and then they gave each other some kind of handshake that ended with them bumping fists. The girls just stood there staring at me like they didn't recognize me from earlier in the night.

I looked down at Ruby; she'd turned around and was looking

at them too. When I looked over at Wade I saw that he was staring at the boys with a crazy smile on his face like he thought what they'd said was funny.

"Y'all play ball?" he asked. I couldn't believe he'd even talk to them, much less try to make friends with them. He had to know they were making fun of us: the way we were dressed, the way we looked.

I turned back to the cage and stared at the catcher's mitt, trying to concentrate on it—trying to picture the ball smacking right up against it—but the longer I stared at it the more I felt like I might start crying. Instead I threw the ball as hard as I could. I didn't care if it was a strike or not; I just wanted it to hurt whatever it hit. It smacked the curtain about three feet to the left of the catcher again, but this time the screen said forty-five. I turned around to make sure Wade had seen it, but he hadn't even been watching me. He'd walked over to the two boys and was talking to them.

"Are you serious?" the tall boy asked. He looked at the shorter boy standing next to him and smiled. He looked back at Wade. "All right," he said. I looked down at Ruby. She'd been watching me the whole time like she was waiting to see how hard I was going to throw the next pitch.

"Come on," she said. She pointed to the forty-five that was still on the screen. "You can throw harder than that," she said.

"I don't want to pitch anymore," I said. I handed the two balls to Ruby and stepped back.

"You sure?" she asked. I nodded my head. She walked into the cage and stopped at about the same spot where she'd thrown her first five pitches. I turned to my left and faced the beach, and I stood there wishing I could look right through the building across the street so I could see the ocean instead of being able to just barely hear it. Ruby's first pitch smacked against the curtain, and then a few seconds later I heard the second. I didn't hear Wade say a word to her once she finished, and I knew he hadn't been watching her either.

But I turned around as soon as I heard what Wade said next. "Me and my buddy here are going ten more." Wade held out a five-dollar bill to the fat man on the stool. He took it and fished out his roll of dollars again and started unfastening the rubber band. The tall boy had left his friends and was standing beside Wade in front of the cage. He looked nervous to be standing so close to Wade, but he smiled like he was trying to hide it.

"Come on, Evan," the other boy said, clapping his hands. He and the two girls were standing in the same spot. The girls looked like they didn't know quite what to make of what was happening. I didn't know what to make of it either. Wade gathered up the three baseballs and sat them down by Evan's feet, and then he picked up one and handed it to him.

"All right," Wade said. "Five pitches apiece." He raised his hand and pointed at the two girls. "And whoever throws the hardest gets to take that teddy bear home." Now I knew why one of the girls didn't look as excited as her friend and the boy who was standing beside them.

"This is all you, Evan," the boy said. "You got this." Evan rolled the baseball around in his hand, and then he turned his cap around to face forward. He squeezed the baseball with both hands like he was trying to make it smaller, and then he moved his head in a circle and rolled his shoulders forward and backward. Then he just stood and stared at the curtain where the catcher squatted with his raised mitt. It wasn't until he brought the ball to his chest and cupped his left hand to hide his grip that I knew for certain that he'd thrown a pitch before. My heart sank into my stomach, and I think it might've sunk even lower after I heard the ball smack that rubber curtain. I looked at the screen: it said sixty-nine.

"There it is," the short boy said. "That's what I'm talking about." Even the girls seemed interested, and they took a step toward the cage to get a better look.

The fat man leaned forward on his stool and took a look at the screen and snorted out a laugh. Then he sat up straight and crossed his arms. "That's the fastest I've seen tonight," he said, looking at Wade like he was letting him know he didn't have a chance against this kid. I looked at Wade too, and then I looked at Evan where he was squeezing another ball with both hands, just like he'd done to the first one. He was bigger than Wade, and he actually looked like an athlete; Wade was at least twenty years older and looked like a skinny man with a belly who'd probably never played a single sport in his entire life. Now that he was clean-shaven I could see where the skin sagged under his chin, and I wondered how his body could seem so skinny and soft at the same time.

Evan went through his windup just like he had before, and this pitch smacked the curtain even louder, and it hit the catcher right in the chest. Seventy-one flashed on the screen. He stepped back and looked at Wade, but Wade just stared at the spot where the ball had hit.

"That was a nice pitch," he said. "You've got a good arm." Evan smiled like he'd already won the bet, and every one of us knew he was right. His next three pitches were just as fast. The last one hit the catcher in the mask and came in at seventy-four. The short boy laughed after he saw where the ball hit the curtain. He and Evan gave each other a high five, and the girl who'd ridden through the haunted house with him went over and put her arm through Evan's.

I watched them celebrate, but then something caught my attention out of the corner of my eye; it was Wade. He was walking back and forth on the sidewalk, swinging both his arms like helicopter blades. The group of teenagers noticed it too. They stopped talking and watched him.

"What the hell?" Evan said. They all laughed. I looked down at Ruby; she was staring at Wade too. He walked up to the cage and stopped and stared down at the catcher, and then he bent down and picked up one of the baseballs. He rolled it around in his left hand, and then he squeezed it between both hands just like Evan had done. He stood up straight and let his hands hang at his sides, the ball cupped in his left hand. I'd never thought about him being left-handed until then. He brought it up to his chest and cupped his right hand to hide the ball, and then he just froze.

He stood there like a scarecrow in a cartoon, and he looked like a scarecrow too; his shirt and his shorts suddenly looked like they were a size too big for him. The sound of the traffic and the voices of people on the street got quieter the longer he stood there until the only sound was the giggling of the two boys where they stood over on his right side. I couldn't take my eyes off Wade.

When he started his windup, he looked down at the sidewalk in front of him and brought his right knee up so high that I thought it would touch his forehead, and when he threw himself into the pitch I swear you could see his arms and his legs come loose from his body and freeze in the air for just a second before reattaching themselves. And I swear I heard something too: a sound like an ironing board unfolding or an old, squeaky gate being opened and slammed shut. But looking at it all, I couldn't tell if Wade's pitch was going to drop at his feet or bust through the curtain and fly down the street into the night.

As soon as the ball hit the curtain above the catcher's right shoulder I knew it hadn't been thrown as hard as any of Evan's pitches. And I was right; the screen said sixty-four. I saw it before Wade did because he was bent at the waist and staring at the ground like he couldn't stand up straight because he'd given that pitch all he had. The two boys saw the screen too. Evan just smiled, but the other boy clapped his hands like he was cheering on a batter that wasn't there. "That's all he's got, baby," he said. "That's all he's got."

Wade stood up straight and massaged his left shoulder with his right hand, and then he shook his left arm like it'd gone to sleep and he was trying to wake it up.

"We can go on home," the short boy said. "This guy's done." Ruby had been watching Wade, but now she whipped her head around and stared at the boys.

"No," she said. "He's got four more. Y'all have to wait." The two boys seemed just as surprised by what Ruby had said to them as I was, and they stood there and stared at her until she turned back around.

"He's got four more," the short boy said, making his voice high and squeaky. Ruby acted like she didn't hear him; she just stared at Wade. Sweat ran down his forehead from his hair, and he narrowed his eyes and wiped it away with his right hand. He looked exhausted after only throwing that one pitch. I wanted to tell him to stop, that he was too old and out of shape to be messing with kids half his age, that most grown men didn't get a kick out of challenging high schoolers in pitching contests, that he was embarrassing me more than he already had. But then he turned his head and looked at me, and when he did I saw that he wasn't having fun, that he hadn't thrown that pitch to try to impress those two boys or show off in front of me or Ruby. He'd thrown it because he knew those two boys were laughing at me, at us. It was the first time in my life that I felt like Wade wanted to be my dad.

"Focus on the catcher's mitt," I said. "And bring your shoulder in so it's pointing at him." He smiled and nodded his head.

"You got it now," he said. "I'm just getting warmed up." Wade went through his windup a second time: the same scarecrow pose, the high knee, the crazy sound I thought I heard again. The ball hit the curtain right on the catcher's mitt, and this time the screen said seventy.

"Yes!" Ruby said. The fat man on the stool raised his eyebrows and folded his arms across his chest again. He looked over at the two boys like he expected them to say something, but they didn't. Wade turned back and stared down the cage at the catcher like he was thinking about his next pitch.

"Bring the heat," I said. "Come on, Dad." He didn't look at me, but he smiled when he heard me call him that, and then he wiped the sweat off his forehead. I looked over at the two boys and saw that neither one of them was smiling anymore. Evan had his hands in his pockets, and the short boy had his arms folded across his chest, and his hips were rocking from side to side like he had to go to the bathroom.

Wade bent down and picked up another ball and went into his windup again, but this time it looked different, smoother, more like the pitchers you see on TV in the major leagues or on posters and baseball cards. It was the first time I could remember thinking of Wade as a baseball player instead of someone who just talked about playing baseball.

And I was right to think that, and I was right to think that pitch would be his best. I don't know if it was a strike or a ball because I was staring at the screen, but I heard the pitch snap against the rubber curtain, and then I watched the screen light up and say seventy-eight.

Ruby saw it too, and she jumped into the air and ran toward Wade, but he stepped right around her on his way to the two boys. He reached out with both hands and snatched the teddy bear away from the girl, and he turned and handed it to Ruby so hard it almost knocked her over. He faced the two boys. "Y'all have a good night," he said. "Don't get in no trouble."

Me and Ruby and Wade were already laughing by the time the taxi pulled away from the Pavilion. It felt like a movie, like we were leaving the scene of a crime after robbing a bank or holding up a gas station, and we didn't care one bit if anybody'd seen us because we knew we were going to get away with it.

My chin rested on the teddy bear's head, and I closed my eyes and buried my face in its fur. I could smell the perfume of the girl who'd been carrying it, and I could smell something else too—something sugary and sour—and I knew it was the lemonade that boy had been spitting into my hair. I prayed that those kids wouldn't call the police or tell their parents about what Wade had done to them. And then I remembered that I'd gone and done that very same thing by calling Marcus. I closed my eyes even tighter and squeezed that bear as hard as I could. I wasn't as ready to go home as I thought I was, but that didn't make no difference. We were already on television by the time we got back to our room.

Brady Weller

CHAPTER 13

On Wednesday, I met Sandy at a new place called Pepé Frijoles for lunch. While I waited for him I stood in the heat out in the parking lot, leaning against the hood of my car and staring up at the restaurant's sign on Garrison Boulevard. A cartoon Mexican wearing a poncho and sombrero smiled down at me like an idiot.

Sandy pulled up beside me in the old Ford Taurus. When he got out I saw that he'd already loosened his tie and left his blazer draped across the passenger seat. His shirt was dark with sweat.

"The a/c out again?" I asked.

"Again? When's the damn thing ever worked?"

He had a manila envelope in his hand. I nodded toward it. "Is that for me?"

"Depends," he said. "You buying lunch?"

We found a booth in the back away from other people in the restaurant. Through the window, a couple of guys shot basketball across the street at Lineberger Park, wavy lines of heat coming up from the asphalt. Our waitress brought two waters and a basket of nacho chips and a little bowl of salsa. Sandy ordered a sweet tea. I opened my menu and looked up at him. "So, what's in the envelope?"

"A present for you," he said.

He opened it and pulled out a card made of construction paper; it looked like something a kid might've drawn in school. "You shouldn't have," I said.

"I didn't," he said. "Easter did."

I dipped a chip in the salsa and popped it into my mouth, and then I took the card from his hands.

"Jesus," he said. "Would you at least *act* like it's evidence?" He gave me a rubber glove. I used it to hold the card between my thumb and finger.

"Is that Sosa?" I asked.

"It looks like him," he said.

I opened the card and read it out loud. " 'Dear Marcus: I'm sorry. Can we talk tonight? Love, Easter, your girlfriend (I hope!).' " I looked up at Sandy. "So what?" I said. "It's a love letter."

"Look on the back," he said. I turned the card over and saw a phone number written in pencil. "Easter's boyfriend wrote that."

"Boyfriend?"

"Yeah, 'boyfriend,' " he said. "Your Easter's all grown up. The kid said the number was on the back of the perp's shirt when he left with the girls."

"How'd he see it?"

"He said he was walking by the house."

"In the middle of the night?"

"He wouldn't cop to it, but he was sneaking over there; his prints were all over the window." I opened the card again and saw where Easter had written *Can we talk tonight?* It looked like she'd invited him.

"How'd you find this kid?" I asked.

"That's the interesting part," he said. "We didn't. His dad called us. Turns out Easter called Marcus last night from Myrtle Beach."

"Did she say who she's with?"

"Wade Chesterfield," Sandy said. "And this morning Marcus was able to identify him as the one who took the girls."

"Just like we thought."

"Just like we thought," he said. "Looks to me like he wants his girls back and didn't know what else to do."

"Looks to me like he's breaking the law."

Sandy shrugged his shoulders. "It's nothing we haven't seen before."

"Did y'all send anybody down to Myrtle last night?"

"No," he said. "Sergeant's not pulling anybody off this missing money. We called the Myrtle Beach PD. They put out an alert last night and got it on TV. They're looking into it."

"Yeah," I said, almost laughing. "I'm sure they are." I looked at the number on the back of the card. "You call this yet?"

"Of course I did," he said. "I called it this morning. It's a cell phone that belongs to a contractor named Lane Kelly."

I held up the card. "Can I hang on to this for a little while?"

"Hell no, Brady," Sandy said, snatching the card out of my hand. "It's a valuable piece of evidence in a police investigation." He dropped the card and the glove into the envelope and sealed it. "Besides," he said, "Marcus wants it back."

"Oh, Sandy," I said, "you're breaking my heart. I didn't know you were so sweet." I found an unused napkin and took the pen from Sandy's breast pocket. I wrote the phone number down on the back of it. "Is that all you've got?"

"Is that all?" he repeated, laughing. "We found prints on the windowsill that matched the ones we have on file for Chesterfield, so we know this kid, Marcus, is telling the truth."

"That's a busy window," I said.

"Tell me about it. They got out of there in a hurry. It looks like the father didn't touch anything in the room, and nothing was taken: no clothes, no toys or books—nothing."

"So, the girls have been out there for about thirty-six hours in their pajamas?"

"I guess so," he said.

When we finished eating, I picked up the check and paid for lunch, and then I came back to the table and left a five under the salt-shaker. I smiled at the waitress where she stood by the busing cart.

"Gracias," I said.

"You're welcome," she said, no hint of the accent I thought I'd heard earlier.

By the time I got outside, Sandy had already tossed the manila envelope onto the passenger's seat, and he was standing by the open driver's-side door.

"You got anything out on the dad's car?" I asked.

"Nothing great," he said. "We put out a call to the highway patrol in North and South Carolina to be on the lookout for a brown car driven by a white man with two white girls inside, and we've got a couple of officers tooling around town here. If we pull over every car matching that description then that's all we'll do all day; same for the guys in South Carolina. We just don't have that much manpower right now, especially without any real leads except for what this kid's given us."

"I'll take care of it for you," I said, smiling. "The next time we talk it'll be about where you can find these girls."

"Right," he said. "I look forward to it."

I turned onto Franklin Avenue and then took a left into Franklin Plaza, a nearly abandoned strip mall that now only housed a dis-count store, a beauty supply chain, and my office. I parked out front and sat looking at the big glass window that made up the front wall of my office. White curtains kept people from looking in. *Safe-at-Home Security Systems* was spelled out in red letters, trimmed in white, and pasted on the glass. Under that were both the local num-ber and the national hotline: *1-800-SAF-HOME.*

I unlocked the front door, turned on the lights, and walked

through the reception area. I tossed my keys onto my empty desk and pulled the napkin out of my back pocket and dialed the number the kid had seen on Chesterfield's shirt. It went right to voice mail.

"You've reached Kelly Renovation, LLC," a man's voice said. "Please leave a message and someone will return your call as soon as possible. Thanks, and have a great day." I cleared my throat before it beeped.

"Hi, Mr. Kelly," I said, trying to sound as unthreatening and kind as possible. "My name is Brady Weller. I'm a guardian ad litem here in Gastonia, and I'm calling about two children who may be the daughters of one of your employees. If you have a minute, give me a call back." As I was leaving him my number I realized that I'd been staring at the picture of Jessica and me the whole time I'd been on the phone. "I hope to hear from you soon," I said before hanging up.

I sat and looked at Jessica a little longer and tried to see the sixteen-year-old's face in the picture, but it was hard to do. I looked to her left, where the forty-year-old version of me stood beside her, still holding on to the saddle horn.

"Hold on tight," I whispered to the guy in the picture.

The phone rang on the desk. I picked it up and looked at the caller ID: a local number I didn't recognize.

"Hello?" I said. "Safe-at-Home." The other end was quiet. "Hello?" I said again.

"Is this Brady Weller?" a woman's voice said.

"Yes," I said. "Who's this?"

"My name's Cynthia Kelly," she said. "I'm Lane Kelly's wife. You called him a second ago."

"Hi, Mrs. Kelly," I said. "Is your husband around? I really need to speak with—" She cut me off.

"He can't come to the phone," she said. "But he wanted me to call you."

"Okay," I said. And then she started asking me questions; her tone was formal and nervous, and the questions she asked seemed like she may have written them down or had somebody write them down for her.

"Why are you calling my husband?"

"I'm calling about someone named Wade Chesterfield. I'm not sure if he works for your husband or not, but I'd like to ask Mr. Kelly about him." The line was quiet, and I figured she was either whispering my response so quietly that I couldn't hear her, or she was writing it down under the question she'd just asked. I waited.

"Are you a cop?"

"No," I said. "I used to be, years ago, but not anymore. I install security systems, and I'm a volunteer in family court." Another long pause.

"Is this about the money?"

"What money?" I asked, but she didn't say anything. The air over the phone line changed, and I could tell she'd put her end on mute. She was doing something she didn't want me to hear. Her voice came back on the line.

"My husband will meet with you," she said. "Tonight."

"Great. Where?"

"You know Tony's Ice Cream?" she asked. I wanted to tell her that everyone in town knew Tony's Ice Cream. It wasn't even a five-minute drive down Franklin Avenue from my office.

"Yes," I said. "What time?"

"Six," she said.

"I'll be there."

CHAPTER 14

Around 5:30 P.M., I left the office and drove down Franklin to Tony's Ice Cream and found a spot in the near-full parking lot. I'd arrived about a half hour early, but something about my conversation with his wife told me that Lane Kelly would be there early too. I rolled my windows down and listened to the music coming from the car garage that shared a parking lot with Tony's. For a second I watched people leave the old blond-brick building, carrying white paper bags full of hamburgers and hot dogs, tall wax-coated cups with milk shakes inside.

And then my eyes scanned the parking lot until I found what I was looking for: an oversize Ford F-150 with a huge toolbox sitting in the bed. I leaned forward to get a better look, and I saw a woman sitting in the front seat. She was scanning the parking lot too. On the driver's-side door, you could tell that someone had removed the lettering, but the paint around where the letters had been was a little faded, and you could still make out *Kelly Renovation* and the phone number beneath it, the same one I'd called earlier. The woman in the driver's seat caught me staring at her truck, and she shifted her eyes and hunkered down in the seat as low as she could without lying down. I watched her window slide up until it closed. Mrs. Kelly, I thought. The truck's windows were untinted, and I saw her eyes dart back over in my direction; I gave her a little wave, but she just hunkered down even lower. After seeing her in the parking lot, I was certain that Mr. Kelly was inside waiting for me.

The smell of frying burgers and boiled hot dogs hit me as soon as I opened the door. Tony's had a full dinner crowd as usual, and I walked through the line in front of the order window and stopped with my back to the ice cream counter. Booths lined three walls, and my eyes hopped from table to table until I found the only man who seemed to be alone: a pretty big guy in blue jeans and a button-down shirt, which surprised me because it was so hot outside. He had short brown hair and a beard. His thick fingers were interlocked on the table in front of him and his head was turned to the right, where the cars on Franklin Avenue passed by the window.

I walked over and stood by the bench seat across the table from him. He didn't look up.

"Mr. Kelly?" I asked. His eyes darted upward, but his head didn't move.

"Who are you?" he asked.

"I'm Brady Weller," I said. "I spoke with your wife a few hours ago. We're supposed to meet at six P.M." I looked at my watch. It was 5:46. "Looks like we're both early."

His face seemed to relax, but his eyes still looked a little nervous.

"Let's get something to eat," I said. "You hungry? I'm hungry."

"No," he said. "I'm okay."

"We've got to eat," I said. "It'll look weird if we just sit here without eating anything." I took a step toward the line of people at the order window. "Let me get you a cheeseburger." He didn't say anything; he barely looked up at me. "I'll get you a cheeseburger," I said. "I'll be right back."

I ordered two cheeseburgers all the way, two fries, a Sun Drop and a Cheerwine, both in the can. I carried the tray over to the booth where Kelly was sitting and divvied up the food before gesturing toward the two sodas. "You can have whichever one you want," I said.

"Thanks," he said, but he didn't make a move for either of them, and he didn't unwrap his cheeseburger. He finally picked up a french fry and put it in his mouth. I was starving, and I didn't hesitate. I unwrapped my cheeseburger and took a bite, and then I emptied my little bag of fries on a napkin I'd opened beside my cheeseburger.

"So, Mr. Kelly," I said, "I figure you know Wade Chesterfield."

"Why are you looking for him?"

"I already told your wife," I said. "His two daughters have gone missing, and somebody identified him as the last person seen with them. I'm looking for those two little girls."

"I don't know them," he said.

"That's fine," I said. "I just want to know about Chesterfield. How long has he worked for you?"

"Maybe two years," he said.

"And what does he do?"

"Whatever needs to be done," he said. "Carpentry, painting, drywall." He took a few french fries and popped them into his mouth. Then he opened the Cheerwine and took a sip.

"When's the last time you saw him?" He looked at me for a second, and then he took another sip of his soda. He picked up a napkin and wiped his hands.

"Friday afternoon," he said. "We were on a job."

"Where was the job?"

"Calder Mountain," he said.

I raised my eyebrows and took another bite of my cheeseburger. "That's a pretty swank place. What kind of job was it?"

"Some guy'd just finished hanging drywall in his basement. He wanted us to mud it, tape it, come back and paint it when it dried."

"Y'all didn't hang it?" I asked.

"No."

"Why not?"

"Because the guy had already done it."

"He sounds like a pretty handy guy."

"Not really," he said. "The job was shit. The pieces were cut all wrong. That's why Wade—" but he caught himself and stopped.

"That's why Wade *what*?"

"Wade couldn't stop talking about how bad the drywall job was," he said. "And it was. I mean, the guy'd cut some of the sheets too long, and he'd used nails instead of screws. He'd beat that drywall all to hell trying to sink some of those nails." He stopped talking and took his hands off the table and leaned back against his seat. "But that wasn't the weird part."

"What was?"

"The walls," he said. "They were everywhere. It was like a maze down there: no outlets, no overhead lights. We had to run work lights so we could see. It was weird. Gave me the creeps as soon as we went in."

"Did you ask the guy about it?"

"No way," he said. "The last thing you want to do is tell a customer he's done a bad job. That's why I got pissed when Wade started messing with the walls."

"Fixing them?"

"The guy had a few leftover pieces of drywall stacked on a pallet in one of the rooms. Wade wanted to fix the worst walls before we mudded and taped them."

"And you didn't want to?"

"No way," he said. "That wasn't *our* leftover drywall. I wasn't going to use it without asking, and then do extra work I might not get paid for."

"But Wade?"

"I went to get something out of the truck, and when I came back Wade had a pry bar and was jerking nails out of one of the walls."

"And what did you do?"

"Nothing," he said. "I didn't have time to do anything before the drywall came down. It just exploded off the wall. Wade barely got out of the way." He leaned forward and put his elbows on the table, and then he put his hands over his eyes and rubbed them. He looked at me. "That's when we saw it."

"Saw what?"

"The money," he whispered.

"The money?"

"Shhhh," he said, looking around to see if anyone had heard me. "Yeah," he whispered, "money—stacks of it. It just came pouring out of the wall. There must've been thousands of dollars back there." I couldn't believe what he was telling me.

"And that's why the guy had hung the drywall himself," I said.

"That's why," he said.

"And that's why he wanted you to finish it. To hide it."

"Yep," he said.

"What's the guy's name?"

"Broughton," he said. "Tommy Broughton."

Tommy Broughton: I almost coughed my Sun Drop up into my nose when I heard that name. Sandy and I had spent years dealing with him in one way or another; he was nothing but a small-time crook, but if Gaston County had had a hillbilly Mafia then Tommy Broughton would've wanted to be its Don Corleone. But he'd also spent plenty of time turning over evidence in investigations and trying to buddy up to the police. I'd always thought of him as one of those fat catfish swimming in the Catawba River, trudging along the bottom with his belly in the mud, his mouth open, feeding on whatever he came across. There was no way he'd earned that kind of money honestly, and even though he'd gotten this far he wasn't smart enough to get away with an armored car heist, but he was stupid enough to hide money in his walls and then invite somebody like Wade Chesterfield to come over and admire his work. But I knew how dangerous stupid could be when stupid got scared, and Broughton scared easily.

"Had you met Broughton before this?"

"Yeah. A couple months ago at a bar he owns on Wilkinson. I did some work for him."

"Was Wade on that job?"

"No," he said.

"What's the name of the bar?"

"Tomcat's."

I smiled and shook my head. "Tomcat's? That's cute. Find any money hidden in the walls there?"

"No," he said, trying to smile. "Not there."

"So, what did y'all do when you saw that money?"

"Me? I didn't do anything. But Wade just freaked out."

"How?"

"He started talking about how this could change our lives," he said. "About how we could take the money and use the extra drywall to hide it. Said it would take Broughton forever to find out, especially if the rest of the walls had money in them. He said we could be long gone before he noticed anything."

"What did you say?"

"I said, 'No way.' I wasn't getting involved in something like that."

"But Wade?"

"But Wade wanted to," he said. "So he did, but I tried to stop him. I swear."

What he'd just said made me stop and think, and I suddenly realized how quiet we'd been talking. I sat back and sized up Mr. Kelly: he was at least six feet tall, easily over two hundred pounds. I remembered the description on the back of Chesterfield's baseball card: six-foot-one, 162.

"You couldn't stop him?" I asked.

"No," he said. "I tried." I narrowed my eyes and smiled at him to let him know I didn't believe him.

"Come on, Mr. Kelly," I said. "You're a pretty big guy; you look like you can handle yourself. You've got what, thirty, forty pounds on Chesterfield?"

"He had a gun," he said.

"He had a gun?" I asked, almost laughing. "Where'd he get a gun?"

"I keep one in the truck," he said.

"Why do you have a gun in your truck?"

"I've had a lot of stuff stolen over the years," he said. "You drive around all day in a truck with thousands of dollars of equipment in it, year after year. People tend to steal it sometimes."

"Okay," I said. "He had a gun. He had a gun that he went outside and got from your truck *after* he found the money. And then he held you up and took it."

"Yes," he said, not showing any signs of being aware of just how lame his story sounded. "He's got a duffel bag that he carries some of his gear in, and he dumped it out on the floor and filled it with money. He could barely zip it, and then it was almost too heavy to carry."

"Did he tie you up, then take your truck?"

"Yes," he said.

I laughed, but he acted like he didn't notice.

"He used zip ties and got my hands behind my back, and then he used them to tie me to a support post under the deck just outside the basement. He put duct tape over my mouth." Now I knew he was lying.

"So," I said, "you want me to believe that you watched thousands of dollars tumble out of a wall, and then you watched your buddy go outside to your truck and get a gun. And *then* you stood there while he fastened all those zip ties together to get them long enough to go around both your wrists, and then you waited for him to make another set to go around the post? And then he put duct tape over your mouth?"

"Yes," he said. "That's what happened."

"Did Tommy Broughton believe your story?" I asked.

"Yes," he said.

"You better hope so," I said.

"He found me down there after Wade left," he said. "He cut me loose and I told him what happened."

"Did he call the police?"

"No," he said. "He never even mentioned the police. It was like somebody'd found his stash of kiddy porn and he didn't know what to say. He just freaked out, started acting all nervous, asking me all about Wade: what kind of guy he is, where he lives, that kind of thing."

"Did you tell him?"

"Yeah," he said, "I told him everything he wanted to know. I mean, I felt bad and I didn't want to, but Wade dragged me into this. I didn't know what else to do. I was scared because the guy was so freaked out."

"Did you ask Broughton where the money came from?"

"Hell no," he said. "He said something about his wife's inheritance, about a will being contested. Said that's why he was storing the cash."

"Did you ask if the other walls had money in them?"

"Hell no," he said again. "I know better than that. I acted like I believed him, and I called somebody to pick me up, and then I got the hell out of there. I mean, there was money everywhere; probably hundreds of thousands of dollars inside that one wall." He raised his eyes to mine, and we just looked at each other.

"Did you call the police?" I asked.

"No way," he said. "That's the last thing I'm going to do. A cop called my phone this morning, but there's no way in hell I'm calling him back."

"You should call him back," I said. "I know him; he's a good guy."

"No way," Kelly said again. "The police show up over at Broughton's and ask about that money, who do you think he's going to suspect of ratting him out? Who's he going to come looking for?" He closed his eyes and sighed, and then he opened them slowly and looked at me. "Somebody broke into our house a couple days ago— kicked in the back door. We've been staying at my mother-in-law's because I knew we couldn't stay at home."

"You think the break-in was related to this?" He looked around and then leaned toward me.

"Yes," he said, "because they didn't take anything—nothing

except a picture of me and my wife." He leaned back like he was out of breath; his face had turned white.

"Did you call the police?" I asked.

"No," he said. "I already told you: no police."

"Okay," I said. "No police. Why are you willing to talk to me?"

"I don't know," he said. "Maybe because you're not a cop. I don't know. I just wanted to tell somebody that I had nothing to do with this. Nothing. You can tell it to whoever you want, but I'm not getting mixed up in this with the police and all that."

"I think you're already pretty mixed up in it," I said.

"Whatever," he said. "The police are going to have to drag me in kicking and screaming. People who testify about stuff like this end up dead in the movies. That ain't going to be me."

We sat looking at each other for a second, and then I leaned forward and put my elbows on the table. "I don't believe your story, Mr. Kelly. At least not all of it."

"You can believe whatever you want," he said, "but that's what happened."

"I can tell you it didn't," I said. "Go in the bathroom and look at your beard. If Wade had put duct tape on your face tight enough to keep you from screaming you would've had to cut it out of your beard. Also, how'd you get your truck back so quick? Did Wade leave you an anonymous message about where to find it?" Kelly closed his eyes, and then he opened them slowly.

"It's not my fault Wade took the money," he said.

"I agree," I said. "It's not your fault. I'm not the one blaming you."

"Wade's a good guy," he said. "He's got a good heart. He just gets carried away and does stupid shit sometimes." I looked at him for a second until the irony of what he'd just said had time to sink in. He sighed. "I know," he said.

My heart was racing, but I tried to keep my cool. I knew I was sitting at a booth in Tony's Ice Cream with one of three people who knew where the stolen armored car money was or at least where it had been on Friday afternoon. Kelly must've sensed the tension.

"Broughton's going to have somebody looking for Wade, isn't he?"

"Yes," I said.

"And it's going to be bad when they find him, isn't it?"

"Probably worse than you can imagine," I said.

"Jesus," he said. He put his hands over his eyes, and then he dropped them to the table. "What should I do?"

I took the last bite of my cheeseburger. "Well," I said. I swallowed and wiped my mouth with my napkin. "If I was you, I'd do one of two things. One, I'd get those letters back on my truck as soon as possible. Then I'd go back to work and act like nothing happened. The minute you start acting weird is the minute more weird stuff happens." I balled up all my trash in the cheeseburger wrapper and picked up my drink. "Or, two: I'd pack up as much as I can, pick up the mother-in-law, and leave town until all this blows over."

"How will we know it's 'blown over'?" he asked.

"I don't know," I said. "I guess the day the cops stop calling and people stop kicking in your back door."

"Great," he said. "Thanks."

I stood up from the table and tossed the balled wrapper and my soda in the trash can beside the booth. Kelly just sat there, his untouched burger on the table before him. I looked down at him. "Do you own a gun?"

"Yes."

"Good. Make sure it's loaded and that you know how to use it. And if you're not going to eat that cheeseburger then take it out to your wife."

What was Mrs. Kelly thinking when she saw me jump in my car, start the engine, and tear out of the lot onto Franklin and head for my office? What was her husband thinking as he sat there in that booth, a cold cheeseburger in front of him, the biggest confession of his life over and done with, a wife waiting in the car with more questions than he'd have answers for?

When I got back to my desk, I picked up the cordless and dialed Sandy's office. I sat down on the edge of my desk, and then I stood up again. "How's it going?" I asked him.

"Fine," he said. "Why?"

"Just calling to check on you," I said. "That's all."

"Yeah, right," he said. "What's up? I'm busy."

"Just want to let you know that you can call in the cavalry."

"What are you talking about?" he asked.

"I solved your case."

"You found the girls?"

"No," I said, "not that case."

"You found Wade Chesterfield?"

"No, not that one either."

"What the hell, then, Brady?"

"I found your money," I said.

"What money?"

"The armored car," I said. "I found out where it made its last deposit." His chair squeaked, and I pictured him sitting up straight at his desk, grabbing a pen, and flipping a pad open to a clean page.

"Go ahead," he said.

I told him what Kelly had seen: the unfinished basement, the bad drywall job, the money behind it. But I really got his attention when I told him who'd put it there.

"Tommy Broughton?" he asked. "I haven't heard that name in a while."

"Now you know why: he's been busy in his basement. It looks like he owns a club too." Then I told him how Wade Chesterfield had gotten himself involved.

"Jesus," he said. "This guy must be an idiot."

"I don't know," I said. "Not if he manages to disappear. It worked for the driver of that armored car."

"*Might've* worked," he said. "Jury's still out. I don't know if Broughton's capable of murder, but he knows people who are."

"Case solved."

"Yeah, right," he said. "On what information? I can't tell the FBI that I leaked all that info to you and you came back and busted this thing wide open. I can't even tell Sarge that. I *like* my job."

"You better move on Broughton, though," I said. "You know how he is; he's lost a whole lot of money, and it's been a few days. He has to figure somebody's onto him. He might feel the need to hit the road."

"We'll figure out a way to start watching him," he said. "If he's dumb enough to hide millions of dollars in a wall then I'm sure he's done something stupid along the way. If he has, we'll find it."

"Take another swing at talking to Lane Kelly," I said. "Find him before *he* does something stupid."

"I'll bring him in," he said. "But there's one thing you should keep in mind."

"What's that?" I asked.

"The FBI's going to have to be in on this," he said. "I'm sorry, but your volunteer work just got a lot more complicated."

Easter Quillby

CHAPTER 15

We spent all day Wednesday in a hotel outside of Charleston. Early that morning, a taxi had dropped us at the garage in Myrtle Beach where Wade had left the car. It looked like they weren't even open yet, but Wade knocked on the door until we finally heard a lock turn on the other side. He'd already told me and Ruby to stay outside so nobody would see us. A few minutes later, his car pulled around the building; it was light blue instead of red like he said it would be. He stopped in front of us and got out and opened the back door. "Ruby, get in," he said.

"Why isn't it red?" she asked.

"Get in," Wade said again. "Hurry up." I went to climb in behind her, but Wade stopped me. "You're getting in front."

No one said anything until we were out of the Myrtle Beach traffic and turning onto the highway. Wade had been checking his rearview mirror every few seconds like he was worried that somebody might be following us. He looked over at me, and then he looked back at the road. "How could you do it, Easter?" he finally said.

"Do what?" Ruby asked. Neither one of us had told her about me calling Marcus.

"Nothing," Wade said. I looked out the window as we drove up over a bridge on the highway: the land was flat as far as I could see, and the grass was dry and brown-looking. Skinny pine trees ran along the road beneath the bridge. In the side mirror, I could see Ruby's face where she was looking out her window too.

"What color is our car?" she asked.

"It's primer," Wade said.

"What color is that?" Ruby asked.

"It's not a color," he said. "It's nothing."

Once we got to the hotel, Wade told us to stay in the room with the door locked, and he walked across the parking lot to Bojangles' to get us something to eat. The parking lot was full of tractor trailers. Last time I'd eaten something from Bojangles' I'd walked up there with Ruby and Mom—Mom walking down the sidewalk counting money and pushing nickels and dimes around in her palm, saying, "Y'all go ahead and tell me what you want, and I'll let you know if you can have it. I ain't going to wait for y'all to make up your minds once we get up to the counter and you see pictures of all that food and I have to say no." A couple times I climbed off the bed and looked out the window to see if I could see Wade coming across the parking lot, but all I could see was a bunch of tractor trailers and the highway off in the distance.

When Wade came back with our food, me and Ruby ate sausage biscuits sitting on our bed while Wade ate sitting on his. Me and him still hadn't hardly said a word to each other since the night before. All he'd said to us was "Don't touch anything" after he hid his bag under the bed when we checked in and "Keep this locked" before he closed the door behind him.

After he finished eating, Wade stood up and tossed his wrapper and napkins into the trash can. "Y'all sit there and watch some TV," he said. "I need to step out for a little bit." He walked around to the far side of the other bed and bent down, and I knew he was getting something out of that gym bag.

Wade lifted the chain on the door and looked back at me. "Lock this behind me," he said. "And don't open it for nobody. I'll be back in a little bit."

He opened the door and stepped outside and closed it behind him. I climbed off the bed and locked the chain on the door. I turned the doorknob and yanked on it to make sure it was locked.

I flipped through the channels until I found some cartoons, and then I looked over at Ruby. "You want to watch this?"

"I want to go back to the beach," Ruby said.

"Well, we ain't going to do that," I said. "Not today anyway."

She climbed down from the bed and walked into the bathroom and shut the door behind her.

As soon as I heard the bathroom door lock, I scooted across the bed and dropped down to the floor and felt around under Wade's bed. My hands found the gym bag and pulled it out far enough to see the zipper. The room was suddenly too quiet, and I realized that Ruby hadn't made a sound from the bathroom. I turned up the TV and unzipped the bag, but I stopped when I saw a bunch of hundred-dollar bills. I knew without even having to look that the bag was full of them, and that was why Wade had broken into our room and taken us in the middle of the night. That man who'd been hiding out in the woods was searching for this money, and that's why he'd come looking for Wade. My heart was beating in my ears and my skin had gone cold.

I pictured myself reaching into that bag for one of those bundles of hundred-dollar bills, beating on the bathroom door until Ruby came out, and then going outside and catching a taxi that would take us all the way back to Gastonia, far away from Wade Chesterfield, and far away from this bag of money that he'd hidden under the bed in a hotel room with us in it.

The teddy bear Wade had won for us was sitting on our bed, and I took a packet of money over and stuffed it down in the bear's overalls. When the toilet flushed, I ran around the bed and dropped to my knees and zipped up the bag and pushed it back under the bed. Ruby walked into the bedroom just as I made it back to our bed.

"What's wrong?" she asked.

"Nothing," I said. I crossed my legs Indian-style and looked at the TV like I was interested in those stupid cartoons.

"You look mad," she said. "Your face is red."

"Well, I'm not mad," I said. "I'm just sunburned." That part was true. But Ruby wasn't sunburned at all. Her skin was an even darker brown than it had been that morning, and her hair looked even thicker after being in the ocean with me and Wade. She climbed up on the bed and sat beside me.

"I don't feel like watching cartoons," she said.

I tossed the remote on the bed in front of her. "Put on whatever you want to," I said. "I don't care what you watch." I picked up the bear and held it to my chest, and I leaned back against the headboard and closed my eyes and thought about how much I hated Wade for sneaking into our room and convincing us to go with him. I couldn't believe that it all had happened just two nights before, and I couldn't believe that in just two days I'd gone from hating Wade, to wanting to believe in him, all the way back to hating him all over again.

A key turned in the lock a little while later, and Wade tried to open the door and walk into the room, but the chain was still on and it only opened a little bit. He closed the door and knocked.

I climbed off the bed and slid the chair over and looked through the peephole. Wade was staring right back at me. "Who is it?" I asked.

"It's your dad," Wade said. "Open the door—hurry up."

"Who?"

He cracked the door again. "It's me, Easter," he said. "Open the door." I hopped down from the chair and moved it back under the table, and then I undid the chain. Wade walked in with a bag from Eckerd's in his hand. "Hey!" he said like everything was just fine.

"Where'd you go?" I asked, but what I really wanted to know about was the bag of money he'd stuffed under the bed, but that question was going to have to wait until we were alone.

"I went shopping," he said, smiling. "I got us some disguises."

"Disguises?" Ruby said. She climbed down off the bed. Wade pulled out a little box of something and handed it to me.

"What's that?" Ruby asked.

"It's hair dye," I said, looking at Wade. "What's this for?"

"It's for you," he said. "You're dying your hair brown."

"Am I dying mine too?" Ruby asked.

"No," Wade said. "That's for you, Easter, but I got something for you." He pulled out a pair of pink sunglasses, and Ruby put them right on. "Now," Wade said, "you have to make sure you wear those glasses whenever we go somewhere. I don't want anybody to know I'm traveling with the world-famous Ruby Chesterfield."

"Quillby," I said. Wade turned around and looked at me.

"What?"

"Quillby," I said again. I stared right back at him. "Her last name is Quillby, and mine is too."

I'd always wanted my hair to be brown, and I hoped it would be as dark as Ruby's, as dark as Mom's.

After reading the directions, I put on the plastic gloves and stood in the tub with the shower off and squirted the dye all over my head, and then I used my fingers to rub it in. I counted off the minutes, and then I turned on the shower and rinsed it out.

When I finished bathing, I wrapped a towel around me and opened the bathroom door. The mirror in the bathroom had been too fogged over to look in, and that was fine; I wasn't ready to see myself anyway. Wade and Ruby were sitting side by side on one of the beds. Ruby was wearing her new sunglasses. She had her head leaned up against Wade and he had his arm around her.

"Cardinals are playing tonight," Wade said. "McGwire's going for fifty-eight." I acted like I didn't hear him, and I looked at Ruby and gathered my hair over my left shoulder so she could see it.

"What do you think?" I asked. "Is it brown?"

Ruby just stared at me, and then she lifted up her sunglasses to get a better look. She wrinkled up her forehead like she was thinking of exactly how to put it, and then she dropped her sunglasses back over her eyes. "I don't know," she finally said. "It's too wet."

That was the last thing I wanted to hear, and I went back into the bathroom to put on my T-shirt and shorts, which I realized were the only clothes we had with us except for our nightgowns. I heard Wade out in the bedroom. "I think it looks great," he said. "I really do."

I walked out of the bathroom in my towel with my wadded-up shirt in my hand. "We need clothes, Wade. And underwear. We can't wear the same thing every day." I went to unfasten my towel and put on my shirt, but then I caught myself. "And we need our own room too. I bet you've got enough money to pay for it." I picked up all my clothes and walked toward the bathroom.

"Hold up," Wade said. "I need a shower. You go ahead and get dressed out here." He picked up a couple of things and walked toward the bathroom, but before he closed the door he looked back at me. "We'll go shopping for more clothes tomorrow," he said. "I promise." He smiled at me and closed the door.

I rolled my eyes and sighed and hung my towel on the back of one of the chairs and started getting dressed. I looked at Ruby. "Is my hair brown or not?" I asked.

"It's wet," she said. "I told you it's too hard to tell."

"You probably can't tell because you're wearing those stupid sunglasses."

"You're just jealous that he didn't get a pair for you," she said.

"No—I'm not," I said.

There was a little sink and a counter just outside the bathroom, and I walked over and opened one of the drawers. I heard Wade turn the shower on. I found a hair dryer and stood up and plugged it in, careful not to look in the mirror; I didn't want to see myself until my hair was dry and I knew for sure just what it was going to look like. It took a few minutes to blow-dry my hair, and then I turned the dryer off and brushed my hair back with my fingers. I walked around in front of the bed where Ruby was sitting. She lifted up her sunglasses and looked at me for a second, and then she took them all the way off.

"It's brown," she said, smiling. "It's definitely brown."

I wanted to believe her, but I just couldn't, not after seeing how much dye had been washed out of my hair and down the drain. I walked back to the mirror and stood in front of it with my eyes closed. I took a deep breath and held it, and then I opened my eyes.

Ruby was right; my hair was brown. I turned my head back and forth, looking at myself from all the different angles I could. The girl in the mirror didn't even look like me, and I saw that with the brown hair and all the sun I'd gotten yesterday that I looked more like Ruby than I ever had before, and I finally looked like Mom.

Ruby had crawled off the bed and come over to get a better look. She stood beside me and both of us stared in the mirror. We looked like sisters for the first time in our lives.

"You look different," she said, "but I like it."

"I do too," I said, still turning my head and looking at myself out of the corners of my eyes. "I love it."

The shower had turned off in the bathroom, and now the toilet flushed. The knob turned and the door opened. Me and Ruby both looked over. Wade stepped out of the bathroom, smiling, already dressed like he was ready to go somewhere.

"What do y'all think?" he asked. I couldn't believe it; he'd shaved off his whiskers and gone and dyed his hair brown too, and he'd gotten just as much sun as I had. He kept smiling and turned around slowly like he was a model. Ruby laughed and clapped her hands; I felt like crying.

The three of us finally looked like a family.

Pruitt

CHAPTER 16

The first thing Lane Kelly saw when he woke up was me standing at the foot of the bed. The room was dark except for the faint green light coming from the alarm clock on the table by his head. He'd opened his eyes to the sound of me tapping the Louisville Slugger's barrel against the footboard. His wife lifted her head from the pillow and stared out into the darkness.

"Get up." Neither of them moved, as if they hoped that lying still would make me disappear. The bat tapped the footboard again. "Get up."

In the green glow, I watched Kelly's hand feel around for the pistol he'd left sitting beside the alarm clock. He didn't know that while he was sleeping the room had already been cleared, the gun found and moved to the dresser behind me, just like he didn't know that a stranger had been in his house for twenty minutes, moving from room to room after coming through the front door with one of their spare keys. I reached into the darkness for the pistol. My thumb cocked the hammer. "No use looking for that gun. It's right here."

Kelly's hand froze when he realized what he'd heard, and then it lifted up toward the lamp. "No lights," I said. His hand kept moving, and I set the pistol back on the dresser and closed both hands around my bat. The lamp on the table clicked on just as I was in midswing. The bulb exploded with a *pop* and the base of the lamp shattered against the wall. His wife screamed in the one second that light filled the room before it fell into darkness again.

My eyes readjusted after the blast of light as Kelly's face and shoulders set themselves off in blurred edges. The bat came to rest barrel down against his neck, pinning him to the bed, his Adam's apple sending a vibration through the wood when he swallowed. His wife whimpered beside him, the sheets rustling as her hand searched the bed, reaching out for him. I slid the barrel of the bat from his neck to his chest, pushing the covers off him and his wife and down toward the foot of the bed until reaching the footboard. "Both of you. Get up. Now."

The inside of the house was pitch black as Lane Kelly and his wife inched down the hallway in front of me, their fingertips tracing the wall, grazing both the framed photographs as well as the empty frame whose picture was still folded and tucked inside my glove compartment along with the picture of Wade Chesterfield's kid.

Their back door was newly repaired, and it squeaked when Kelly pulled it toward him. His wife stumbled when she stepped out onto the deck, and she fell to her knees and stayed that way, crying, her hands covering her eyes. He bent down and whispered to her, and then he helped her to her feet and down the steps into the grass.

Neither of them seemed surprised to find that the door to the garage was unlocked or that the blinding construction lights had been turned on and pulled into a circle with a folding chair in the center. It wasn't until Kelly was sitting in the chair in that bright light with his wrists bound together that he thought to ask a single question. "What do you want?"

His wife was also sitting in a chair somewhere in the dark in front of him, just far enough outside the light that he couldn't see her. I'd already fastened her wrists behind her back, and her ankles were now being duct-taped to a chair just like the one he was sitting in. "Who are you?" she asked.

"It doesn't matter."

She was crying and trying to see my eyes through my sunglasses where I knelt at her feet, my hands tearing strips of duct tape from the roll. Her short white gown left her legs exposed.

"Are you going to hurt us?" she asked.

"That depends."

"On what?" Kelly asked behind me.

"On what you know." I used my teeth to tear off a long piece of tape that wrapped twice around his wife's head, covering her mouth. She screamed into it.

"If you hurt her I'll kill you," Kelly said.

"You shouldn't be worried about her."

He wasn't wearing anything but a pair of white jockeys, and his stomach sagged slightly over his waist. In the bright light, both his underwear and his skin were whiter than they should've been. An industrial table saw sat eye level with him in the center of the lights. He stared past it in the direction my voice had come from, and then his eyes focused on the saw as if he'd never seen it before.

But his wife must have seen it before, and she must've been thinking about what she'd seen it do, because she began to grunt and toss her head from side to side, rocking her chair back and forth off the concrete floor. Kelly looked in her direction and called out, "Honey! It's okay!" She either didn't hear him or didn't believe him, because she didn't stop rocking. "If you hurt her—"

"Stop talking and listen." My shadow fell across him, blotting out the light. "Do you know why this is happening?"

"The money?"

"Yes. This is definitely about the money."

"Let her go, and I'll talk."

"I don't think so."

"I don't know anything," he said.

"You haven't been asked any questions yet."

"I saw Wade take it. That's all."

"See? You do know something." I'd taken off my batting gloves earlier to string the zip ties and tear off pieces of duct tape, but my right hand found them in my back pocket and slid them on before removing the safety guard from the saw. Kelly's eyes followed my gloved hand while it moved, but his eyes stayed on the blade once it was exposed.

"I don't know anything," he said again. "I swear." His voice had changed, gone higher, more desperate.

"How much was it?"

"How much what?"

"How much did he take?"

"I don't know," he said. "A lot. Couple hundred thousand—maybe more. It was too much to count."

"Where is he now?"

"I don't know," he said. "I swear. I have no idea."

"You need to have a better answer than that." When the saw turned on, a sharp, guttural whine came from the darkness behind me and immediately melded with the scream of the blade until the two sounds were indistinguishable. My fingers closed around Kelly's forearms and pulled him out of his chair. His wrists slammed down on the bridge of the saw. "Wait!" he screamed. "Wait!" His hands clenched themselves in tight fists, but they weren't strong enough to keep his right index finger from being pried loose and pushed toward the blade. "Charleston!" he screamed.

My hands let go of his wrists, and Kelly fell back against the chair, knocking it over onto its side. The saw powered down and the sound of it faded away.

"What about Charleston?" He laid at my feet in the fetal position, his right hand tucked against his stomach as if it were already missing. He wasn't going to answer, so my hand closed around his face and squeezed his cheeks together before the question came again. "What about Charleston?"

"His mom," he finally said. When my hand let go of his face his head bounced against the concrete floor.

"Is that where he's going?"

"I don't know," he said. "I just can't think of anything else. Please."

The sounds of his wife's crying came out of the darkness, and he raised his head and looked toward her. The saw turned on again, and the sound of it sucked the air out of the garage. When he heard it, Kelly closed his eyes and lowered his chin to his chest, but he opened them when he felt my hands on his again, and he screamed when his wrists hit the saw's bridge.

My mouth was right by his ear, the wind from the saw blowing across my face. "Is that where he's going?" But if he answered, I didn't hear him.

My eyes opened into the blinding construction lights, and my hands reached out on either side of me and searched the concrete floor for my sunglasses. When my fingers closed around them and lifted my sunglasses to my eyes I felt something warm and wet. Blood.

When I stood, I stepped on the heavy framing hammer she'd used, and the toe of my shoe kicked it, sending it skittering across the floor and into the darkness.

The garage door was open, and Lane Kelly and his wife were gone.

Outside, the floodlights showed two sets of footprints in the shiny, damp grass that led to the woods behind Kelly's house. They'd known better than to go back inside. They must've also known that those woods would go on for miles and miles before crossing the South Carolina state line, that they'd be walking barefoot and barelegged in the pitch black for hours before stumbling upon another house. There was no one coming to help them, and there was no one they could go to for help.

My truck was parked in the grass about a quarter mile down the road, but within minutes it was rolling through Lane Kelly's front yard on the way behind his house. It came to a stop at the spot where the sets of footprints disappeared into the woods, the high beams and the lights on the roof rack piercing the darkness and throwing long shadows out away from the trees.

The truck idled in neutral for a few seconds, and then my foot eased on and off the gas and the sound of the engine revving echoed back toward the house from the woods. My eyes scanned the trees where they were lit up like a stage, looking for any sign of movement, any flash where the light caught an open eye or a piece of white fabric. Lane Kelly and his wife were out there somewhere in those trees, hunkered down, holding their breath, listening to the sound of the engine and praying to hear it die away. It could've taken hours to find them, and it would be near daylight before they were marched back into the garage. And that would be time taken away from the search for Wade Chesterfield and the money.

I dropped the gearshift into reverse. It was still full dark in Gastonia, North Carolina, but in less than three hours the sun would be rising over Charleston.

Easter Quillby

CHAPTER 17

In the middle of the night, I woke up with Ruby beside me, but Wade's bed hadn't been slept in yet. He stood by the window, peeking between the curtains with the light from the parking lot shining on his face. I whispered his name, and he looked over.

"Did you hear something too?" he asked.

"No," I said.

"What woke you up?"

"I don't know." He looked out the window again, and then he let go of the curtains and they closed. Two chairs sat beside the door, and one of them faced the window. I knew that's where Wade had been all night. He turned the chair around toward the bed, and then he sat down and crossed his legs.

"You not going to sleep?" I asked. He held a finger to his lips, and then he pointed at Ruby. I kicked the covers off and got out of bed and went and sat in the other chair. Wade grabbed one of the legs and pulled my chair closer to his. We'd gotten our nightgowns out of the trunk, and I had mine on. I pulled my knees up to my chest under my gown. "Are you not going to sleep?" I asked again.

"No," he said.

"Why not?"

"Because I'm not sleepy," he said.

"Are you worried?"

He smiled. "What would I be worried about?"

"That the police are going to find us," I said. "Or maybe he'll find us first."

"That's not why I was looking out the window," he said. He put his legs out in front of him like he was stretching, and then he crossed his ankles.

"Then why were you looking out there?"

"I already told you," he said. "I thought I heard something."

"What?"

"I don't know. Could've been anything: a ghost, a vampire." He pointed to the bed. "The kind of things that wouldn't bother you if you were asleep."

"I'm too old for that to scare me," I said.

"You're too smart for that, aren't you? You're starting to remind me of your mom."

"Really?"

"Yes, really," he said. "You're starting to look like her too."

My new brown hair hung over my shoulders. I picked up a piece of it and looked at it up close in the dark room. "Not for long," I said.

"It's not your hair that's making me say that," he said. "Your mom was tough—tougher than me—and you're just like her. The things you've done?" He shook his head. "I couldn't have done any of that when I was your age—taking care of Ruby like you have. I can barely take care of y'all now." He smiled. "And now you've got a boyfriend?"

I could feel my face getting hot, and I looked down. "I think so," I said.

"You think so?"

"I think so," I said again.

"How'd y'all meet?"

"At school. He's in my grade, but he's in another class."

"What's his name again?"

"Marcus Walker."

"Marcus Walker," he whispered. "Trying to steal my little girl away from me."

"No he's not," I said.

"Serves me right if he did," Wade said. "Your mom was only seventeen when I met her."

"How'd you meet her?"

"She never told you?"

"No," I said. "She didn't like to talk about you."

"I can't blame her," he said. "I wouldn't have liked to talk about me either."

"Then tell me now," I said. "How'd you meet her?"

"I was playing ball in Gastonia for the Rangers when I met her. I guess it was probably the 'eighty-four off-season. A bunch of guys I played with that year decided to go up to Alaska and work these terrible jobs to make as much money as they could before the season started back up in the spring: canning work, refinery, oil field—all kinds of cold, miserable jobs. Dirty jobs too. But you could make good money fast, and that's all we cared about.

"I worked in an oil field outside Anchorage, and my first day at work some of the guys took me to a little restaurant that was supposed to have the best hamburgers in the world." He smiled. "And that's where I saw your mom for the first time. She was working as a waitress that summer; I think it was probably the first job she'd ever had. I can tell you I ate more hamburgers that fall and winter than I'd ever eaten in my life. When it was time for the season to start, I convinced her to come back to North Carolina, and the rest is history. You were born about a year later."

"And when did you leave?" He looked surprised that I'd asked him that, but I'd never had the chance to ask him before, and I didn't know for sure if I'd ever have this chance again.

"I don't know," he finally said. "I don't know when the first time was. I think I did a lot of leaving during those years when you were growing up."

"There's a lot I don't remember about you," I said. "Same with Ruby. She was little when you finally left for good."

"I know," he said. "But it's probably a good thing that y'all don't remember much about me. I'd forget it all myself if I could. I did a lot of things I'm not proud of, but all that's behind me. Behind us."

"But what about the money?"

"What money?"

"The money under the bed."

"What are you talking about?" he asked.

"I found it today," I said.

"Okay."

"Is it his?"

"Whose?"

"The guy looking for you. The guy who came to my school."

"No," Wade said, sighing. "It's not his. I don't know why he's out there looking for me, but we don't need to worry about him. I've already told you that. And I've also told you that we have to start trusting each other. You shouldn't have been going through my stuff."

"I can't trust you," I said. "Because that money's not yours, is it?" I knew it wasn't, that it couldn't be. He seemed ashamed to have to answer that question, and I could tell he was thinking of what to say.

"I asked you to tell me the truth about calling Marcus last night," he said, "so I guess I'd better tell you the truth too, right?"

"Right."

"It's not my money," he said, "but I took it anyway. I don't think it even belongs to who I took it from. I don't know whose it is."

"Why'd you take it?"

He looked past me at Ruby where she slept, and then he reached out and took my hands into his. "Easter, I've only ever wanted two things in my whole life. The first was to play baseball, and I was good at it—real good—but I screwed up. I did stupid stuff and I didn't work hard enough, or maybe I didn't want it bad enough. I don't know what happened, but something got in the way."

"Did we get in the way?"

He squeezed my hands a little. "No, not at all. You and your sister are the second thing I want, something I never thought I'd have. When y'all were born, my dream changed, and I wanted to be a good dad, but I screwed that up too." He let go of my hands and leaned back in his chair. "And then here comes this money," he said, closing his eyes like he was picturing it. "When I took it I thought that at least one of those dreams could still come true." He opened his eyes and looked at me. "My dream is here. It's you. You and Ruby. I just want a normal life, a normal house, a normal family."

I wanted to tell him that I'd always dreamed of having the exact same thing.

A few minutes later I got back into bed and pulled the covers over me. I looked over at Wade where he still sat in the chair. "When are you going to sleep?" I asked.

"Soon," he said. "Any minute now."

I laid back and closed my eyes, and before I knew it I was asleep. In the morning, when I woke up, Ruby was asleep beside me. Wade was still sitting in that chair. He'd turned it away from us to face the window, but he was still there.

Brady Weller

CHAPTER 18

I was a divorced father with almost no relationship with my teenage daughter, and I'd been forced to resign from my job after more than twenty years on the police force. But I never felt like I'd hit rock bottom until the first time I owed money to a guy named Roc. He was a pretty reliable informant back when I was on the force, and I still leaned on him from time to time whenever I had to deal with a deadbeat I figured he'd know. He worked as a fry cook at a dive restaurant called the Fish House. His real name was Pete, and he was an overweight white guy in his midforties who wore black skullcaps and spoke in hip-hop slang and chewed on Philly blunts. If you let it, it could really bother you to owe money to somebody like that.

I'd been wrong about McGwire going homerless Tuesday night—he'd actually hit two—and now $250 of my hard-earned money would be finding its way into the dirty kitchen of the Fish House and right into Roc's greasy hands.

The Fish House sat by some abandoned railroad tracks on the edge of downtown. I pulled into the parking lot a little before 9 A.M.

The place was only open for lunch between 10 A.M. and 2 P.M., and the parking lot was empty except for a few old cars on the far corner of the lot by the broken sidewalk.

Just as I stepped out of my car, the kitchen's side door flew open and slammed against the outside wall. Roc, wearing black sunglasses and his black skullcap and oversize white T-shirt, dragged a trash can from the kitchen toward a set of Dumpsters beside the restaurant. He stopped pulling the trash can and fished a lighter from one pocket of his sagging blue jeans and a cigar from the other. He lit it and went back to dragging the trash can across the pavement. He looked up and smiled when he heard me close my car door.

"Oh, snap," he said. "What up, playa?"

"Nothing," I said. "What up with you?" I walked up to him and he shook my hand and pulled me into one of those half hugs guys like to share when they pretend to be "homies." I felt the grease on his fingers where they wrapped around mine, and when he turned my hand loose I put it in my pocket and wiped my fingers on the lining. I looked down at the trash can. "You need a hand?"

"Hells yeah," he said.

He took one handle and I took the other, and then we half dragged, half carried the trash can to the Dumpster, where we heaved it up, tipped it over, and poured the garbage inside.

"You watch the Cardinals Tuesday night?" he asked.

"No," I said. "It's bad luck, but looks like it didn't matter. I know what McGwire did off Hernández."

"He did it off Pall too," he said.

"I know," I said, "but I only owe you for Hernández."

"Damn," he said. "I thought I'd try anyway."

I pulled a bank envelope from my back pocket and counted out the bills and handed them over.

"My man," he said, smiling. He counted the money quickly, and then he pulled a wad of bills wrapped with a rubber band from one of his front pockets. He unwound the rubber band and shuffled through the bills like he'd already marked out a spot for the money I'd just given him.

"You're killing me," I said. "I'm down, like, what—four hundred dollars?"

"More like four-fifty," he said, smiling, still thumbing through the bills. "But I ain't mad at you, baby." He fitted the new bills into the spots where they must've belonged, and then he started counting all the money in the roll. A guy like Roc always knows exactly how much money he has on him at any given time, but he also wants you to see just how much money there is, how much money one could make running a small gambling empire in west Gastonia out of the Fish House's dirty kitchen.

"Can I ask you something?" I said.

"Shoot."

"You ever run numbers on the Gastonia Rangers back in the day?" He stopped counting his money and looked at me over his sunglasses.

"Why?"

"Just want to drop a name on you," I said. "See if it means anything." He stared at me for a second, and then he went back to counting his money.

"Go ahead," he said, smiling. "Anything for my best customer."

"Do you remember a guy who played for them about ten years ago named Wade Chesterfield?"

He stopped counting the money and put his head back and forced out a loud, fake laugh. "Hell yeah, I do," he said. "Rowdy? You needed a game fixed, you called Rowdy."

"Rowdy?"

"Hell yeah," he said again. "That's what they called him."

"Why?" I asked.

He wrapped the rubber band around the wad of cash and dropped it back into his pocket. "Because," he said, "when that dude couldn't pitch no more they made him play the mascot: Rowdy. You know, man, the damn Ranger—Rowdy the Ranger. After he got the yips, that's all they'd ever let his ass do, and he'd do it just to keep getting paid, to stay around the game. But damn, when he was playing—he could fix it for you. Old Wade Chesterfield." He laughed again.

"The yips?"

"Yeah," he said. "The yips. He plunked this guy in the face one time, and the dude just lost it and charged the mound. Beat. Wade. Down. It was bad; nobody could stop him. Dude just went insane. After that, Wade couldn't throw a strike to save his life, whether he had a batter or not. He didn't last long after that." He spit onto the cement and rubbed it in with the toe of his boot. "Why you asking about him?"

"Because he kidnapped his two daughters from a foster home on Monday night," I said. "I'm looking for them."

"Damn," he said, like he was impressed. "I never thought ol' Wade had something like that in him." He sighed and looked down into the empty trash can, and then he looked up at me. "You know, Wade played with Sosa before Sammy got called up to Texas."

I'd completely forgotten that Sosa ever played in Gastonia, but I nodded my head at Roc like I remembered it well.

"Good thing Sammy got out of here when he did," he said. "He's got old teammates snatching up they kids, and him out there chasing Maris with Big Mac." He shook his head like it was the most profound thing he'd ever thought, much less said.

"Do me a favor," I said. "Let me know if you hear anything about Wade Chesterfield."

"Some birdies sing for they supper," he said, rubbing his fingers together and smiling.

"We can do it that way," I said. "But only if there's any songs worth listening to."

He smiled and took a drag off his cigar. "You want to put something on Sammy getting number fifty-seven against the Pirates Friday night?"

"I don't think so," I said. "No use pressing my bad luck."

"All right," he said. We shook hands and I faked my way through a long, awkward handshake that ended with us bumping fists. "Holler at your boy if you change your mind."

"You bet," I said, not catching my own pun. Roc laughed.

I turned and walked back to my car while listening to him slowly dragging that empty trash can across the lot back toward the restaurant. When I reached the car, I turned around and saw him looking at me from the open kitchen door like he'd been waiting on me to change my mind.

"What are the odds against Sosa homering Friday night *and* Saturday night?" I asked.

Roc smiled. "You serious?"

"I am."

"Hold up," he said. He fished a small notebook from his back pocket and flipped through it; he found what he was searching for and looked back up at me. "They're bad," he said. "Real bad. But I can make it sweet for you. Want to say twenty to one? That's pretty sweet."

"That is pretty sweet," I said, even though I knew I should've been back inside my car and pulling out of the parking lot by now. "Put me down for a hundred," I said.

"That's it?" he said. "Come on, playa."

"That's it," I said. "And let me know if you hear anything about anything."

He nodded his head, flicked the tip of his cigar, and opened the kitchen door. Rap music blared from inside. The door slammed shut and swallowed the music. The only noise was the sound of me jingling the keys in my empty pocket.

CHAPTER 19

The first Thursday night of the month was my one night with Jessica. Whenever I picked her up from her mother and stepfather's house, I always pulled into the circular driveway in front of the white-brick mansion and gave the horn a quick "I'm here" beep. I'd only been inside the house once, years ago, when it had been raining and I'd carried an umbrella up the steps and knocked on the front door. Dean had answered. I'd only stood inside the front door and waited for Jessica to come down, but from what I could see, the house's interior matched its exterior. The foyer was floored in white marble, and a wide, wooden staircase curved up to the second floor. Over Dean's shoulder was what must've been the kitchen, and beyond that a living room. Darkened rooms sat on either side of us, and all I remember is seeing more marble floors and white pillars and thinking that Tina was hidden away somewhere that I couldn't see, counting her blessings that she was married to Dean and not to me.

Tonight, Jessica was already waiting outside when I pulled up. She looked taller, older, and thinner every time I saw her. She had her mother's soft face and my blond hair, and she wore it long and wavy like a girl who might be showing off her hair in a shampoo commercial. I put the car in park, left it running, and opened my door to step out and give her a hug, but she'd already opened the passenger's-side door and climbed in before I could even get both feet out. I closed my door and looked over at her just as she clicked her seat belt.

"Hey," I said, leaning over to give her an awkward hug, noting that she only put one arm around my neck.

"Hey," she said. She smiled, and then she turned around and tossed her purse into the backseat.

Chili's was crowded and noisy as usual, and Jessica and I stood outside, waiting for a table. It wouldn't be dark for another half hour, and the night was humid even though there was something in the air that said it was more fall than summer.

"I drove past the school yesterday," I said. "It looks like they're hosting a college fair Saturday night. You going?"

"Yeah," she said. "I think Mom's taking me."

"Oh," I said. "Good. Because I was going to say I could take you if you wanted the company, but if she's already going, then good."

It was quiet for a second, and I looked around at all the other people and families who were talking and laughing, and I wondered what they could be talking about with their kids.

"I'm still leaning toward Peace," Jessica finally said. "They have a good English major, and the classes are small. I know you're not wild about it, but it's where I want to go."

"It's not that I'm not wild about it," I said. "I'm sure it's a great school. It's just really expensive. But NC State, UNC-Charlotte— shoot, my tax dollars are already going there, right?"

"Yeah, Dad," she said. "You've said that before. You don't have to worry about it; Mom and Dean are paying for school."

"And you've said that before, and I've told you that I'm going to help," I said. "It's my job. I'm still your dad. I just want you to consider all of your options. That's all."

"Sure," she said.

The pager the hostess had given me vibrated in my hand, and Jessica heard it and looked down and saw that it was glowing. She turned and walked inside, and I followed.

Once we were seated a waitress came by and dropped off some menus, and a few minutes later she returned with our drinks. I studied my menu even though I already knew what both of us would order: the black-and-blue burger for me and the Cajun chicken pasta for Jessica.

I looked up and saw that the waitress was standing at our table, pen and pad in hand. "Are y'all ready?" she asked. I looked at Jessica, and she nodded.

"I think so," I said. "I'm going to have the black-and-blue burger, medium please, and she'll have the—"

"Grilled chicken salad with just oil and vinegar," Jessica said. "No croutons, please."

"Are y'all good with water?" the waitress asked.

"I am," Jessica said.

"Me too," I said. The waitress smiled and walked toward the table behind me. I heard her ask them the same questions she'd just asked us.

"Grilled chicken salad?" I said. "That's new."

"I'm trying to eat better," Jessica said. "Trying to be healthier."

"Is that going to be enough?" I asked. "You want to get an appetizer or something?"

"No," she said. "I'm not very hungry."

The waitress brought our food a few minutes later, and while we ate I tried to think of things to ask Jessica about school or college or about other things she was interested in. "English major," I said. "So, what's your favorite book?"

She'd stabbed a piece of grilled chicken with her fork, and she held it in midair and stared at it like she was thinking long and hard about my question. "I don't know," she said. "I have a lot of favorites: *The Catcher in the Rye, To Kill a Mockingbird*."

"What's *The Catcher in the Rye* about?"

She popped the chicken into her mouth and sat her fork down while she chewed. Then she took a sip of water. "I don't know," she said. "It's hard to explain. It's not really *about* anything. The narrator is this kid who's going home from boarding school for Christmas break, and he just kind of tells the reader about it."

"And that's it?" I asked.

"Pretty much," she said.

"It doesn't sound like a very interesting book. What makes you like it so much?"

"I don't know," she said. "I guess I just understand where he's coming from. I understand how he feels."

"How does he feel?" I asked.

"I don't know. Alone?"

"Do you feel that way?"

"No. Not really." She sighed loud enough for me to hear it. "So," she said, "what's been up with you?"

I stopped eating and looked at her, but she didn't raise her eyes from her plate. "Just work mostly. The exciting world of home security." I wiped my mouth and dropped my napkin back onto my lap.

"What's it like working with Uncle Jim?" she asked. "I haven't seen him in like two years."

"I don't really see him that much either," I said. "We don't really work together. It's more like I work *for* him."

"He's your boss?"

"Yes," I said. "I guess so."

After we finished eating, the waitress came and cleared our plates and left the bill on the table. I slid my credit card into the sleeve, and she came back and picked it up.

"Did you hear about those two little girls? The ones who were kidnapped a couple days ago?"

"Maybe," she said. "Was it on TV?"

"All over the news."

"What happened to them?"

"Their father kidnapped them," I said. "Took them from a foster home. I was their guardian."

"Why do you say it like that: that you *were* their guardian? Do you stop just because they got kidnapped?"

"No," I said. "Their dad took them down into South Carolina, and now the FBI's getting involved. It's a mess."

"But that doesn't mean you just stop," she said.

"Stop what?"

"Guarding them, or whatever."

"You're right," I said. "I'm still their guardian. And I'll still be their guardian when they come home."

The waitress came back with the receipt, and I left a tip and signed my name. And then I slid my credit card and the receipt into my wallet.

"How can a father kidnap his own kids?" Jessica asked.

"This guy gave up his parental rights a couple of years back. He broke the law by taking those girls."

"But he's their dad."

"It doesn't matter," I said. "I'm your dad, but that doesn't mean I can just carry you off somewhere without your mom's consent. I'd be breaking the law if I did that."

"What happened to their mom?"

"She'd dead," I said.

"Then maybe it's good that nobody's found them," she said. "Maybe they want to be with their dad. Maybe they feel safe."

"Maybe so, but that doesn't make it legal." I folded my napkin and set it where my plate had been. "What would you do if you were me?" I asked.

"About what?"

"About these two little girls. Would you let them stay with their dad, or would you follow the law and make sure they got back where they're supposed to be?"

"I don't know," she said. "I guess I'd try to think about what they want. Nobody ever does that. Kids just want to be happy."

"Were you happy?"

"I guess," she said. "I don't remember being *un*happy."

"Being happy and being unhappy are very different," I said. "Those two little girls might not have been happy in foster care, but maybe they weren't unhappy either. You know?"

"Yes," she said. "Then I was happy."

"Did you feel safe?"

"Of course I felt safe," she said. "Why wouldn't I have? My dad was a cop."

"I know," I said. "But that's not what I mean. Did you feel secure, even after what happened?"

"Yeah," she said. "I think so. But I don't remember much about all that. I was just a little kid, and that was a long time ago."

"You were ten, Jessica," I said. "It was barely six years ago."

"Yeah?" she said. "Then maybe I just forced myself to forget."

"But you remember feeling safe?" I asked. "And happy?"

"Yes," she said. "Safe and happy. I remember."

"So, what would you do: leave them alone or bring them home?"

She sighed. "I don't know," she finally said. "I'm not a dad."

Pruitt

CHAPTER 20

Her neighborhood in North Charleston was made up of small houses surrounded by brown grass and scrubby pine trees. To the east, planes from the city's airport and jets from the air force base beyond it rose over I-26 in the hazy morning. On the first pass by the house it looked almost identical to the homes on either side of it: a squat brick ranch with windows and a front door trimmed in green, a green garage door, black shingles on the roof already radiating heat.

I parallel-parked my truck on the side of the road five houses down from hers, and my eyes moved between my mirrors and the street in front of me, checking to see if anyone was passing on foot or looking out doors or windows to see who was sitting out in front of their house on a white-hot morning.

On my way up her driveway my eyes weren't so much looking at her house as they were looking at the houses and yards around it, searching for an indication of who was at home and who was not. There were no cars in the driveways of the houses on either side of hers, and the front doors were closed and the shades were pulled.

There was no car in her driveway either, and through the garage door's windows it was clear that there was also no car in the garage, meaning she was either not at home or did not drive and that someone may be coming by to check on her at any moment. Or perhaps Wade Chesterfield himself had already come by and picked her up or warned her about who or what may be coming, and she had left on her own, gone to stay with friends a few streets over or family members whose names and addresses I hadn't yet discovered.

But then the curtain moved in the window by her front door. Someone had been watching me approach the house, and they pulled the curtain closed when they saw me come to a stop in the driveway. None of the other curtains stirred. My right hand moved instinctively to the handle of the Glock that was tucked into the back waistband of my shorts. I moved slowly up the driveway and stopped at the front door.

My hand left the Glock and raised itself to knock, but the door suddenly flew open, and she stood there, looking out from behind a thick pair of sunglasses with blacked-out lenses. She was tiny, barely five feet tall, her thinning white hair permed in frizzy, tight curls against her head, a white blouse tucked into a long tan skirt, and hose that ran into a pair of black lace-up shoes. She stood there looking at me for a few moments, and my fingers unfolded themselves from the gun and my hand came to rest at my side.

The street was quiet. Nothing but the noise of a dog barking a few houses down and the soft sounds of the airplanes taking off and landing in the distance.

"Come in, come in," she finally said, backing away from the door and then turning, waving over her shoulder for me to follow. "Let me get my coat and my umbrella. I know what it looks like and feels like out there right now, but this is summertime in Charleston, and you can't ever tell about the summertime in this godforsaken city. And don't get me started on how cold that office is."

I closed the door behind me, and my hand reached back and locked it quietly.

"Leave it unlocked," she said. "We're going to be heading right back out." She disappeared down a hallway, and my eyes scanned what must have been the living room. It was tidy and clean, and looked as if nothing had changed since the house had been built. Brown shag carpet covered the floors, and a mint-green sofa sat beneath windows that looked out on the front yard behind heavy curtains. There were two cream-colored sitting chairs opposite the sofa, a coffee table in front of them. There was no television. The room, and maybe the entire house, smelled like something I couldn't quite place, but it was something that seemed familiar, something on the front end of a memory.

I heard her open and close a closet door somewhere down the hall. When she walked back into the living room she wore a jacket and carried a small umbrella, her purse slung over her shoulder, the blacked-out sunglasses still on.

"Are you ready?" she asked. She stood there as if waiting for an answer. When none came, she leaned forward as if trying to smell me, and then she leaned away as if she'd discovered something she didn't want to know. "Well," she said. "You can say something." She waited. My eyes followed her purse as it slid slowly down her right arm, stopping at the bend in her elbow. She held her umbrella in front of her with both hands. Her posture made her seem like someone who was used to waiting and was willing to wait forever.

"Where do you think we're going?" I asked.

As soon as the words were out she dropped her purse at her feet and her right hand shot up and spread itself out across the bridge of my nose, pushing my sunglasses up against my eyes. The touch of her hand was shocking, and I pulled away from it, but her hand moved too, and her fingers kneaded my lips and cheeks, slowly working themselves up to the bill of my hat.

I realized that she couldn't see me. The muscles in my body relaxed, and my face leaned heavily toward her.

"Who are you?" she asked, barely above a whisper.

"A friend of your son's. Of Wade's."

"What's your name?"

"Pruitt."

"I've never known him to mention you," she said.

"He wouldn't have. He hasn't seen me in a long time." Her hand came to a rest on my left shoulder, and she left it there for just a second before touching my chest, right above my heart.

"I'm sorry if I scared you," she said. She took her hand from my chest and lifted up her glasses so that her eyes could be seen; they were both covered in a murky blue film. "These don't let me see as well as my hands do." She smiled and dropped the glasses back into place. "I thought you were someone I'd already arranged to take me to an appointment on Friday morning, but I knew today is Thursday, and I was confused because of that." She bent down and felt along the floor until her hand closed around the strap of her pocketbook. She stood again and put the strap over her shoulder, and then she turned away and walked back toward the middle of the room before stopping. "It *is* Thursday, right?"

"Yes. It's Thursday."

"Humph," she said as if she'd discovered something. "Then my doctor's appointment is tomorrow. They will come tomorrow, and they will pick me up then." She gestured toward the sofa. "Please sit down. Be comfortable." She walked through the living room and into the hallway back to the room she'd been in earlier.

Dust motes floated up from the sofa cushions and drifted through a shaft of sunlight shining through a gap in the curtained windows behind me. The light disappeared as the curtains were pulled tight. My body sunk down into the old cushions, and the gun dislodged itself from my waistband. My back leaned against it so that it rested nose down behind me.

She walked out of the hallway and stood in the middle of the room, her hands on her hips. "Let me get us some tea," she said. "And then I want to hear all about how you know my Wade." She turned to walk into the kitchen that was off the right side of the living room, but she stopped and turned back. "Is sweet tea okay with you?" she asked.

"Yes. But this won't take long."

She waved her hand as if dismissing my words. "Nonsense," she said. "You stay as long as you'd like. I have nowhere to be; we've already decided that." Her shoes squeaked over the linoleum in the kitchen, followed by the sound of her opening cabinets and getting down glasses, opening and closing the refrigerator and getting ice out of the freezer. "Would you like coffee instead?" she asked, her voice curving around the half wall that separated her from me.

"No." But her question made clear the smell in her house, and a memory forced itself into my mind. It was not the smell of freshly brewed coffee but the stale scent of coffee after it has permeated everything. And it is there in my mother's kitchen, the smell of stale coffee in a hot room with the windows closed. My mother has dropped the glass coffeepot and the sound of its shattering has made me cry. And the smell of that memory lived here in this house now.

When she walked back into the living room she carried a small wooden tray with both hands; on it sat two tall glasses of tea and a small stack of napkins.

"I was confused when I heard you at the door because my appointment is on Friday," she said. "And I knew today is Thursday, so I couldn't understand why someone would be at the door." She laughed to herself. "Even when I'm right I think I'm wrong. Old age can be a very good prankster." She stopped walking when her knees brushed against the coffee table. "You'll have to set this down for me," she said. "There are some things I cannot trust myself to do."

When the tray was out of her hands and had been set down, she moved around the coffee table and sat in one of the armchairs. She reached forward and picked up her glass from the tray and brought it toward her. Her hand shook and the ice cubes clinked together softly. She took a drink from her tea and picked up a napkin and wrapped it around the glass. She crossed her legs and smoothed out her skirt.

"So, Mr. Pruitt," she said, "you know Wade."

"We played baseball together."

"If I were a betting woman, I'd bet you played first," she said, smiling. "You're tall. Most first basemen are tall and right-handed, and usually very strong. Am I right?"

"Yes."

"Did you make it to the majors, Mr. Pruitt?"

My fingers had closed around one of the napkins on the tray, and now it was balled up in my hand. "No."

"That's too bad," she said. "I'm sure you wanted to become a professional ballplayer. I'm sure you worked very hard."

"Very hard." The napkin had become rock-hard from my squeezing it, hard enough to be thrown through the glass window behind me or tucked into a fist to make the fist heavier and more solid. The memory wasn't of me crying after all, but of my mother crying instead. Her forehead is bleeding from where the coffeepot has been shattered across her face, splattering me and the walls and the floor with cold, stale coffee. The old man has slammed the door behind him, and now the lawn mower is sputtering, finally catching and firing. My mother doesn't look up from where she cleans the floor, but each time the lawn mower passes the windows it kicks up gravel and sticks against the glass, and my mother ducks lower as if my father has aimed those things at her.

"Well," she said, reaching out and setting her glass on the tray. "Sometimes you need a little luck. Wade didn't have the career he wanted to have either, certainly not the career I wanted him to have. Especially not considering his talent."

"That's too bad." But those were just words, and she knew it. She leaned forward as if preparing to ask something or say something that no one else should ever hear, even though there was no one else in the house and there probably hadn't been for a long time.

"Does he owe you money, Mr. Pruitt?"

"Money?"

"Does Wade owe you money?" she asked. "Is that why you're here?"

"No. He doesn't owe me money."

"Well," she said, smiling, "good for you, because he sure owes me money." She leaned away and opened the palm of her left hand, showing that she'd balled up her napkin too, and she tossed it onto the table before picking up her glass from the tray. "I ask you that question because he owes a lot of people money," she said. "They've come here looking for him over the years."

"That's not what this visit is about."

"What's it about?" she asked, before saying, "I'm sorry. I'm sorry to ask you so many questions. I don't get very many visitors, and I forget how to act." She smiled. "Forgive me."

"Business. This is just about business."

"Well, I won't ask you what kind of business you're in," she said. "I've asked enough questions."

The room grew quiet, and the ice cubes popped and resettled themselves in the glasses. She stared at the table before lifting her eyes toward me. "I have to tell you that I haven't seen my son in years, Mr. Pruitt. I honestly can't remember the last time I even spoke with him."

"Do you know where he is?"

"Why?" she asked. "In case your business takes you there as well?"

"Perhaps it will."

"That doesn't sound good to me, Mr. Pruitt," she said. "It seems that you want to find my son to do more than catch up and talk about baseball. But it doesn't matter what it seems like to me. I've already told you I don't know where he is, and I have no idea how to contact him."

"It's just old baseball stuff. That's all."

"Old baseball stuff," she said. "Of course." She looked down at her glass as if trying to remember what it was she was drinking. "Would you like to see something, Mr. Pruitt? I think it will bring back good memories of 'old baseball stuff.'" She set her glass back on the tray and stood. "Come on," she said, turning toward the hallway. "Follow me."

After standing with her and stepping around the coffee table, I stopped before walking down the hallway. The Glock had been left behind, stuffed down behind the cushion. She must have heard my feet turning away from her.

"No," she said. "Leave it. I'll get the glasses later. Follow me."

She shuffled past what must've been her bedroom with its made bed and framed photographs on the dresser, past a small, dark bathroom to the end of the hall where two closed doors faced each other. She went to the door on the left and ran her hand along it until her fingers closed around the doorknob. She looked back toward me without saying anything, and then she opened the door and stepped inside.

The room was hot and bright from the sun that poured through the windows in the far corner of the room. It was a boy's room, clearly the room Wade Chesterfield had grown up in, and it hadn't changed since he was a boy. Posters of baseball players from the 1970s covered the walls: Jim Kaat, Ron Guidry, Tommy John before his elbow surgery, and Steve Carlton—all of them lefties like Wade had been. Trophies sat on every flat surface, most of them crowned with tiny gold figurines either poised with bats on their shoulders or in the middle of their windups, their knees raised against their chests and the ball tucked into their mitts. The bed was made neatly and the burgundy carpet showed the tracks left by a vacuum cleaner. It smelled old and closed off like places smell when no one visits them for a long time.

She stood in the doorway with me standing behind her, and like mine, her eyes seemed to take inventory of everything in the room, even though she was only seeing it through a memory. When she stepped farther inside her right hand reached out and felt along the wall to a desk that was covered in trophies. Her fingertips flitted across the tops of each one, stopping when they found the tallest. Her hand rested there as she turned to face me.

"All of these before he graduated from high school, Mr. Pruitt," she said. She turned back toward the trophies as if assessing them in some way. "It's all here. Right from the very beginning: every single bit of it." She lifted her hand from the trophy and let it drop to her side. "And now I'm the only one who ever comes in here."

She stood there for another moment before shuffling across the room and skirting the bed under the windows. Her hand lifted to touch the bedside table as she drew closer to it. Once she touched it she stopped and reached down for something hidden between the table and the bed, and when she stood up straight she held a twenty-six-inch Louisville Slugger; it was almost black with age and use and the barrel was chipped and dented. She held it with both hands in front of her and stared down at it like an offering.

"This was his first bat," she said. She looked toward me. "I bet you haven't seen one this small in a very long time." She held the bat out to me, and when my right hand took it my left hand searched my back pocket for my batting gloves, finding them and slipping them on. To swing it made the bat feel even smaller and lighter, almost like a nightstick a police officer would carry on a belt. She still faced me, and my mind wondered what she thought at that moment while standing in this dusty old bedroom that was still decorated for a boy's life with a boy's things, not speaking but just listening to the sound of the tiny bat cut through the air. My feet set themselves as if stepping into the batter's box.

"Wade's father bought that bat for him on his sixth birthday," she said. "He was so happy to have a boy, and he was even happier when he saw that Wade was going to be a lefty." She turned and raised her right hand and pointed toward the window that looked into the backyard. "His father would take him to the ball field behind the elementary school at—" My eyes caught sight of it a split second before it happened, a split second before the bird's body smashed against the window. The sound startled her, and she stumbled against the table; her left hand came down and knocked a lamp onto the floor, her right hand reaching out for the bed as she tried to steady herself.

The room was quiet now. The only sound was her breath coming in short bursts. She brought her hand to her chest as if feeling for a heartbeat. The child's bat hung down by my side.

"What was that?" she asked.

My mind replayed the memory of the bird smacking the window, my eyes watching it gather itself a half second later before flying away. But she hadn't seen any of that, and now, in the silence afterward, her heart raced and her mind spun, struggling to imagine the unknown. She stood there, not looking at me but looking for me, waiting for me to say something. Instead, my feet stepped closer to her at the center of the room and set themselves while my hands raised the tiny bat to my shoulder. When my eyes closed, a picture of Wade Chesterfield as a boy in this same bedroom flashed before them—perhaps he'd stood in the very same place where she stood now. But when my eyes opened they saw past the boy in this room and decades into the future to the place where Wade Chesterfield the man waited to be found.

Easter Quillby

CHAPTER 21

The next morning, Wade checked us out of the hotel and then drove across the parking lot to Bojangles'. He went inside by himself and told us to roll the windows down. The heat was killing me after a cold night in our room, and it was miserable inside that car with me and Ruby both sweating and wondering where Wade was taking us next. He came out and handed us sausage biscuits and orange juice, and then he started up the car and didn't say a word until an hour later when he parked it on the side of the road in a neighborhood full of little brick houses that all looked the same, and even then he didn't say nothing but "This is the street I grew up on."

"Which house was it?" I asked, but it seemed like he didn't even hear me.

"The one with the green garage door," he finally said. "It looks nice, doesn't it? Somebody's been taking care of things."

"Is that thunder?" Ruby asked.

"No," Wade said. "Those are planes. There's an airport back there."

Me and Ruby sat up on our knees and looked out the back window. You could see a plane taking off over the trees down the road behind us.

We sat there for a long time, me and Ruby watching the planes and whispering to each other, Wade just staring straight ahead at the house he'd come all the way down here to see.

Finally, Wade unclicked his seat belt, and then he turned around and looked at us in the backseat.

"Y'all stay in the car until I come back," he said. "And keep the doors locked. You can keep the windows cracked a little bit, but don't roll them all the way down. And stay in the car. I'm serious." He looked at us like he was waiting for us to say something. "I'm serious," he said again.

"Okay," I said.

"Okay what?"

"Okay, we'll stay in the car."

Me and Ruby watched him walk down the street. The day was so hot that heat waves came up off the ground and made his body look all fuzzy the farther away he got from us.

"What do you think he's doing?" Ruby asked.

"I don't know," I said. "There's no telling."

We watched him until he stopped in front of his old house and just stood there and stared up at it. Then he looked up and down the street. He walked up the driveway and rang the doorbell and waited for a minute, and then he reached out for the doorknob, looked up and down the street again, and then went inside.

"You think that's really his old house?" Ruby asked.

"I don't know."

"Maybe his mom and dad still live there," she said. "Think they're still alive?"

"I don't know," I said again. "I've never seen them."

On the other side of the street a Mexican girl a little bit younger than me was helping her little brother ride a bike back and forth in their driveway. She'd turn his seat loose and then run and catch up with him before he fell. She kept looking at me and Ruby where we sat in the car. She said something to her brother, and he looked up at us too.

"Those kids are looking at us," Ruby said.

"That's okay," I said. "Let them look. They're not hurting us."

"But I hate them staring at us," she said.

"Close your eyes, then. You won't even know."

I closed mine and laid my head back against the seat. I was mad at Wade for bringing us down here without telling us why and for parking outside a house in a neighborhood without hardly any shade. Maybe he had lived here, maybe he'd come back to find something else he'd left behind, just like he'd done when he came and took me and Ruby.

How long I had my eyes closed or whether or not I drifted off to sleep I don't know, but the next thing I heard was Ruby's voice saying my name, quiet at first and then louder and louder until I finally opened my eyes and saw what it was that made her scream: it was Wade, running up the street toward us, his hands and the front of his shirt covered in blood, the front door of the house he'd gone into flung wide open. His mouth was moving, but from inside the car I couldn't hear what he was saying, but by the time I opened the door and stepped out, he was screaming for me to get back inside.

It wasn't the blood that covered Wade's hands up to his elbows as much as it was the look on his face as he ran toward us that kept me from reaching over the front seat and unlocking the car door to let him in. He must've seen it in my eyes—or maybe he heard Ruby screaming inside—but something made it clear to him that he'd have to get that door unlocked on his own; that didn't keep him from yanking on the handle and pounding on the glass with one hand and searching through his pockets with the other. Each time he beat against the window it left a bloody handprint until the glass was so full of them that we couldn't hardly see him on the other side. He found his keys and got the right one into the lock and opened the door—but Wade climbing inside only made Ruby scream louder. Wade slammed the door shut and acted like we weren't even there, like he couldn't hear what was going on in the backseat. He started the car and put it in gear without even turning his head to look at us. He pulled into traffic, and I saw that the steering wheel was smeared with blood too.

We stopped at a red light, and Wade sat there with his hands in his lap like he was trying to hide them from the cars going by. "Hold on," he said to us even though he hadn't turned around to look at us yet. "Hold on," he said again. "Just let me think for a second." Hearing his voice made Ruby stop, and maybe that's why he turned and looked at us; his face was covered in sweat and his eyes were wide open and crazy-looking. Ruby screamed and pushed her face into my shoulder. "Ruby, baby," he said. "Please stop. I'm sorry. Please." His hand came over the seat toward us, and when Ruby looked and saw it she screamed even louder. He pulled it back like we'd smacked at it. "I'm sorry," he said. "I'm sorry." He turned around and held the steering wheel with both hands like he was trying to think of what to do or say next. Then the light turned green, and he wiped his hands on his shirt and kept on going.

We pulled off the street and into a convenience-store parking lot. Wade stopped the car and turned off the engine, and then he sat there staring at the side of the building.

"Easter," he said real quiet and calm, "I need you to get out of the car and see if the ladies' room is unlocked. If it's not, then I need you to go inside and get the key." I didn't know what he was talking about, but when I leaned forward and looked out the windshield I saw that he'd been staring at the doors to the men's and women's bathrooms the whole time we'd been sitting there. He turned his head and looked at me. "Did you hear me?"

I nodded my head yes, but all I could think about was leaving

Ruby in the car all alone and that money that I'd tucked down into the bear's overalls. It was sitting right in between me and Ruby, and if Wade hadn't been watching I swear I would've fished it out, grabbed Ruby's hand, and made a run for it. But he never took his eyes off me.

"Go on, then," he said. "I need you to do this for me."

I reached for the door. Ruby grabbed my arm and tried to keep me from opening it. "It's okay," I said. "I'll be right back." She turned me loose, and I opened the door and got out. The ladies' room had one of those big silver door handles with a dead bolt on it, and I knew it was going to be locked before I even reached out and tried to open it. I gave it a tug, and then I turned around and looked at Wade. His eyes were just as wild-looking as they'd been when he got into the car, and he looked at me for a second before nodding his head toward the convenience store.

The store was empty except for a fat blond-headed woman and a guy with a ponytail who were both standing behind the counter. When I walked in the woman was trying to light a cigarette, but she kept laughing at something the guy had said to her. I stood in front of the register until she'd lit her cigarette and tossed the lighter onto the counter.

"Can I help you?" she asked. The guy laughed again like he remembered what was so funny about what he'd said before I came in. He turned and walked back into a little office, and the woman watched him go. She looked at me again. "What do you need, baby?"

"I need to use the bathroom," I said. "It's locked."

The woman reached under the counter and pulled out a long piece of wood with a key attached to the end of it. "Don't leave this in there," she said. "The door locks behind you." I took the key and walked back to the bathroom. When I had the door unlocked Wade stepped out of the car and went inside. Before I could get back in the car with Ruby, he opened the bathroom door and hollered for me. He was holding some wadded-up paper towels that he'd run under the sink.

"Wipe off that window," he said. "And then wipe down the steering wheel. I'll be out in a second."

The window was sticky and the blood had started to turn brown, but I got most of it off and you couldn't tell what it was by the time I was finished. I opened the door and started wiping down the steering wheel as good as I could, but I knew it would take another handful of paper towels to get it all clean. I sat down in the driver's seat and waited.

"What's he doing in there?" Ruby asked from the backseat.

"Getting cleaned up," I said. "He can't let nobody see him like that."

"Why'd he have blood on him?"

"I don't know," I said. "I ain't had a chance to ask him yet."

I tossed the paper towels into a garbage can by the curb and got into the backseat with Ruby. She sat on the passenger's side, looking out the window.

"You think it was his blood?" she asked.

"I don't know," I said. "It could've been."

"You think he hurt somebody?"

"No," I said.

"I don't either," she said.

A few minutes later, the door to the ladies' room opened and Wade stepped out. All the blood had been washed off his hands and his shirt and his jeans were wet where he'd tried to clean them. He walked around to the back of the car and opened the trunk; I heard him opening his bag and moving stuff around. The trunk slammed shut and he walked back toward the bathroom carrying new clothes. When he came back out he was wearing tan-colored shorts and a clean T-shirt. He opened the trash can and tossed his old clothes inside, and then he waved me out of the car and handed me the bathroom key.

The woman was alone behind the register when I went back into the store. I set the key on the counter.

"You okay?" she asked.

"I'm fine."

"You were in there a long time," she said. "I almost came looking for you."

"I'm sick," I said. "Sorry."

"I hope you feel better," she said.

"Thank you," I said. "I hope so too."

Wade was on a pay phone in the corner of the parking lot out by the road when I came out. I stood there watching him for a second, but when he hung up and started walking back toward the car I knew I'd better get back inside there too. Wade pulled out of the parking lot and across the road right into the parking lot of a Waffle House. He shut off the car and turned around in his seat. "Are y'all hungry?" he asked.

"No," me and Ruby both said at the same time.

"Well," he said, "that's too bad, because we're going to go inside here and sit down for a few minutes and we're going to eat something. Okay?"

"I want to go home," Ruby said. Even though she was staring down at the floorboard and I couldn't see her eyes, I knew by the way her voice sounded that there was a chance she might start crying again.

"That's not going to happen, Ruby," Wade said. "So right now we're going to go inside here and eat instead."

"I want to go home!" Ruby said again, but this time she kicked the back of the passenger's seat and raised her voice.

"Hey," he said. "Hey." He waited for Ruby to look up. "You're not going to talk to your dad like that. Not right now, not ever."

"You're not my dad!" Ruby screamed. "We don't have one!" Wade looked at me like I'd told her to say it, and then he looked back at Ruby. He started to say something, but then he stopped. When he finally spoke his voice was lower and quieter.

"I'm sorry I yelled at you," he said. "And I'm sorry I scared you back there. I was helping a friend do something and I got cut and it bled a little bit, and I just wanted to get cleaned up before we ate. That's all."

"I don't believe you," Ruby said. Wade sighed.

"I do," I said. "I believe you." He looked at me and smiled. Ruby looked at me too.

"You do?" she asked. I nodded my head yes.

There wasn't hardly anybody inside the Waffle House except for the people working there. We'd come in right between lunchtime and dinnertime, and even the waitresses seemed surprised to see us. "Y'all have a seat wherever you want," one of them said.

We sat down at a booth right inside the door. Somebody'd left a newspaper on the seat, and Wade picked it up and tossed it on the table. It was opened to the sports section; the headline read SHOW-DOWN IN ST. LOUIS? with side-by-side pictures of McGwire and Sosa swinging at pitches just below it.

"What can I get y'all to drink?" the waitress asked. Me and Wade both ordered waters, but Ruby wanted an orange juice.

"I have to go to the bathroom," Ruby said after the waitress left. The bathrooms were right inside the door, and you could see them over Wade's shoulder. Wade turned around and looked at them, and then he looked at Ruby.

"Go ahead," he said. I got up and let her out of the booth, and then I sat back down and acted like I was looking at the menu.

"I want you to know that I don't believe you," I finally said. "I don't believe that you got cut back there helping somebody. I know you made all that up. I just said I believed you so Ruby wouldn't start crying again."

Wade just stared down at the menu. "Well, I appreciate that," he said.

"So," I said.

"So what?"

"What happened?"

He sighed and dropped the menu on the table, and then he closed his eyes and rubbed them with his fingers. They were bloodshot when he opened them again. "Telling you isn't going to do any good."

"I know you're worried about scaring Ruby," I said, "but you can't scare me. Nothing can." He stared at me for a second, and then he turned and looked to make sure Ruby wasn't out of the bathroom yet. He leaned across the table to tell me whatever he was about to tell me.

"My mother lived in that house," he said.

"Does she live there now?" He raised his hand like he didn't want me to say anything until he'd finished.

"I hadn't been inside that house in years, and I hadn't seen her for a long time." I opened my mouth to ask him why not, but he held up his hand and stopped me again. "And today, when I got there and knocked, nobody came. The door was unlocked, so I went inside." He looked back at the restroom, and then he looked around the restaurant too. "And that's when I found her," he said. "And she was dead. Somebody'd come in and beat her up, Easter. I couldn't even hardly tell who she was." After he finished he sat there leaning across the table, and then he sat back against the seat and laid his hands flat on top of the menu. "I didn't know what to do," he said. "I just knew that you and your sister were out there in the car, and all I could think about was getting back to you."

My mind pictured what he'd just seen, and I felt myself getting dizzy. The smell of the food cooking on the grill and the sound of the country music coming from the jukebox made me feel sick. I took a drink from my water to push down what was trying to come up out of my stomach. "Who do you think did it?" I asked.

"I don't know."

"You think it was *him*?"

"I don't know," he said again. "I don't know how he could've found her."

"He found me," I said. We sat there staring at each other for a second, but then the sound of the waitress's voice made me jump. My knees hit the underside of the table and the ice rattled in our glasses.

"Y'all ready to order?" she asked.

Wade ordered a patty melt with hash browns, and I ordered waffles for me and Ruby and a bowl of cheese grits for us to share. I didn't know how I was going to eat any of it.

Ruby came back to the table and sat down beside me. "I got you a waffle," I said. "And I got some cheese grits for us to share."

"I wanted pancakes," she said, smacking the table with her hands. "I didn't want a waffle. Why didn't you ask me?"

"Because you were in the bathroom," I said. "Besides, a waffle's no different than pancakes. A waffle's just a big pancake with dents in it." I smiled, hoping she'd laugh.

"But I wanted pancakes," she said. "And nobody asked me." She crossed her arms on the table and put her head down. She said something else, but I couldn't understand her. I touched her back, and she started crying.

"Hey," Wade said, reaching out and putting his hand on the back of her head. "We'll get you some pancakes. It's no big deal."

"I don't want pancakes now," Ruby said, looking up at Wade. "I want to go home!" She screamed it so loud that the people working behind the counter turned their heads and looked at us.

"You can't," Wade said. "I'm sorry, but you can't. But we can go anywhere you want to go. Just name it. I'm serious. Anywhere you want to go, that's where we'll go."

Ruby wiped at her eyes with her hands, and I took a napkin out of the holder and gave it to her. She wiped her nose with it. "Anywhere?" she asked.

"Anywhere," Wade said. Ruby smiled and looked over at me. The newspaper was still sitting on the table, and I picked it up and showed it to her.

"How about St. Louis?" I said. Ruby looked at the picture of McGwire and Sosa, and then she looked over at Wade.

"St. Louis," she said. I turned the paper around and showed it to Wade. He took it from me and looked at it for a second.

"Okay," he said. "Okay. That's what we'll do. We'll go to St. Louis, and we'll go see a game—maybe two."

We sat there talking about the trip and all the things we'd see on the way. Wade told us we'd have to drive up into the mountains and it would be chilly at night and that we'd have to buy jackets and long pants. Ruby said she wanted a blanket or a sleeping bag, and Wade said he didn't see any reason why she couldn't have them both. He laughed and smiled, and it was like he'd forgotten all about whatever he'd seen inside his old house.

But when the food came it was a different story. Wade took one look at that patty melt, and something about it made his face turn white. He slid out of the booth and stood up. "I'll be right back," he said. "Y'all go ahead and eat." He just about ran to the bathroom. Ruby didn't even seem to notice. She just ate her waffle and looked at that picture of McGwire and Sosa.

"Who do you think's going to break the record?" she asked.

"I don't know," I said. "Probably McGwire. He's the closest."

The waitress came back over and stood at the table. "Can I get y'all anything else?" she asked.

"No," I said. "Not right now."

She looked down at Wade's plate and saw that it hadn't been touched. "Is everything okay?"

"Yes," I said. "He just went to the restroom."

She smiled and looked at Ruby. "You a baseball fan?"

Ruby looked up at her. She had a little bit of syrup on her chin. "Yes," she said, pointing at the newspaper. "We're going to St. Louis to see them break the home-run record."

"Well, that sounds fun," the waitress said.

Wade came back to the table and the waitress stepped aside so he could slide into the booth. His face was still white and his hair was damp where he'd splashed himself with water. It made it look like he was sweating.

"Doing okay?" the waitress asked.

Wade nodded his head. The waitress smiled and walked back toward the grill. I took another bite of my waffle and looked out the window. Something caught my eye across the street in the convenience-store parking lot where we'd been just a few minutes before.

I recognized him as soon as he opened the door to his truck and put one foot out onto the asphalt. I knew him without even seeing his face, but when he turned and looked around I knew for certain it was him: the baseball hat, the sunglasses, the huge arms, and the skinny legs. I dropped my fork onto my plate and reached across the table for Wade without taking my eyes off the parking lot.

"It's him," I said.

"Who?" Wade said. He looked at me, and then he turned his head to see what I was staring at.

"*Him,*" I said. "In that black truck." The guy slammed the truck's door and stood there looking around the parking lot. Then he walked toward the store and went inside.

Wade looked at me, and then he looked over at Ruby. He reached into his pocket and pulled out his wallet; he grabbed some money and tossed it onto the table. "Get in the car," he said. "Now. We've got to go."

Pruitt

CHAPTER 22

Her side of the street was lined with police cars, their lights flashing. A fire truck sat half in the driveway. An ambulance had backed up into the yard, its back doors open, a couple of paramedics standing by the front door. My truck coasted down the street toward the house where a cop waited before stepping off the curb and shouting for me to stop. I rolled my window down to hear what he said.

"You're going to have to turn it around," he said, looking up at me. He was maybe forty years old and overweight. A bead of sweat ran from his blond buzz cut down the side of his face. "This street's open to emergency vehicles only." He slapped the truck's door and stepped away like he'd said all he had to say.

"What happened?"

He walked back toward me. "Somebody died who lives here."

"Mrs. Chessman?" He nodded his head. "What happened?"

He turned to look at the other cops he'd been standing with at the curb; they were too far away to hear him. "Looks like she was murdered."

"My God. Why would somebody do that? She never bothered anybody."

"Did you know her?" he asked.

"Yes. My house is just up the street."

He fished a pen and a pad out of his breast pocket and opened it and turned to a clean page. "Mind if I ask you some questions? It'll save us both time later."

"Sure."

"What can you tell me about her?" he asked.

"She was blind. And she was scared to death of her son, always talking about how he owed her a bunch of money. He seems like a bad guy."

"You know his name?"

"Wade Chesterfield."

"Wade Chesterfield," he repeated.

"He changed his last name. Isn't that strange?"

"Anything else you can tell me?"

"No. Nothing comes to mind. Just hope you catch whoever it was that did this." He scribbled something onto the pad, and my eyes raised to spy the paramedics as they carried a gurney into the house. "Who found her?" The cop stopped writing and looked up at me. "Just asking since she lived alone."

"We don't know," he said. "The call came in from a gas station up the street." He raised his eyes and looked up the road behind me, and then he looked back at his pad. "We're checking on it."

He stood there jotting down notes on his pad. It must have been Wade Chesterfield who'd found her, and it must've been him who'd driven to a gas station to make the call. Anyone else would've called from inside the house. Anyone else would've waited for the police to arrive. "Which one?"

"Which one what?" the cop asked.

"Which gas station?"

He raised his eyes and looked at me, and then he turned his pad to a new page. "What did you say your name was?"

"Why?"

He shook his head like I shouldn't worry about what he'd just asked me. "Just in case we need to get ahold of you."

"No reason to get ahold of me. There's nothing else to tell you." The Glock was tucked under my seat, the doctor's kit full of syringes and vials stuffed somewhere under the passenger's side.

"Just give me your name and address just in case," he said, tapping the pad with his pen, trying to see my eyes through my sunglasses. "You never know what can come up." He stared at me for another second, and then he pointed at me with his pen. "Your nose is bleeding."

"Yeah. It's cut." The back of my hand wiped at my nose, and the amount of blood left behind told me it wouldn't stop.

"It's cut?"

"Don't involve me in this." My foot stepped on the brake and my hand pulled the gearshift down. My foot lifted off the brake and the truck rolled back slowly.

"Whoa, whoa," the cop said, stepping toward the yard.

After going back about fifty yards, I eased the truck into a driveway and then pulled onto the street. In the rearview mirror the cop stood in the middle of the road watching me, his hand lifted to his face like he was trying to keep the sun out of his eyes. At the first stop sign, my hand felt along the door panel for something for the blood, and my other hand flipped down the visor to check the mirror. The blood around my nose was still damp, but it was already starting to harden and turn brown.

The closest gas station had a pay phone in the corner of the parking lot. The girl's picture was somewhere in the glove compartment, and my hands riffled through the papers looking for the same face that had been stapled to the cafeteria wall back in Gastonia.

Inside the station, a tall, skinny kid with a ponytail and an older woman stood behind the counter and stared while the picture was unfolded on the counter in front of them. My finger pointed down at the photo. "Have you seen this girl?"

The kid with the ponytail took his eyes off the photo and looked at me, but the woman put on a pair of glasses that hung from a string around her neck and stretched her neck until her face was close to the picture. She took her glasses off and looked up. "And who are you?" she asked.

"It doesn't matter. Have you seen this kid or not?"

"It certainly does matter," the woman said, leaning her hip into the counter and folding her arms across her chest. "Are you the police, or are you just some kind of weirdo?"

"Police."

"Well," she said. "I'd like to see a badge."

Both the kid's and the woman's eyes followed my hand as it reached for my back pocket. They waited, expecting to see a badge, but instead they saw five twenties laid out on the counter. "Have you seen her or not."

The kid looked at me, and then he looked down at the money. He reached out and scooped it up and folded it into his pocket. "She was in here," he said. "It wasn't even twenty minutes ago."

"Damn it, Cody," the woman said. She smacked his arm.

Cody raised his finger and pointed out the door behind me. "They went across the street."

Inside the Waffle House, a young blond-headed waitress was cleaning a booth by the door. She turned and looked when she heard the door close, a newspaper folded under her arm. The girl's picture was still in my hand, and when the waitress saw it the newspaper fell out from under her arm, and she lifted her hands to cover her mouth.

"Oh my God," she whispered. "They just left. They were sitting right here." She turned and pointed to the booth she'd been cleaning, the plates still full of food, two crisp twenties in the middle of the table.

"Did you see them leave?"

"Yes," she said.

"Do you know where they went?"

She looked down at the newspaper at her feet. It was open to the sports section, a picture of McGwire and Sosa looked up at her. "St. Louis," she said. "To see a baseball game."

Brady Weller

CHAPTER 23

Sandy's car was parked out in front of my office on Friday morning, and when I pulled into my spot he stood up from the sidewalk like he'd been waiting on me. He had a cigarette in his hand, and he looked like he'd been awake for hours. I opened my car door and stood up. "When did you start smoking again?"

"I've got some bad news, Brady," he said.

"What is it?"

"It's bad," he said.

"You already said that. What is it?"

"It's about Wade Chesterfield."

"What about him?"

"The cops in Charleston found his mother's body yesterday afternoon." He took the last drag off his cigarette and flicked it into the parking lot behind me. Then he fished a pack out of his breast pocket. "It's bad, Brady: the way they found her." He held the pack out to me. I took a cigarette and so did he.

"What happened to her?"

He lit his cigarette, and then he held out the lighter and I lit mine.

"She was murdered: blunt force to the head. She had a lot of injuries. Somebody took their time."

"Any idea who?"

"That's the thing," he said. "Doesn't seem to be much of a motive. Nothing taken, nothing damaged, no sign of a break-in. But there is something else."

"What?"

"They found her in Wade's room," he said. "The room he grew up in. It still had his posters and shit all over the walls. And she was beaten with a kid's baseball bat." A train engine blew its horn on the tracks a few streets over, and Sandy smoked and waited for it to pass before he said anything else. "Wade's prints were all over the scene too: the front door, the bedroom. They think he might've been the one who called it in."

"How do they know?"

"His prints were on a pay phone at a gas station down the street from his mom's house. And that's where the call came from."

"Anybody ID him?" I asked.

"No," he said. "But they saw one of the girls: the oldest one."

"Easter."

"She came into the gas station looking for a key to the outside bathroom right around the time the call was made."

"Did she seem okay?" I asked.

"They said she might've seemed a little nervous, but they didn't think anything of it. They forgot all about it until somebody came in a little bit later with a picture of Easter, asking if they'd seen her. Whoever it was didn't seem like a cop: black baseball hat, sunglasses, black clothes—had a blown-up picture of Easter he was carrying around folded up in his pocket."

"Who the hell is this guy? And how'd he get Easter's picture?"

"I don't know," he said. "No one knows. Right now all they have is a dead body with Wade Chesterfield's fingerprints all over the scene. It doesn't look good."

"Come on, Sandy. Of course his fingerprints are there; it's his mother's house."

"I'm not saying he did it, Brady. But we both know he's capable of kidnapping, and now he shows up at a murder scene. I mean, for somebody to beat that woman like that would take real anger, Brady—maybe his mother said something or tried to do something he didn't like."

"Or, 'the man in black' killed her," I said. "You don't know who this guy is. He could've done it."

"Sure," Sandy said. "Anybody *could've* done it. But Wade was there. That's all I'm saying."

"And all I'm saying is there's room for doubt—a lot of room. Broughton could have somebody out there; this guy carrying Easter's picture around could be him. Maybe Wade's mother got in the way."

"What? Have you turned into a conspiracy theorist on me?"

"No. I'm a realist. And I'm thinking like a cop. You should be thinking like one too."

"Look, Brady: I just wanted to let you know what I heard," he said. "I told you I'd keep you in the loop. Consider yourself looped in."

"Are you headed down there?"

He looked at me, and then he dropped his cigarette on the sidewalk and stubbed it out with his toe. "No," he said. "I got my hands full up here with the Feds. You know that. This is South Carolina's mess now. We've got a mess of our own to worry about."

"Those girls were taken from Gastonia, Sandy," I said. "And I know they ain't worth millions of dollars, but they're worth something. And they deserve to be found before anything bad happens to them."

"What do you want me to do, Brady? Just take off across the state line and swoop in like the FBI's done here?"

"Somebody should. Maybe I will."

He stood there looking at me for a second, and then he laughed. "This is a real investigation now, Brady; the Feds are all over it. Why in the hell would you get involved in this?"

"I'm already involved," I said.

"Really?" he asked. "Says who? The court? That old woman who runs the home? This isn't a game, man; you can't play your way back onto the force. The last thing you need to do is get involved and step on somebody's toes."

"Whose toes are you worried about, Sandy: yours?"

"I'm just trying to keep you from getting in over your head. Again."

"You're not thinking about me. So far I'm the only one who got your witness to talk about this money. You can't even find him. Now we're the only ones who know about it, and you can't stand it, can you? You can't stand sharing this case with me." I flicked my cigarette butt against the glass door to my office.

"Look, Brady, I came over here to give you an update. I'm trying to help you out."

"I don't need your charity, Sandy."

He stepped back and took a look at the window where *1-800-SAF-HOME* was printed on the glass. "Yeah, Brady," he said, smiling, pulling his car keys out of his pocket. "It looks like you're doing just great on your own."

CHAPTER 24

Saturday night was the college fair over at Jessica's school, and I spent most of that time at home, watching baseball and thinking about the decision Jessica was going to make about going to Peace. I could picture her, Tina, and Dean moving from table to table, talking to all of Jessica's friends who I didn't know anymore about a graduation party that I probably wouldn't be invited to.

And I just felt stuck, like I couldn't even get out of my chair to turn off the lights or the TV to go to bed.

So maybe that explains why I don't quite remember going to the closet for my .38, then going out to the car and hiding it under the driver's seat. But I definitely remember sitting out in the parking lot at Tomcat's, staring at the building and wondering who or what I'd find inside and exactly what I was going to do once I found out. I had a feeling that whoever had killed Wade's mother was the same guy carrying around a picture of Easter, and I had no doubt that he was really looking for Wade, and I was even more certain that Tommy Broughton was the one who'd sent him. I'd never met Wade Chesterfield, but by all accounts he sounded more like a fool than a murderer. But I had met Tommy Broughton, and I knew if he'd had that much money hidden in one wall then there was no telling how much he had hidden in others—every single cent of it stolen. He'd be desperate enough to do just about anything to cover his ass.

The bass from the music inside the club pounded in my chest as I walked through the parking lot, and it pulsed against my hand when I touched the door. Inside, the club was dark and smoky, and it looked exactly like what you'd expect a place to look like on Wilkinson Boulevard in the no-man's-land between Belmont and Charlotte: purple neon lights shone over the bar, and glaring red light lit the dance floor. The place was filled with people of all ages, but most of them were grizzled-looking men in their forties and fifties, drinking beer and staring up at the TV screens. None of them seemed surprised or interested that I'd shown up to join them.

There were a few empty stools around the bar, and I walked over and sat down and leaned my back against the counter. Someone tapped my shoulder a few minutes later, and I turned around and saw the bartender. His mouth was moving, but it was so loud that I couldn't make out what he was saying. I screamed, "Budweiser," and he nodded and walked down the bar; a few seconds later he came back and twisted off the cap and sat the beer in front of me. I opened my wallet and fished out a five-dollar bill and slid it across the counter. He picked up the money and turned to the register, and when he turned back around he slid a one-dollar bill across the counter to me. It dawned on me that maybe some of the money hidden in Broughton's walls came from selling four-dollar bottles of Budweiser to lonely middle-aged guys. I slid the dollar across the bar, and he nodded and picked it up and dropped it into a glass tip jar. Before he could turn away, I motioned for him to lean forward.

"Is Tommy here tonight?" I yelled.

"Who?!"

"Tommy!" I screamed. "Is he here?"

"He's not here tonight!" he screamed back. He stepped away and shrugged his shoulders, and then he walked to the other end of the bar, where a waitress had been trying to get his attention.

I turned around and leaned against the bar, and then I lit a cigarette. The beer was barely cold, and I took a few more sips before leaving it on the bar and crossing my arms.

A shaft of light spread across the back of the club where someone opened and closed a door, and I watched a tall skinny guy walk toward the bar. He stopped a few feet to my right and held up his hand until the bartender saw him and came over and took his order. When the bartender walked away, I leaned toward the guy.

"Tommy here?" I screamed.

"No," he yelled back. He turned toward the bar, but then he seemed to think better of it, and he looked at me again. "Who wants to know?"

"Just wondering," I said. "Just want to meet him—that's all."

"Tommy's not here," he said. The bartender brought over the guy's order: a Bud Light and what looked like whiskey on the rocks. The guy looked at me again, and then he picked up his drinks and walked toward the back of the club. Light poured from the door when he opened it and stepped inside. I sat there for a couple of minutes, smoked another cigarette, and then I snubbed it out, got up, and followed him.

The hallway was black and the door was painted black too just like the doors on the men's and women's restrooms that sat to the right of it. A strip of light glowed beneath it. I thought about knocking, but I couldn't think of a good reason, so I turned the knob and opened the door instead.

The guy I'd seen out at the bar sat in a chair against the wall on the right side of the room. Facing me was the kind of desk you'd see at a used-car dealership with a faux-wood tabletop supported by black aluminum sides. Behind the desk sat Tommy Broughton. He was fatter than he was the last time I'd seen him, and his black mustache and black hair had clearly been dyed to hide the gray. Both he and the guy sitting against the wall looked shocked that I'd opened the door, much less had dared to step inside.

"There you are," I said, staring at Broughton while closing the door behind me. The guy sitting against the wall made to stand up, but I held up my hand to stop him. "No, no, no," I said. "It's okay. I just want to talk." I pulled out one of the chairs facing the desk and sat down. The guy on my right sat back down too.

"So," I said, looking at Broughton, "it's been a while." I crossed my legs and let my hands rest in my lap.

"What the hell are you doing here?" Broughton asked.

"I'm just out on the town on a Saturday night," I said. "Just like anybody else, but when I found out that you were the Tommy in Tomcat's, I was just dying to see you. So I asked your buddy here if he knew you, but he said no." I sat up straight and turned to the guy sitting in the chair. His face was almost white and he looked nervous, like he didn't know what was going to happen; I didn't either. I pointed at Broughton. "This is Tommy," I said. "You should get to know him. He's a real stand-up guy. We go back a long way, don't we, Tommy?"

"What do you want?" Broughton asked.

"I just want to talk," I said. "Ask a few questions."

"About what?"

"Oh, I don't know," I said. "Where do I start?" I looked over at the guy to my right and smiled. He smiled back before catching himself, frowning, and looking over at Broughton to make sure he hadn't seen him smile. I looked at Broughton too. "Who do you have out there?"

"Out where? At the bar?"

I laughed. "No," I said. I pointed my finger like I was pointing through the wall toward Wilkinson. "Out *there*—looking for Wade Chesterfield."

"I don't know who you're talking about," he said.

"Really?" I said. "Then you're a better man than me. If somebody stole that kind of money from me I'd want to know where they were. But that's just me." I looked toward the guy on my right again. "That's probably just me," I said. I turned back to Broughton. "I think whoever you've got out there just murdered an old woman who had nothing to do with this." I waited a second while I watched Broughton's face turn whiter and whiter. Out of the corner of my eye I noticed the other guy fidget in his seat. "If you sent someone to do that, Tommy, that's just like murdering that woman yourself. That's how the police will see it anyway—once they catch you. You need to call him off before this thing gets worse." Broughton snorted, leaned back in his seat, and interlocked his fingers over his bulging stomach.

"Don't talk to me like a cop," he said. "You aren't a cop anymore, remember? And if anybody in this room is guilty of murder, it's you."

He rocked back in his chair and smiled, but his smile slowly widened and he actually started laughing. The guy sitting to my right laughed too. I looked down at my hands and waited for them to finish, but they just kept on. When I looked up I saw that Broughton was looking at the guy on my right, and before he could turn back to me I'd already left my chair, reached across his desk, and grabbed him by his hair. I slammed his face on the desktop. His buddy jumped up from his seat, his chair slamming against the wall, but I'd already pulled my .38 and had it pointed at his chest before he could stand up all the way.

Broughton couldn't catch his breath, and he wheezed and coughed under my hand, leaving a trail of spittle on the desk. The room was quiet except for the music from the club vibrating through the walls. I kept my gun on the guy to my right. "Lift up your shirt," I said. He lifted it, and I could see he didn't have a piece tucked down in his front waistband. "Keep it up and turn around." He did; there wasn't a gun in the back either, but I saw something else: a thin black wire ran from his waist and disappeared up his back. Broughton's head was facing away where I had him pinned to the desk, and he hadn't seen what I'd seen. I looked down at him. "You *are* in over your head, aren't you, Tommy?"

"You're a dead man," he said.

"Okay," I said. I looked up at the guy on my right. He'd dropped his shirt and was staring at me with a look of pure fear on his face. "Let's get some music going," I said. "Let's get some of the tension out of this room." With the barrel of my gun, I pointed at a radio that sat on top of a file cabinet on the guy's right. "Turn that on," I said. He just stood there. "Turn it on," I said again. He reached over and turned the radio on. The Eagles' "Life in the Fast Lane" came out of the speakers. "Perfect choice," I said. "Turn it up." He reached over and slid the volume dial toward himself. "Louder," I said. He turned it up as loud as it would go. I stared at him until he sat down, and then I looked at Broughton where I held him to the desk.

"I want to know who you sent after Chesterfield and those little girls," I said, barely above the music.

"I'm going to kill you," he said.

"You mentioned that already," I said. "I got it. Let's move on: who'd you send after Chesterfield and those little girls?"

"He's dead," Broughton said, his cheek flat against the desk. "His kids too." When I lifted him by his hair, he made the mistake of looking down, and I felt his nose break when I slammed his face against his desk. Blood spread across either side of his desk like a Rorschach test.

"That wasn't a nice thing to say," I said. I took my gun off the guy sitting down and pressed the barrel firmly against the top of Broughton's head. "Let's try it again: who's out there?"

"A guy named Pruitt," Broughton said, his voice trembling under the nose of the gun.

" 'Pruitt' who?"

"Bobby Pruitt," Broughton said.

"He works here," the guy in the chair said. "He bounces."

"Is that true?" I asked Broughton.

"Yeah," he said.

"Where's he at now?" I asked.

"I don't know," Broughton said. I raised him by his hair like I was going to slam his face on his desk again. "St. Louis," he said, spitting blood onto the desk. "He said he's going to St. Louis." I lowered his head down and let him lay his cheek against the desk.

"Is he following Wade Chesterfield?"

"I don't know," he said. I took the butt of my gun and cracked Broughton on his spine; his feet splayed in opposite directions behind his desk, and I had to grab the collar of his jacket to keep him from falling. I kneeled down toward the desk and spoke right into Broughton's ear so he could hear me clearly.

"Your boy's carrying around a picture of one of Wade's little girls. If something happens to her, or if he touches either one of those girls, so help me God, Tommy, I will come back here and butcher you." I stood up and cracked him on the spine again. His body convulsed. "Is he following Wade?" He muttered something, but I couldn't quite make it out, and I bent lower to hear him.

"Yes," he said. He was breathing heavy and sweating through his clothes, and I was afraid he might pass out if I didn't turn him loose. I let go of his neck, and he crumpled to the floor in front of his chair. I looked over the desk at him. Blood covered his face and ran over his forehead and into his hair. He lay there with his eyes closed, facing the ceiling. The guy in the chair just sat there, waiting for whatever happened next.

"Is there something you want to say?" I asked. He shook his head. I thought about punching him in the face just to do it, but I had no idea why he was wired or who he was working for, and I figured I was probably in enough trouble as it was. I reached back and stuffed my .38 down into my pants waist, and then I opened the door and stepped into the dark, loud hallway.

I pulled the door closed and walked back toward the front of the club. When I came out of the hallway I looked toward the bar to see if anyone had noticed me leaving the office, and that's when I saw what was on the TVs hanging on the wall: Sosa was trotting slowly around the bases in Pittsburgh, which meant that he'd hit a home run for the second night in a row and that Roc now owed me $2,000. My luck had finally changed, but that's not what made me stop dead in my tracks; it was an ESPN graphic that showed the remaining games Sosa and McGwire had left to break Maris's record. Their paths would cross in St. Louis on Monday afternoon, and something told me that Wade and those two little girls might just be there to see it.

CHAPTER 25

A black Chevy Lumina started tailing me almost as soon as I turned out of the parking lot at Tomcat's and made a left onto Wilkinson. It would hang back two or three cars and switch lanes when I did, trying to keep me in view. I tried not to pay attention to it and drive like it was any other Saturday night, but I knew it could be just about anybody in that car: Broughton and a couple of his thugs, the FBI, my own paranoia. My .38 was hidden beneath my seat, and I couldn't decide whether to reach for it or use my heel to push it back even farther.

Wilkinson turned into Franklin Avenue when I got back into Gastonia proper, and by the time I'd turned onto New Hope Road the black Lumina was right behind me. When I pulled into my parking spot at Quail Woods the car pulled in parallel to my back bumper, making it impossible for me to leave. In my rearview mirror, I watched the driver open his door slowly like he had all the time in the world. He wore a dark suit and had a military haircut and was a little older and shorter than me. When the passenger climbed out I saw that he was tall and thin, and when he stepped into the light I realized it was Sandy. I watched him first in my rearview and then in my side mirror as he walked up to my window and knocked on the glass. The driver hung back like he was waiting to see how it went. I sighed and turned off the engine and rolled my window down.

"Go ahead and step out, Brady," Sandy said.

"Jesus, Sandy, really?"

The driver pounded my car's trunk once with his fist. "Get out," he said. "Now!"

I rolled my window up, opened the car door, and stepped out. Sandy backed away. "Do you have a weapon on you?" he asked. He looked me up and down like he was sizing me up.

"Who's your angry friend?" I asked, nodding toward the back bumper where the driver was still standing.

"Agent Barnwell," the guy said. "Federal Bureau of Investigation."

"Oh," I said, turning to look at him. "Welcome to Gastonia." I turned back to Sandy. "I've got a .38 under my seat, and I've got a license to carry it."

"I told you he had a gun," Barnwell said. Sandy looked at him, and then he ducked down and reached under my seat and felt around until he found the gun. He opened the cylinder, dumped the bullets into his hand, and dropped them into his pocket.

"Is that it?" he asked.

"That's it," I said.

"No it's not," Barnwell said. He walked around the other side of the car, so I couldn't see him without turning my head. "We've got some questions for you."

"I'm ready when you are," I said, my back still to him.

"Not out here," he said. "Inside."

I turned to face him. "What makes you think I'm letting you in my house?"

He smiled and put his hands in his pockets. "We can do it down at the police station if you'd like," he said. "Give you a chance to see all your old friends. Detective Sanders was just telling me on the way over about what a huge fan club you've got down there." I looked at him for a second, and then I turned back to Sandy.

"Y'all have to take off your shoes if you're coming inside," I said. "I won't get my security deposit back if you track bullshit everywhere." I turned and looked at Barnwell and took my keys out of my pocket. "And you'd better move your car before one of my neighbors sees that you don't know how to park. Director Freeh's not going to appreciate you getting his car keyed."

The inside of my apartment was dark, and I flipped on the lights and Sandy and Barnwell followed me into the small kitchen.

"Nice place," Barnwell said, looking around and smiling.

"Thanks," I said. "I love hosting parties."

"You mind if we go into the living room and sit down?" Sandy asked. "We just need to talk for a bit. It won't take long." They followed me into the living room, and I turned on the light on the ceiling fan and sat down in the recliner. Barnwell looked around the room, and then he took a seat on the sofa beside Sandy.

"Y'all see Sammy get fifty-eight tonight?" I asked, but they just sat there staring at me. I looked at Barnwell. "You not a big baseball fan?"

He pulled out a pad and pen from inside his jacket. He flipped through the pad until he found an empty page. "What were you doing at Tomcat's tonight?" he asked.

I shrugged and raised my eyebrows. "Having a four-dollar beer," I said. "That's what you should be investigating."

Barnwell looked up from his pad. "How do you know Tommy Broughton?" he asked.

"The same way Sandy knows him. We used to run into him from time to time. You meet all kinds of people in this line of work," I said. "Gangsters, thugs, FBI."

Barnwell laughed and closed his pad. "You're a piece of work, Weller," he said. He looked over at Sandy. "He's a piece of work, isn't he?" He stood up from the sofa and walked past me and stopped at the sliding-glass door. He pulled back the curtain and looked out onto my tiny, cluttered patio. He acted like he was looking at something, even though I knew it was too dark out there and too bright in here for him to see anything besides my rusty, old grill and folding chairs. The curtain swished closed when he let it go, and then I felt his hand rest on the back of the recliner. I looked up and saw him staring down at me.

"That was cute," he said. "Turning up the music: they teach you that in alarm school?"

"No," I said. "I saw it on *Law & Order*." Barnwell snorted again, and then he looked at Sandy. "I can't believe you got to work with this guy," he said, smiling. Sandy was leaning forward, staring at me. "We should take you down to the station and let you do some stand-up," Barnwell said. "Maybe you could sign some autographs for your fan club."

"They're a devoted bunch," I said. I stared at him until he looked away.

"Brady," Sandy said, "what the hell were you doing there tonight?"

"No," Barnwell said before I could respond. "No more questions." He stepped in front of me so that I couldn't see Sandy anymore. "If you do that again, if you piss on this investigation again, I will do everything in my power to bury you," he said. "You can take that to mean anything you'd like, but you should know that I mean it. We don't need you out there playing cop. Those days are over."

"What he's saying, Brady, is that we've got everything under control," Sandy said.

"It seems like it," I said. "Y'all are really doing a great job."

Barnwell laughed and walked back over to the sliding-glass door and stood staring at the closed curtain, his hands making fists in his pockets.

"Brady, I'm telling you: don't do this again," Sandy said. "That's not going to help anybody: not those girls, not us, and definitely not you."

Barnwell turned around and pointed at me. "You pull some shit like that one more time and I won't come back here looking to talk," he said. "You're in the way, Weller, and I've been on this case for too long for you to waltz in and blow it here at the end."

"In the way of what?" I asked. "Finding the money or finding those girls?"

"We think we'll find both of them if you let us do our jobs," Sandy said, standing up.

"I hope so," I said. "I also hope you know what's out there."

"We know more than you think," Barnwell said.

"I doubt that."

They both stood there looking at me, but then Sandy reached into his pocket and brought out a closed fist that held the bullets he'd taken out of my .38. He lined them up slowly one by one on the coffee table. When he was finished he looked up and smiled. "Have a good night," he said. "We'll be in touch."

I kept my seat and watched them leave, and I didn't move until I heard the car crank and pull away from my apartment. It was only then that I walked to the small hall closet, opened the door, and pulled down my old suitcase from the top shelf.

Easter Quillby

CHAPTER 26

The first night after leaving Charleston we pulled off the highway at a rest stop in North Carolina. We got out and used the bathroom and got some snacks and some Cokes from the vending machines and went back to the car. Wade pulled around back behind the bathrooms, hoping we could stay there for the night, but just as we got settled in a man in a uniform came and knocked on the windshield with a flashlight and told us we couldn't spend the night there. Wade rolled the window up without saying anything, started the car, and pulled back onto the highway.

Friday morning I woke up with the light hitting my eyes through the windshield. When I sat up I saw that the sun was just rising and that Wade had covered me and Ruby with a couple of sweatshirts dotted with paint stains and one of his old coats. It was chilly inside the car, and I knew it was early by the way the light looked outside — all soft and glowing.

The car sat in a paved parking lot surrounded by mountains that were covered in fog; that fog could've even been clouds for how high it seemed like we were. Ours was the only car in the parking lot. I slipped my shoes on as quiet as I could and wrapped one of Wade's sweat-shirts around my shoulders, and I opened the door and slipped out and pushed it shut behind me. Wade was laying across the front seat, his eyes closed and his arms pulled up inside the sleeves of his T-shirt.

A little sidewalk ran around the edge of the parking lot, and just beyond it a guardrail kept you from getting too close to the edge. I walked right up to it and leaned against it and looked down into the valley, where the fog was thicker than it was up where we'd spent the night. When I was in the fifth grade my class took a field trip to Crowders Mountain in Gastonia, and that seemed like the tallest thing I'd ever seen, especially after we hiked all the way to the top. But now, standing where I was standing and seeing what I was seeing, I realized that I'd never seen anything like these mountains before.

Behind me, a car door opened and closed quietly, and when I turned I saw Wade standing there looking around like I'd just been doing a few minutes before.

"Where are we?" I asked.

"We're on the Blue Ridge Parkway," Wade said.

"What's that?"

"It's a road that runs through the mountains from Virginia clear down to South Carolina." He rubbed at his eyes. "It's the country's most visited national park," he said, his words turning into a yawn that finished with him stretching his arms over his head.

"You wouldn't know it right now," I said, looking around at all the empty parking spaces.

"It's early," he said. "People will be up here soon enough to check out the leaves."

I hadn't noticed the leaves yet. You could see their color through the fog in the valley right below us: gold and red and some green here and there. It seemed like the fog couldn't cover the tops of the tall mountains, and up on top of them almost all the leaves were gold. I couldn't believe that just last night we'd been down in Charleston, where the air was salty and hot and sticky, and now we were up here looking at these mountains, my breath coming out of my mouth like smoke every time I breathed.

"Look back here," Wade said. "Back behind us." He pointed to a huge mountain on the other side of the parking lot that you could just barely see through the clouds. A red-and-white antenna tower sat up on top of it. "That's Mount Pisgah," he said, looking up at it with his hands cupped around his eyes even though the sun wasn't hardly out yet. He dropped his hands and looked over at me. "You know where that name comes from?"

"No," I said.

"From the Bible," he said. "God told Moses to climb to the top of Mount Pisgah so that he could finally see the Promised Land." He looked back over at the mountain. "It wasn't *this* mountain—that one was out in the desert somewhere—but that's where the name comes from."

"Did you make that up?"

"No," he said.

"Then how'd you know it?"

"What?" he said. "You think I can't know things just because I know them?" He stood there looking at me like I'd hurt his feelings, and then he smiled and pulled a brochure out of his back pocket and showed it to me. "I got this at the rest stop last night," he said. "I needed a little bedtime reading." He opened it and spread it out on the hood of the car. "The early explorers who found this mountain climbed to the top of it and thought they'd found the Promised Land when they saw what waited for them on the other side. Those guys were heading west, just like us."

"Where are we going exactly?" I asked.

"St. Louis," he said. "I thought y'all wanted to see some baseball."

"After that."

"I don't know," he said. "Oklahoma? Texas? California?" His eyes got bigger as he listed the names. "We could keep going clear on to the Pacific Ocean if we wanted to."

"Then what?" I asked. "We can't live in this car forever."

"I don't know," Wade said again. "I guess that's why they call it an adventure."

Ruby opened the car door and climbed out. Wade's other sweatshirt was wrapped around her shoulders. She looked around the parking lot at all the mountains and the fog; she'd never even been to Crowders Mountain like I had, and I couldn't imagine what she was thinking.

"Where are we?" she asked.

"Mount Pisgah," I said.

"Why?"

"Because we're looking for the Promised Land," Wade said, folding up the brochure and sliding it into his back pocket. He winked at me. "And we're almost there."

The next couple days passed by like blurry dreams of riding in the car on back roads and getting lost late at night in places like Paducah, Kentucky, and Cookeville, Tennessee, where no stores or restaurants were ever open and there was never any place to use the bathroom. Wade had told us it would take about fifteen hours to drive from Charleston to St. Louis, but we were in the car a lot longer than that. It began to feel like we were just driving in circles, and it seemed like there were times when Wade had no idea where we were going or what we were going to do once we got there. We went long stretches without talking, me and Ruby looking out the windows and Wade trying to tune in baseball games on the radio to see where McGwire and Sosa were in the home-run race. It seemed like Wade hadn't hardly closed his eyes since we'd left Myrtle Beach, and while he drove he told us long stories about playing for the Rangers and throwing batting practice to Sosa: how Sammy couldn't hit any of his pitches except his fastball; how, back then, Sammy was just a skinny little Dominican kid who didn't even speak English. The stories and the radio games all ran together, and before long I started picturing Sammy Sosa as a poor, skinny teenager in a Cubs uniform catching McGwire's pop-ups out in the outfield.

By Saturday night, McGwire had hit sixty home runs to Sosa's fifty-eight, which meant that McGwire only needed one more to tie Maris's record. Saturday's game was in Cincinnati, and Wade said there was no way McGwire would tie the record there; he said that was the kind of thing a ballplayer wanted to do on his home field, and he had no doubt that McGwire would wait on the record until him and Sosa were both in St. Louis on Monday, and he promised us that we'd all be there to see it.

Wade didn't have tickets to Monday's game, but he told us he had a feeling they wouldn't be too hard to come by. The radio had been saying that just one ticket might cost as much as $1,000, so I knew Wade's hope for a ticket had more to do with the money he had hidden in that black bag than any kind of luck or know-how he pretended to have.

Late Monday morning we drove into St. Louis. Just as we were crossing a river, Wade slowed down and pointed at something on the other side of the bridge. "See that right there?" he asked. It was a huge white half circle that looked to be sitting in a field off to our right. "That's the St. Louis Arch." He looked at us in the rearview mirror. "They call it the 'Gateway to the West.'"

Ruby moved over to my side of the backseat to see it better. "What is it?" she asked.

"It's a sculpture, kind of," Wade said. "And it's a monument too."

"How's it a gateway?" I asked.

"That's just symbolism," he said. "Like a metaphor or an analogy. You know what that means?"

"No," I said, shaking my head.

"It means when something stands for something else. That arch stands for the gateway to the West. Like the old-time settlers, we've left everything behind in the East and we've crossed the mountains, and now we're pointing our horses west." The car was quiet, and the three of us sat there looking at the Arch as it got closer and closer, and before I knew it we'd driven right past it.

"Like Oregon Trail," Ruby said.

"What?" Wade asked.

"Oregon Trail," I said. "It's a game you play on the computer."

"I want to go see it," Ruby said, turning and climbing up on her knees to look out the back window at the Arch.

"We will," Wade said. "Maybe tomorrow. But today we're here to see a baseball game. Tomorrow, we head west."

Brady Weller

CHAPTER 27

Before leaving town on Sunday morning I'd gone by the Fish House to get the $2,000 Roc owed me. He must've known I was on the way over to see him because he was sitting on an overturned trash can and smoking a Black & Mild outside the kitchen door when I pulled up.

"Damn, son," he said when I got out of the car. "Don't you know we don't open for lunch until eleven on Sundays? I know your ass isn't on the way to church."

"I thought I'd come by here and collect my money so I'd have something to drop in the offering plate," I said, taking his hand and fumbling through another awkward handshake.

"Sammy and McGwire *mono y mono* tomorrow afternoon," he said. "You sure you don't want to let that two thousand steep in the pot?"

"No way," I said. "Not the way my luck's been going."

He laughed, jumped up off the trash can, and pulled a wad of cash out of his pocket, counting out twenty one-hundred-dollar bills and handing them to me. I folded the bills and tucked them into my breast pocket. Roc stuffed what was left of the wad back into his jeans.

"I can't believe you carry that kind of cash," I said.

He smiled. "Come on, man," he said, lifting up his shirt to reveal a compact 9mm tucked into the waistband of his jeans. "Everybody knows the Fish House is the safest place to work in town."

"Yeah, I see that," I said. "Before I take off, you mind if I run another name past you?"

"Hey." He spread his arms like he was about to give me a hug. "That's what I'm here for, baby: to share my wealth of knowledge with my community."

"Have you ever heard of a guy named Bobby Pruitt?"

"Robert Pruitt?" he asked.

"Yeah," I said. "Sure."

"Old baseball player?"

"That's him."

"Shit, man," he said, "that's the dude who took Wade down. That's the one I was telling you about."

"The guy he hit?"

"Yeah, man, and I'd stay away from that dude if I was you."

"I think he's looking for Wade and those girls."

"Well, you'd better find Wade before he does."

I took the keys out of my pocket and nodded toward my car. "That's what I'm hoping to do tomorrow."

"Where you off to?"

"St. Louis," I said.

"For what?" he asked, smiling.

"A baseball game."

He laughed. "Shit, you got tickets?"

I held up the folded bills he'd just given me. "I do now."

Pruitt

CHAPTER 28

A ll that money, and you're calling me collect," the Boss said. "You should've paid it in quarters."

"Where are you?"

"It doesn't matter."

"You'd better have good news," he said.

"He's been found."

"Then why don't I have what I want?"

"Because it's not time yet."

"When will it be time?"

"Monday. In St. Louis."

"Why St. Louis?"

"That's where he's headed. And that's where this will end."

"It's Thursday. Why should I have to wait that long?"

"Because the terms of the deal have changed."

"What the hell makes you think that?"

"Because the cards aren't in your hands anymore."

"What do you want?"

"A hundred thousand."

The other end of the phone was silent. "No way. That wasn't the deal."

"The deal has changed."

"No. It hasn't."

"He's going to be found, and what belongs to you is going to be found with him. It's up to you if you want it back. Getting it back means the terms have changed."

"I'm cutting you loose. We're done. This is over."

"No, it's not. Not for me."

The forty-dollar lot at Busch Stadium was already slam full of people an hour before the first pitch: college kids, families, hundreds of people wearing T-shirts and hats with "61" on them, carrying posters and signs with McGwire's name and face on them. Outside the lot, scalpers littered the sidewalk, holding signs, looking into car windows, walking back and forth in the street during red lights.

A group of scalpers stood on the corner of Clark and Eighth, and a tall skinny black guy stepped away from them and waved me over. "What do you need, man?" he asked. "Whatever it is, I got it: dugout, left field, right field, everything but the box."

"Just a ticket to get in. Doesn't matter where."

"Get in where you fit in, right?" he said, smiling, looking around like he expected somebody to be following me or trying to get close enough to hear what we were saying.

"What's the cheapest you got?"

"You a cop?"

My eyes turned toward the group of guys still standing behind him. "Do they ask questions, or do they sell tickets?"

"Hold up, now," he said. He looked around again, and then he nodded his head toward the parking deck behind him. "Follow me." He turned and walked into a parking deck on the corner of Clark and Eighth Street, stopping in between a van and a pickup truck. "A grand," he said, holding up a ticket. "A grand gets you standing room."

The garage was full of cars but near empty of the sounds of people, everyone already headed toward the ballpark. The only sound was that of me peeling crisp bills off the stack. His eyes stayed on me while the money was counted.

"Fifteen," he said

"Fifteen what?"

"Fifteen hundred. The price goes up this close to game time."

The bills were folded and slid back into my pocket. "Okay." But by the time he heard it the Glock had already been pulled from the waistband of my shorts and the tip of its barrel slammed down on top of his head. His knees buckled, and he fell at my feet.

"Do you want to play?" The barrel pushed down on his head until it felt like it could be forced through his skull. "Do you?"

"No," he whispered. "I'm sorry. Take it." He lifted the ticket up toward me, and my free hand closed around it before the sole of my shoe kicked him in the sternum, knocking him back against the concrete wall. He laid there looking up at me, tears in his eyes, his chest heaving like he'd been running as fast as he could. I pulled the grand back out of my pocket and balled it up and threw it at his face. He winced as the money fell all around him.

Easter Quillby

CHAPTER 29

Wade had parked under an overpass and left us in the car while he went to look for tickets. All the parking lots had signs up saying they were full, and we drove away from the stadium, looking for a place to park. The streets were empty because everybody was already inside. Other cars were parked around us under the overpass, and me and Ruby rolled down the windows and watched a family climb out of a minivan. Both boys were younger than me, and they both had on baseball gloves and McGwire jerseys, and their little sister stood behind their minivan and stared up at the overpass, sniffing and wiping her eyes like she'd been crying. The man and the woman were fussing at each other.

"It's not like I meant to leave it," the man said. He was tall and brown-headed just like the boys, and he had on a Cardinals ball cap and a T-shirt with a picture of McGwire on it.

"You'd just better hope it doesn't rain," the woman said. She had the back of the minivan open, and she was stuffing things inside a bag. She looked back at the little girl, and then she looked at the man. "Where are her damn snacks?" The man sighed loud enough for everybody to hear it. "Really, Marty?" she said. She slammed the back of the minivan and grabbed the little girl's hand and started walking toward the ballpark. The man and the two boys followed her. Me and Ruby watched them go.

Wade had promised us he wouldn't be gone long, but now we were the only ones still sitting under the overpass. The game was going to start soon, and I couldn't help but worry while the parking lot got quieter and quieter as everybody headed inside for the game. Soon you couldn't hear nothing but the cars driving on the interstate above us and the music and announcements coming from far away inside the ballpark.

Ruby had rolled her window down all the way, and she stuck out her arm like she was trying to feel if there was any breeze. "You think we'll see Big Mac break the record?" she asked.

Sweat ran down my forehead, and I wiped it with my T-shirt. "I don't know," I said. "I bet he'll tie it at least." My legs were sweating too, and I grabbed a handful of napkins we'd left on the dash and wiped my legs, and then I balled up the napkins and threw them on the floorboard. "There's another game tomorrow," I said. "Maybe Wade will bring us to that one too."

"Where is he?"

"He went to get tickets," I said. "Remember? You have to have tickets to get inside."

Ruby picked at something on her shirt, and then she sighed. "Think we'll stay in another place tonight that has a pool?" She'd been asking that same question ever since we'd left Myrtle Beach, and I'd told her the same thing every time.

"I don't know," I said. "Ask Wade."

"He never says nothing when I ask him," she said.

"It might be because you talk all the time," I said. "You're like background music."

"What's background music?"

"It's music you forget about because you hear it all the time. Like the music they play in elevators and stores."

"But we're not in elevators and stores all the time," she said. "How could he be used to it?"

"It's just something people say."

"That doesn't make any sense," she said.

I didn't say anything because I saw Wade a couple of rows over, walking toward us like he couldn't wait to get back to the car. Seeing him hurry like that made my stomach feel sick, and I reached back and found my seat belt and put it on. But as he got closer I saw that he was smiling. When he saw us watching him he reached into his back pocket and pulled out three tickets and spread them out like he was playing cards.

He leaned into Ruby's window and smacked her leg with the tickets. "Y'all ready?" he asked. "Left field. We're going to catch us a home run."

"A ball can really carry on a bright, hot day like this one," Wade said. "It ain't going to take much for McGwire to knock one out of here." He had both of us by the hand, and we were walking up a concrete ramp toward our seats. "Keep up and stay close," he yelled. There were people everywhere, most of them in Cardinals T-shirts and uniforms, but a couple of people had on Cubs hats and jerseys with Sosa's name and number on the back. I couldn't hardly hear what Wade was saying for all the people screaming and the music and the announcer introducing the lineups over the speakers. I heard the announcer say "Mark," but I couldn't hear the rest of it because the fans were cheering so loud.

Wade led us up the ramps to a long hallway that curved around the field. To our right, shorter tunnels led out to the seats, and whenever we passed the tunnels I could feel the heat from the sun and see the green outfield and the upper-deck seats on the other side of the stadium. The seats were already full. I'd never seen so many people in my entire life.

"You think Sammy Sosa will hit a home run too?" Ruby asked.

"I'd say he probably will," Wade said. "If I know one thing about Sammy it's that he ain't going to let McGwire have all the fun today."

"You think he'd remember you?" I asked.

"Of course he'll remember," Wade said. "He couldn't forget an arm like mine." He gave my hand a squeeze and winked at me.

"I'm hungry," Ruby said. "And I'm thirsty too."

"You want to find our seats first?" Wade asked. He looked at me like he wanted me to say something.

"But we haven't had anything to eat or drink all day," Ruby said. Out on the field somebody started singing "The Star-Spangled Banner."

"We're going to miss it," I said.

"But I'm hungry," Ruby whined.

"It's okay," Wade said, giving my hand a little squeeze. "We've got plenty of time."

"There he is!" Ruby screamed. She pointed at Mark McGwire where he was taking warm-up swings on a huge television screen over the seats in center field. Staring at the screen made her walk even slower down the steps toward our seats.

"Keep going," I said, lifting my knee and nudging her in the back. I was holding a Coke and two boxes of popcorn; Ruby'd already opened her popcorn, and she was stuffing handfuls in her mouth while she took the concrete steps one at a time.

Behind me, Wade carried his and Ruby's sodas and all three of our hot dogs. "All the way down, Ruby," he said.

We found our seats, the first three to the left of the steps in row two, and I stood in between Ruby and Wade because everybody else was standing too so they could get a look at McGwire. Wade passed our hot dogs over to me and Ruby, and then he tapped a guy on the shoulder in the first row. "What did Sosa do?"

The guy turned around and looked at Wade. He had a mustache and a red Cardinals uniform on with a black baseball hat. "Popped it up," he said. "Left Hernández stranded on first."

"I can't see nothing," Ruby said. I folded her seat down and helped her climb on top of it, and then I did the same with mine. I could see everything around me now: the whole outfield with Sammy Sosa standing over in right, the upper deck, and the open white circle of the ballpark above us where the bright blue sky almost looked like a lid that was keeping all the heat trapped inside. I could feel everything around me too: the crowd was so loud that you couldn't even hear the music or the announcers, and when Brian Jordan hit a fly ball to left field and McGwire stepped into the batter's box with nobody on base it was the loudest thing I'd ever heard. Ruby stuffed her hot dog in her mouth and covered her ears with her hands. But as soon as McGwire set his feet and got into his batting stance the whole stadium went totally silent, and you couldn't hardly hear a thing.

Maybe it was all the heat, or maybe it was the breeze coming across the field from home plate, but something about it all reminded me of the first time me and Ruby saw the ocean. It felt like years ago, even though it hadn't quite been a week, but I remembered it now: the way the warm sand felt under my feet, the sound of the tide like the whispering voices I heard all around me now, the sight of the waves moving far out in the ocean like the way people were moving all around the ballpark, trying to get a better look at what might be about to happen.

McGwire swung and missed on the first pitch. As soon as the ball snapped into the catcher's mitt, everybody in the stadium sighed at the same time like the audience does on game shows when somebody says the wrong answer. But it got quiet again when McGwire stepped back into the box. The next pitch was a ball, and everybody sighed just like they had before.

But as soon as the ball left the pitcher's hand on the third pitch it was like we all knew it was the one. The ball cracked off the bat and headed right toward left field where we were sitting, and I stood on my seat and reached for Ruby's hand and saw the right fielder backing toward the wall, and then he stopped and watched it fly just left of the foul pole and over our heads. I turned just as it bounced off the window in the skyboxes above us and fell right down in front of our seats and rolled toward the wall.

It seemed like everyone in the stands dove for the ball at the same time, including Wade. People pushed up against me, and I stepped down off my seat and grabbed Ruby and lifted her down too. "Hold on to me," I said. But then it was over all of a sudden, and the guy who'd been sitting in front of us stood up and lifted the ball above his head, and everyone around us started clapping and cheering.

Wade stood up too. His shirt was smeared with mustard and ketchup from the hot dog he'd been holding, and his hair was sopping wet where somebody'd spilled something—maybe Coke or beer—all over him. But he was laughing. "I almost had it!" he said, lifting his hand and high-fiving me and then Ruby. "I almost had a piece of history." He held his hand in front of me like he wanted me to see it, but I wasn't looking at his hand; instead I was watching Mark McGwire as he rounded third and gave the third baseman a high five, and I watched when he crossed home plate, where his son was waiting for him in a Cardinals bat boy uniform. His dad picked him up and lifted him into the air, and I watched them, thinking about what it must feel like to have your dad reach down and pick you up, lift you up off the ground away from everything while everyone watched and everyone cheered.

"Look!" Ruby said, raising her hand and pointing at center field. "It's us!" Me and Wade both looked up; she was right. The three of us were on the huge screen, standing in the row behind the guy who held the home-run ball over his head, high-fiving everyone around him.

Brady Weller

CHAPTER 30

At first my eyes had been locked on McGwire at the plate, but now I watched him as he rounded first. When he crossed second base, my eyes lifted to the Jumbotron in the center field, and that's when I saw them just before the screen changed to replay McGwire's swing. My hand immediately went to my back pocket, and without looking at it I unfolded the copy of Chesterfield's mug shot. In slow motion, the screen showed McGwire's home run flying just fair and bouncing off the skybox before dropping into the stands. In those couple of seconds, I got a quick glimpse of two girls who looked like Easter and Ruby, and then I saw Wade dive for the ball.

Beside me, an elderly man with binoculars stood by the upper-deck railing behind home plate. "Can I borrow these?" I asked, lifting the strap from around his neck without waiting for him to answer. McGwire had crossed home plate by the time I found them out in the left field, just two rows up from the wall. I pushed the binoculars back toward the old man and pounded down the stairs to the concourse tunnel.

It was empty; everyone inside the stadium had stayed at their seats or gone down the tunnels to watch McGwire at bat. I turned to my right and ran through the stadium faster than I'd ever run in my life, trying to remember the section number they'd been sitting in when I found them through the binoculars, slowing to look down the tunnels to get my bearings from what I could see of the stands. Each tunnel was a flash of sunshine and green grass and deafening cheers.

When I rounded the third-base line for the outfield, I took the first tunnel on my right, and when I saw the yellow foul pole I pounded down the steps toward the field, the grass rising up like the flat face of a green mossy lake.

The girls were alone.

Pruitt

CHAPTER 31

Her picture was in my hand when her face appeared on the Jumbotron, but my eyes were focused instead on Wade Chesterfield where he stood beside her.

But by the time I found them in the stands he was walking up the steps away from their seats.

The concourse was empty, everyone still cheering inside the stadium, the roar carrying down each tunnel where the light crossed my face and my feet hammered the cement on the way toward him. My hand reached back and cradled the gun against my waist, holding it to make certain it didn't work itself free.

He probably heard someone running down the concourse toward him and thought they were rushing back to their seats to see the celebration, but if he'd looked up instead of ducking into the bathroom at the top of the stairs he would've seen me bearing down on him.

Wade stood in the first stall on the left, inside the empty restroom, his back to me, wiping at his shirt with toilet paper. My heart pounded in my chest and the blood surged through my body, and I felt a trail of it trickling from my nose and down onto my lips.

I stepped into the stall, and he turned around to see me standing right in front of him.

"Hey, Wade."

He tried to squeeze past me, but my arms locked around his neck and pulled him back into the stall. He squirmed around so that his back was against my chest, and his feet pushed off from the toilet. We stumbled out of the stall and fell toward the sinks. My shoulder slammed against a bank of automatic hand dryers, turning a few on, the hot air blowing down my arm and across his face. He thrashed around trying to get free, but my arms tightened around his neck and lifted him off the floor, part of me hoping to feel his body go slack so that it would be done. "Do you remember me, Wade?"

"Wait," he said, his voice barely able to make it all the way out of his mouth. "My girls." He was covered in the smells of the ballpark—ketchup, mustard, beer, sweat.

"Where's the money, Wade?" My hold on his neck loosened so he could get enough air to answer. But he squirmed free and faced me, his eyes looking right into mine. My hands flew to either side of his face, my thumbs forcing themselves into his eye sockets. He screamed out and closed his eyes as tight as he could, his fingers reaching out blindly, clawing at my face. His hands came away from me covered in the blood from my nose, and his fingers slid down my arms and to my wrists.

Suddenly there was the sound of my sunglasses hitting the concrete, and the dim light was now brighter in my eyes. My hands turned him loose and my knees bent so that my fingers could sweep the floor. Wade rushed past me, knocking me backward to the ground, the gun coming loose from my waistband and my hand sending it sliding across the room.

I grabbed hold of Wade's ankles and pulled him to the floor, my body on top of him and my hands covering his just as his finger closed around the trigger and squeezed off a round. It skipped off the floor and ricocheted into the ceiling. The noise was deafening.

I got to my feet just as voices echoed outside in the concourse, and then a set of hands were on my shoulders, another set grabbing Wade and pulling him free. Someone yelled, "Gun!" before my fist crushed a jaw, teeth tearing into my knuckles.

"Let's get some help in here!" another voice screamed.

Wade was still underfoot when my shoulders squared to the two guys in orange vests in front of me, my eyes trying to scan the floor for the gun. And then the Mace hit me, and they were on top of me. And in a few seconds there were others.

"Stop!" someone screamed, but they weren't talking to me. From out in the stadium came the sound of people cheering once the game restarted. But my ears caught another sound: it was the echo of Wade Chesterfield's footsteps running away from me down the concourse.

Easter Quillby

CHAPTER 32

When I saw Wade again he was standing just outside the tunnel at the top of the stairs leading down to our seats. I figure he'd stopped walking toward us when he saw the man sitting beside me. Even if Wade didn't know who Brady was he probably knew exactly why he was there. Something must've told him that it was all over, that somebody'd found us and we'd be going back to North Carolina, back to Gastonia, and after that, who knew where.

I don't know how long he'd been standing there when I turned around and saw him, but his eyes were red like he'd either been crying or was fixing to. He waved at me, and I waved back, and that was it—he was gone. I waited a few more minutes—until the bottom of the second inning when the Cardinals were up to bat—before I told Brady that I didn't think Wade was coming back. He asked me if I was sure, told me we could wait just a little bit longer, but I knew there wasn't any use. I was ready to let whatever was going to happen just go ahead and happen.

Brady Weller

CHAPTER 33

Gastonia had exploded by the time I brought Easter and Ruby back to town on Tuesday afternoon, a full week after they'd gone missing. The armored car heist was all over the news again, and so was Tommy Broughton's mug shot. It wasn't just the local news covering the story; cable news was back in town too, and CNN and the morning programs had live feeds going around the clock showing agents up at the house on Calder Mountain, tossing chunks of drywall out the doors of the basement and carrying out black trash bags that I knew were slam full of millions of dollars. The only thing they couldn't find was the missing driver of that armored car. He could've spent the past six months weighted down at the bottom of the Catawba River, or he could've been relaxing on a beach somewhere in Mexico, far away from Tommy Broughton and the mess he'd gotten himself into. But I knew Broughton would eventually cough him up; he wasn't smart enough or hard enough to keep that kind of secret.

Some of his money was found with Robert Pruitt in St. Louis on Monday. They'd found a gun on him too, but that wasn't what had bothered me: it was the picture of Easter he'd had folded up in his pocket that kept running through my mind. I'd been right in thinking it wouldn't be too long before they connected him to the murder of Wade's mother back in Charleston, and who knew what else they'd find once they started digging. He'd only been out of jail for a few months, but it looked like he'd made pretty good use of his time. And now he was back in jail, awaiting trial for murder. Who knows what he would've done if he'd been able to get his hands on those little girls.

Easter and Ruby were back under Miss Crawford's care by Tuesday night, but their heads didn't hit the pillow until I'd installed the Deluxe Delta 6000, which retails at $750 with a monthly subscription of $74.99. But of course there was no fee or subscription rate; it was all taken care of, courtesy of Safe-at-Home and my brother-in-law, Jim. The only hard part was showing Miss Crawford how to turn it off and on, but I wasn't too worried about that because I knew that Easter and Ruby wouldn't be there for long. Their disappearance had kicked their grandparents into overdrive, and once the girls were found, things started to move fast. It was only a matter of days before I was standing in their bedroom, broken-down cardboard boxes tucked under my arm, asking them what they wanted to take with them and what they wanted to leave behind for the other kids.

Once the dust settled, everybody and everything could easily be accounted for except for Wade Chesterfield.

And that's when he called me.

"Do you still have my girls?" he asked. It was a few minutes before nine on Thursday morning, and Wade Chesterfield's voice was the last thing I'd been expecting to hear when I came into the office that morning. I looked at the caller ID. The area code was 704. He could've been calling me from next door, or he could've been anywhere else in this part of the state.

"Is this Wade?"

"Do you still have my girls?" he asked again.

"No," I said. "I don't have them. They're back where you found them three weeks ago. And it's best if you leave them right where they are."

"I got your number from the woman there," he said. "She told me to call you if I needed anything."

"That was before all this happened, Wade," I said. "There's nothing I can do now."

"Were you the one at the game?" he asked.

His question caught me off guard. I never imagined that he'd seen me. "Yes," I said. "I was there."

"Thank you for taking care of my girls," he said.

"You're welcome," I said. "But that's what I'm supposed to do. You just made it a little harder than it should be." I waited for him to say something, but the line went quiet. "Wade? Are you still there?"

"Can you see them whenever you want?" he asked.

"Why are you asking?"

"Because I'll pay you. Two hundred and fifty thousand if you let me get them back."

The bells on the Baptist church a block from my office started tolling for 9 A.M., and before I could respond to Wade I heard those same bells coming through the phone. I jumped up and ran to the windows at the front of my office and looked up and down Franklin Avenue, but there were no pay phones that I could see.

"Hello?" Wade said.

"I'm here," I said. I opened the front door and stepped out into the parking lot. "Listen, Wade, there's no way I can—"

"Three hundred thousand dollars," he said. In the parking lot, the bells and the traffic were so loud that I almost couldn't hear him, and the connection began to fade and static took over the line. I stepped back toward the building and held my free hand over my ear. "I need them to be with me. Please, just think about it. I'll call you tomorrow."

"Wait!" I said. The bells had stopped chiming, and I realized that I was yelling into the receiver. "Wait. If you're in town, somewhere nearby, maybe we could meet up and talk."

But he'd already hung up.

I went back inside and checked the caller ID and dialed the number. It rang for almost a minute before somebody picked up.

"Hello?" a woman's voice said.

"May I speak to Wade?"

"Who?"

"Wade," I said. "He just called me two minutes ago."

"There's nobody here," she said. "This is a pay phone. I was just walking by, and it started ringing."

"Thanks," I said. I hung up and sat down at my desk, and then I leaned back in the chair, took a deep breath, and closed my eyes. *Wade called me,* I thought. Not the police, or the FBI, or the foster home. I was the only one who knew he was in town. I was the only one who knew what he was willing to do to get his daughters back.

When I opened my eyes they were already locked on the photo of Jessica and me that sat in the frame on my desk. I couldn't help but think about what she'd said about nobody ever asking the kids what they want, and I pictured Easter's face at the Cardinals game once she'd realized Wade wasn't coming back for them. I couldn't undo the things I hadn't done right for Jessica, even though I'd spent years and years trying. Maybe I'd spent my life believing in second chances only because I was always the one who'd asked for them. But now I had to make the call about whether or not to give Wade Chesterfield a second chance, and I had twenty-four hours to decide what that call would be.

Easter Quillby

CHAPTER 34

Ever since me and Ruby had been back we hadn't been allowed to go out to the playground after school with the rest of the kids, but on Monday Mrs. Davis came by the classroom where we'd spent the past few afternoons doing our homework and watching movies, and she asked us to line up with the rest of the kids. "Go ahead and bring your things with you," she said. We put everything in our backpacks and followed her outside.

Brady was waiting for us out in the parking lot behind the school, leaning up against the front of his car with his hands in his pockets. He smiled and waved when he saw us. Me and Ruby waved back.

Mrs. Davis was at the front of the line, but she stopped when she got to Brady, and she looked over at Selena. "If anybody wants to go down to the ball field then y'all go ahead and follow Selena. The rest of you can head out to the playground, and I'll be out there in a second." Selena led some of the kids down the stairs to the field, and the rest of them started walking toward the playground. A couple of them turned around and stared at Brady while they walked off. I'm sure they were wondering who he was and why he'd been out there waiting on us. They'd had all kinds of questions for me and Ruby once we'd come back. They'd seen us on the news when we were missing, and a couple of them had brought in our pictures from the newspaper and showed them to us.

But Mrs. Davis already knew who Brady was. Right before school had started in August, Brady had brought me and Ruby to meet all of our teachers, and he told them about us having to move into the home after what happened to Mom. We'd even gotten to meet the principal.

Brady reached out and shook Mrs. Davis's hand. "How are you doing?" he asked.

"Fine," she said, smiling. "I'm doing even better now that we've got our girls back home." She reached down and squeezed my shoulder and put her hand on Ruby's head. Ruby looked at her. "Y'all have fun," Mrs. Davis said. She walked off toward the playground.

"Where are we going?" Ruby asked.

Brady opened the car door and folded the seat back. "I thought we'd do something fun, like go to the park," he said. "Y'all are going to be leaving next week, and I figured this might be one of the last days we'll get to see each other."

Ruby climbed into the backseat and buckled herself in, and I pushed the seat back into place and got in the front. I'd ridden in the back with Ruby on the whole ride from St. Louis back to Gastonia, but now I felt like riding up front with Brady. His car was little and old, not quite as old as Wade's, and it smelled a little bit like cigarettes. Brady started up the engine and rolled down the windows. Then he turned the radio on and looked at the clock. Then he looked at me. "All right, copilot," he said. "Where to first?"

Our first stop was at the Dairy Queen right beside the school. Brady let me and Ruby both order whatever we wanted. I got a vanilla ice cream cone dipped in red shell, and Ruby got the same thing dipped in the chocolate. "Does Miss Crawford let y'all have ice cream?" Brady asked.

"Sometimes," I said. "But only after dinner."

"Well, maybe we shouldn't tell her about this."

We headed down Union Road and turned onto Garrison and headed toward Lineberger Park, but right when Brady turned on his blinker to pull into the parking lot, I decided I wanted to do something else first. "Can we drive past our old house?" I asked him.

Brady sat there with his blinker on for a second, and then he looked at the clock on the radio and turned and looked out at the park.

"It's just right up the street," I said. "It won't take but just a second."

"Okay," he finally said. He flipped his blinker the other way, and he pulled back into traffic and turned left off Garrison and onto Chestnut.

As we turned I looked out at the pay phone on the corner of the parking lot at Fayles' and saw that it had been fixed.

"What are you looking at?" Brady asked.

"Nothing," I said. I turned back around and looked out at the houses as we passed them on the way to our street. "We ain't seen our old house since we moved into the home."

"I bet it feels like that's been a long time," Brady said.

"But everything looks the same," Ruby said from the backseat. She'd taken off her seat belt, and she was leaning forward in between me and Brady and looking out the windshield. I thought about telling her to put her seat belt back on, but we were going so slow now that I figured it didn't matter one way or the other whether she had it on or not.

I showed Brady which house had been ours, and he slowed down and stopped his car in front of it and leaned toward me to look out my window. It still looked like the same little white house it had been when we'd lived there. Aside from the plastic chair that was missing from the porch, it looked like we'd never left. And then I started to notice little things about it that were different. A set of pale blue curtains were pulled closed in the living room, and a red plastic cup sat on the windowsill on the other side of the glass. The screen was missing from the bottom half of the screen door, and a couple of old newspapers that still had the rubber bands around them had been left on the porch. There was no car in the driveway, which wasn't any different because we'd never had one either, but in the high grass at the end of the driveway a new tricycle was turned over on its side. I figured it belonged to whoever was living there now.

We must've been sitting there for close to a minute when a man opened the front door and stepped out onto the porch in his bare feet, letting the screen door slam shut behind him. He was about Mom's age, and he had on a white tank top and blue jeans. He used his shoulder to hold a portable phone up against his ear while he took out a cigarette and lit it. The three of us just sat there staring at him, and I figured he wondered what in the world we were doing out there. He nodded his head at us, and I waved.

"We'd better go," Brady said.

"Okay," I said.

Brady turned around in the neighbor's driveway, and when we passed the house I turned around in my seat to look back at it, and I saw that Ruby was looking back at it too.

Something felt different when we pulled off our old street and turned left onto Chestnut. The day had changed somehow. Brady had turned off the radio and rolled up the windows, and none of us said a word on the way back down to the park. Maybe it was seeing our old house that made us so quiet, or maybe it was seeing a stranger standing on the front porch of a place where we'd never live again, especially now that we were on our way to Alaska, that made me and Ruby feel something that we didn't quite understand.

But as soon as Brady pulled into the parking lot at Lineberger

Park and turned off the engine, it was clear exactly what was on his mind. "I want to go ahead and let y'all know that you might see your daddy today." He looked at me, and then he turned toward the backseat and looked at Ruby.

"Where is he?" I asked.

"He's here," Brady said, nodding toward the park. "I mean, he might be here. I don't know. I just wanted you both to know that you might see him. And I didn't want it to scare you."

"We're not scared of him," Ruby said. "He's our dad."

"I know," Brady said. He reached out and opened his door, and then he looked back at Ruby again. "I know."

It had been two weeks since we'd left with Wade, and now it was the middle of September and the summer was definitely over. Even though the past couple of days had been hot ones, it was almost cool out there in the park with all that shade and all those tall trees around us. The park was full of people, and me and Ruby held hands and followed Brady toward the playground. He sat down on a bench, and we went and stood in front of him. Ruby looked at everybody around her like she expected Wade to walk up and say "hey" at any second, but I only looked at Brady.

"That's why you wanted to bring us out here, isn't it?" I asked. "To see him."

"No," he said. "Well, that's not the only reason anyway. I really did want to see y'all one more time before you have to go."

A bunch of guys were out on the courts shooting basketball up on the hill behind Brady. Down here at the park, kids were playing, running past us and laughing and hollering at each other. I didn't see any police, and I was happy for that, but that didn't mean somebody else might not recognize Wade from the news and call the cops.

"He's going to be in trouble if he comes out here, isn't he?" I asked.

"I don't know," Brady said. "We'll have to see." He looked toward the playground and pointed at the little merry-go-round. It was empty. "Do y'all want a push?" he asked, standing up.

I pulled Ruby toward the playground. "She'll only let me push her," I said. "She don't like to go too fast."

Ruby climbed on the merry-go-round and stood right in the center. "Hold on tight," I said.

"Not too fast," she said.

"I know." I started pushing it around.

Brady walked over and sat down on a bench beside an old woman who was reading a book. He sat there and just looked around at all the other people in the park like he was waiting on something, but he didn't quite know what it would be.

A little girl, maybe a year older than Ruby, came and stood beside me and watched me spin the merry-go-round. "Can I get on?" she finally asked.

"Sure," I said. I stopped it and let her climb on, and I made sure she got ahold of one of the bars before I started spinning it again.

"I'm getting dizzy," Ruby said. She was smiling.

"I'll spin you the other way," I said. "That'll get you un-dizzy." I wanted to laugh at Ruby, but the whole time I couldn't help but look at every single person in the park, half expecting to see Wade. Brady was still there on the bench, looking all around him, and I figured he was probably expecting to see Wade too. The old woman sitting beside him must've been the little girl's grandmother, because she'd set her book down on her lap and was watching me push the merry-go-round.

And that's when I saw Brady lean over and whisper something to the woman. She pulled back and stared at him for a second like she couldn't believe what he'd said, and then she leaned closer. He whispered to her again. She closed her book and stood up and grabbed her purse. Then she walked over to the merry-go-round and reached for the bars to try to stop it from spinning.

"Come on," the woman said. She reached out her hand to the little girl, but the girl didn't move.

"Are we leaving?" she asked.

"Yes," the woman said.

"But we just got here," the girl said.

The woman looked back at Brady, and then took the girl's hand. "It's just time for us to go home," she said. She picked the girl up without saying anything and walked back toward the parking lot. The girl started crying, and the woman turned her head and looked at me and Ruby, and then she looked over at Brady. Other people were looking at us too.

"Why'd she leave?" I asked him.

"I don't know," he said.

"What did you say to her?"

"Nothing," he said. He smiled, but I could tell he was hiding something from me.

I started pushing Ruby again, the other way this time. She was sitting down now, turning her head around and around, watching the old woman carry the little girl back to their car. It felt like a lot of people were staring at me and Ruby after what had happened, but when I looked around I saw that a couple of them were staring at Brady. One of them was a man up on the hill to our right, sitting on a bench, holding a newspaper. He let it drop to his lap so he could see, even though he'd been too far away to hear anything the woman had said. And then I noticed a man closer to us, standing on the bridge that ran over the little creek off to the left of the playground. He was staring at Brady too. When he saw me looking at him, he looked away, and I swear I saw him say something to himself.

Then I saw what looked like a little wire running up into the man's ear. He was way too young for some kind of hearing aid, and as soon as I saw that wire I knew the real reason Brady had brought us out here in the first place, and I couldn't believe he'd do this to us, to Wade. But he had.

I grabbed on to the merry-go-round and ran with it in circles as hard as I could. Ruby hollered out that I was going too fast, but I didn't stop. She was half screaming, half laughing by the time I jumped on. The park moved past me in a blur, and I could just make out Brady where he sat on the bench, the man up on the hill, the one over on the bridge, and all the other people who may have been there for the same reason those three were.

Ruby was still sitting down, and I climbed to the middle and leaned up against one of the bars. I watched everything rush by, and I reached up and touched my nose with each finger, and then I touched both ears before rubbing my hands down my arms one at a time. I kept doing that until the merry-go-round slowed down, and then I hopped off and pushed as hard as I could and jumped back on and kept giving the same sign Wade had showed me.

Brady had stood up from the bench, and he hollered my name. "What are you doing?" he said.

Ruby was lying on her back, staring up at me. "Faster!" she screamed. She was laughing now, and she didn't seem one bit scared anymore. I wasn't either.

CHAPTER 35

We didn't see Wade that day, and we didn't see him before we left Gastonia for Alaska either. I don't even know for certain if he was there at Lineberger Park that afternoon, but I like to think he was.

That night, one of our last nights in the home, I laid there with my head against the pillow and realized I'd been wrong about what Wade was doing after he'd left us in St. Louis. For the past week I'd pictured him headed west in the opposite direction of me and Ruby, that black bag of money on the seat beside him, his brain working and working, trying to figure what to do next. But he'd actually tried to come back for us.

I didn't like what Brady had done, trying to use us to get Wade caught by the police and the FBI and whoever else, and I had a hard time forgiving him after that. But then I remembered that he didn't know Wade like I did, and he'd probably never had his own father disappear on him twice and come back both times. Brady thought he was doing the right thing for me and Ruby, even though I thought he'd been wrong to do it.

It took a few days of Miss Crawford fussing over us to get us all packed, me and Ruby going through our bedroom as slow as we could, trying to decide what things to keep and what things to give away to other kids who could use them: the new bedspreads that finally matched our sheets, the books on our bedside table, the clothes hanging in the closet.

But there was one thing I wanted to make sure I didn't leave behind; it was one of those old baseballs Wade had signed back before he'd left us, back when he thought he might be somebody one day and that baseball would be worth something to someone besides him. As hard as I'd tried to rub his signature off all those years ago, it was still there—even though you couldn't hardly see it. That's a little bit what it was like being Wade's daughter too.

And then me and Ruby were in Anchorage with Mom's parents. When we first got there I'd lie in bed at night in a room that was all my own for the first time in my life, and I'd listen to strange voices coming from strange rooms in a place I knew I didn't belong. But the only thing those voices did was tell me how happy they were that me and Ruby had come to live with them and how much I reminded them of Mom.

But I knew better than that, and I knew that was just something they'd probably said to make me feel at home, to make me feel like I belonged. Once all that brown washed out of my hair and my tan finally faded for good they'd probably stop seeing Mom when they saw me, and that was okay. They'd have Ruby there to remind them of Mom. So would I.

My grandfather's name was Nolan, and he was tall with skin that was even darker than Mom's and Ruby's. You could tell that his hair had been black once upon a time, but now it was silver and longer than mine, and he wore it back in a ponytail. My grandmother's name was Barbara, and she was just the opposite. After seeing her, I realized just why I looked the way I did. Her skin was light like mine, and her hair was the same strawberry blond. She wanted us to call her "Grandma," so we did. Nolan said he wasn't old enough to be anybody's grandpa and that the name Nolan had always suited him just fine, so that's what we called him.

Me and Ruby had been there for almost a month when Grandma went out on the front porch to get the mail and carried a big cardboard box into my bedroom. I was sitting on the bed, listening to my CD Walkman and doing homework, when I looked up and saw her standing there, her eyes just barely peeking out above the top of that box. She set it down on my bed and stood back and looked at it. It was addressed to me and Ruby.

"This came from Cordova," she said. "That's a few towns over. I don't know anybody over that way, and I don't think Grandpa does either. Do you?"

"I don't hardly know anybody in this whole state," I said.

She picked up a pair of scissors from my desk and cut the packing tape and opened the box. There was an envelope sitting right inside on top of some tissue paper. Grandma picked it up and pulled out a letter. "You want me to read this?" she asked.

"Sure," I said. I got up on my knees to look inside.

She started reading.

Dear Easter and Ruby,

Please accept this gift as a welcome to Alaska. I have seen you on the news and read about you in the paper, and I'm very sorry for all that you have been through. But I think you will enjoy living here. It is a very safe place, and the people are very nice and happy to have you. Please know that I am praying for you both.

Sincerely,
A Friend

But I only heard half of what she'd read. I'd already pulled back the tissue paper and seen what was inside the box. It was the teddy bear that Wade had won for us that night in Myrtle Beach. I pulled it out of the box and held it up and stared at it, and I tried to keep Grandma from knowing that I recognized it and that I knew exactly who'd sent it.

"Well," she said, "this is a nice surprise. It was awfully kind of somebody to do that."

"Can I see the letter?" I asked.

She handed it over, and I saw that it had been typed instead of handwritten.

"Your sister's out in the backyard," she said, "helping Grandpa set up the bird feeder. I'll go grab her."

"Okay," I said, folding the letter and sliding it back into the envelope. I listened to her footsteps going down the hallway toward the kitchen, and I heard her open the sliding-glass door and call for Ruby. She slid it closed behind her.

As soon as I heard that I stuck my hand down the front of the bear's overalls and felt around for what I'd left there that night back in South Carolina. My fingers closed around the stack of money, and until I pulled it out and saw it I almost couldn't believe it was still there. But, when I turned it over in my hand, I saw something that hadn't been there before. One of the tickets to the game in St. Louis was tucked behind the band. I slid the ticket out and looked at it; on it was a picture of Mark McGwire tipping his hat to the crowd. I turned the ticket over, and there on the back, scribbled in Wade's messy handwriting, were three words: *Stay on base.*

ACKNOWLEDGMENTS

I wish to thank the following people and institutions for their kindness and support:

David Highfill, my editor at William Morrow, for his honesty, patience, and vision.

Nat Sobel and Judith Weber, my agents at Sobel Weber Associates, Inc. Nat, I wish you could ensure the New York Jets' future as well as you've ensured mine. A heartfelt thank-you to the rest of the Sobel/ Weber team: Julie Stevenson, Adia Wright, and Kirsten Carleton.

The Corporation of Yaddo, the MacDowell Colony, and Highland Springs Farm in Wellsburg, West Virginia, where so much of this novel was written and revised.

All of the amazing people at William Morrow/HarperCollins, past and present: Liate Stehlik, Michael Morrison, Jessica Williams, Sharyn Rosenblum, Stephanie Kim, Abigail Tyson, Shawn Nicholls, Kimberly Chocolaad, Tavia Kowalchuk, Carla Parker, Mike Brennan, Jeanette Zwart, Doug Jones, Caitlin McCaskey, Gabriel Barrilas, Anne DeCourcey, Ian Doherty, Karen Gudmondson, Jim

Hankey, Kate McCune, Cathy Schornstein, Robin Smith, and, holy moly, Eric Svenson.

My colleagues and students in the MFA Program in Fiction and Nonfiction at Southern New Hampshire University.

The friends and family who either read drafts, gave advice, listened, or did all three: Cliff Cash, Amy Earnheart, Walker Barnes, Patrick Crerand, Christian Helms, Michael Jauchen, Thomas Murphy, Chatman Neely, Harry Sanford, Brian Sullivan, and Reggie Scott Young.

Last of all, but most of all, Mallory Brady Cash, my wife, best friend, and first reader: if not for her, then nothing.